A Garland Series

The
Flowering of the Novel

Representative Mid-Eighteenth Century Fiction
1740-1775

A Collection of 121 Titles

A Trip to the Moon

Francis Gentleman

**Two Volumes
Reprinted in One**

Garland Publishing, Inc., New York & London

1974

———————

Bibliographical note:

this facsimile has been made from a copy in the
Beinecke Library of Yale University
(Im.G289.764)

———————

Library of Congress Cataloging in Publication Data

Gentleman, Francis, 1728-1784.
  A trip to the moon.

  (The Flowering of the novel)
  Reprint of the 1764-65 ed. printed by A. Ward for
S. Crowder, York and London.
    I. Title. II. Series.
PZ3.G2884Tr5 [PR3475.G5]   823'.6   74-17337
ISBN 0-8240-1167-8

A

TRIP to the MOON.

Containing an Account of the

ISLAND of NOIBLA.

Its INHABITANTS, RELIGIOUS and POLITICAL CUSTOMS, &c.

By Sir HUMPHREY LUNATIC, *Bart.*

I am but mad North North-West; when the Wind blows Southerly I know a Hawk from a Hernshaw.
SHAKESPEAR.

Y O R K:

Printed by A. WARD, for S. CROWDER, in *Pater-noster-Row*; W. BRISTOW, in *St. Paul's Church-Yard*; J. PRIDDEN and W. GRIFFIN, in *Fleet-street*; G. BURNET, in the *Strand*; G. WOODFALL, at *Charing-Cross*; and J. JOHNSON, opposite the *Monument, London*; C. ETHERINGTON, in *York*; and W. CHARNLEY, in *Newcastle upon Tyne*, 1764.

*W*HEN Alexander *was consulted concerning a Successor to his Crown and Dignities, he replied, Let them be given to the* Worthiest; *on such a Principle, if any one can find a more eligible Patron for the following Work, the* Author *is willing to give up his own Choice of*

ASHLEY COWPER, *Esq;*

Terms and Phrases of the NOIBLAN *Language, which occur in the following Account of the Island.*

NALSINA, a Mediator.
SALMINA, a Temple.
AVOZENS, Priests.
RANEVERS, Vergers.
SNERRUNETS, Servitors of the Temple.
ECARUOCNE, a Religious Ceremony.
NOTLAM, the Spring of Purification.
ARESAL, a City.
NAMREDAL, Father of a City.
SENIRATS, Wards of a City.
RUVENAL, a Square.
REQUECEX, the House of Justice.
SOLARMAN, the common Cryer.
NODNOL, the Capital of NOIBLA.
SNOISSAPANS, public Schools.
NOITOCS, Masters of them.
ASSELANS, Ushers.
RAYAMON, a Year.
REAPAN, a Month.
TOIRTA, a Week.
SILCAR, a Mile.

NE-

NEROMA, a desolate Province.

ERISHNOVER, the Mountains of Blood.

OMYRCHAL, the Valley of Weeping.

SEITNUOCS, Districts or Shires.

ELKNITAN, the Bell of Noon.

SELBATAZA, Dinner.

AZONIA, an Aromatic Liquid.

ELENGAL, Virtue.

ESTRALAM, a Theatre.

ZAMELA, the Plain of Modesty.

NOIGLEVER GENVELA, be grateful to GOD.

MALTRA ENUTHE, the Tree of Health.

MAGINLEB NALSINA ELVERAN YURNE SE-
ZIVED WAL PHAZAZ, remember that the
Mediator sees your Thoughts as well as your
Actions.

BINEDA, OH NAMREDAL, TWANTO SELBEN
TWANTASTEZ, temper, Oh Father, Justice
with the Dew of Mercy.

RETHO ESOL NA LENGALI, a Foe to Virtue.

RETHO ETTIBEM ELBAL, an artful Wife.

RETHO SLINTAT ELBAL, a tatling Wife.

DOSEN ALOPU, Birds of the Garden.

RETHO ESOL NA ITSEDOM, a Foe to Modesty.

ELBIROS, weekly Inspectors.

EFFILAR, }
ATROITA, } proper Names.

A TRIP

A TRIP to the MOON.

CHAP. I.

Containing a short Account of Sir Hum-phrey's Predecessors, from the first Ba-ronet of his Family.

THOUGH the following Piece is not of a Biographical Nature, the Author thinks it neceſſary to give ſome ſhort Account of himſelf and his Family, that thereby forming a Kind of Acquaintance with his Readers, they may purſue their Journey together thro' the LUNAR WORLD with more Cordia-lity and Pleaſure.

It is well known by thoſe who have Skill in Heraldry, that the LUNATICS *have been a conſiderable Family, ever ſince* ENG-

A   LAND

LAND WAS ENGLAND; they have occa-
fionally been at the Helm of State; they
have nodded upon Wooll-Packs in Lawn
Sleeves; they have difpenfed Law from
under Voluminous Wigs; they have ra-
vaged Nations with Armies, and plowed
the Deep with Fleets; in fhort, they have
filled every Station in Life, from Princes
to Coblers; from Duchefles to Cham-
bermaids: To make a complete De-
tail of Genealogical Particulars, would
be a Work of infufferable Prolixity and
Oftentation; wherefore the AUTHOR
will only revert to his Great Grandfather,
the firft BARONET of *his* Part of the Family; and proceed from him in a direct
Line, without Regard to feveral other diftinguifhed collateral Branches.

WHIMSICAL LUNATIC, Efq; afterwards Sir WHIMSICAL, diftinguifhed
himfelf much by his Zeal in Favour of
Royalty, at that Critical Period when the
RE-

REPUBLICAN Party made such severe Attacks upon the weak and unfortunate FIRST CHARLES; nor did he, like the mercenary slaves of Interest, attach himself, till Rebellion had so far gained the Ascendant, that Hope was fluttering on its last Wing; not PERSIAN like, a Worshipper of the rising, but a faithful follower of the setting Sun; pursuing his Beams even into the profound Darkness that ensued, with a Spirit truly heroic he join'd the general Wreck, which depriv'd the Monarch of his Life, and himself, among many others, of his Estate.

Thus reduced, for some Time he comforted himself with the Opinion of CATO; that it is a necessary Compliment in every good Citizen to join the Ruin of his Country: However, Want of Money, which generally gives Time for Reflection, and adds Force to it, soon led him to entertain a different Notion of

A 2   the

the prevailing Party; through the Optics of Neceſſity freſh Notions of Freedom entered his ever active Brain; Non-reſiſtance and Paſſive Obedience, his darling Principles, vaniſhed like Miſts before the Sun, and a new Kind of Patriotiſm ſo enflamed him, that he commenced one of thoſe public-ſpirited Orators, ſince diſgraced by the Title of Fanatic Preachers.

Being poſſeſſed of great Volubility, Force of Expreſſion, and Luxuriance of Fancy, he ſoon became highly diſtinguiſhed in his New Capacity; and as Converts are generally moſt zealous againſt the Cauſe they have forſaken, he was eſteemed ſo valuable an Acquiſition, that CROMWELL cauſed his Eſtate to be reſtored, and had him elected a Member of his firſt PARLIAMENT; in which Situation he made a very conſiderable Figure: No one in the Debates commanded

manded more Attention and Refpect.
Hence he might have been eminently
advanced in the State; but, like a true
LUNATIC, being fond of Oppofition,
and difdaining to run with the Stream
long, he began to find Fault with the
Conduct of Public Affairs; openly declaring, that the Plan of PLATO's RE-
PUBLIC, with fome Alterations and
Amendments of his own, would be the
only fure Foundation for National Happinefs.

His Objections to almoft every Mea-
fure propofed, rendered him remarkably
obnoxious within Doors, but made him
popular without; however, as in thofe
days the VOX POPULI was not efteemed
the VOX DEI, he reaped no other Advantage from his hardy and anxious Endeavours, but fome faint Gales of whifpered
Applaufe; for public Acclamations in
Favour of laborious Patriots, were not

then

then so common or so safe as they have been since.

Plumed up and animated with the Approbation of many as discontented as himself, he gave full Scope to his Zeal, without apparently waking the Dragon Power from his Slumbers, as his Keepers shrewdly foresaw that to lie in Wait for hot-brained Politicians is the surest Method of circumventing them: And even so it happened with the illustrious Personage here spoken of, who grew so extremely violent upon the Motion for constituting CROMWELL LORD PROTECTOR, which he said was only a softer Name for TYRANT, that his Fury knew no Bounds, but hurried him to such Lengths of general and personal Reflection, that he was not only expelled the House as a seditious Member, but was also put under legal Prosecution, and amerced with so heavy a Fine for Defamation, that his Estate could
stretch

ftretch little farther than to fave him from a Prifon.

Thus, once again funk into the unhofpitable and chilling Shade of Fortune, he had no Comfort left but the Uprightnefs of his own Heart, and fome diftant Hopes that Matters might yet take a more favourable Turn; which however did not happen till fome fhort Time before Cromwell's Deceafe; when, a rich Relation dying, he obtained a Legacy that redeemed his Eftate, and enabled him to appear in public with Refpect; for Refpect ufually follows the Circumftances, and not the Qualifications of a Man.

At this Period, as if his Life had not been already fufficiently difturbed, he took it into his Head to marry a fecond Wife, his own Houfe-keeper; who being raifed to the Degree of Miftrefs, poffeffed sed of Youth without Prudence, and Beauty without Underſtanding, made ſuch large Strides to arbitrary Power, that all her Huſband's REPUBLICAN Principles could not ſtem the Torrent of her Pride and Extravagance. This domeſtic Concern kept him from meddling any further in Politics, than addreſſing his Life and Fortune, among the other good People of ENGLAND, to RICHARD CROMWELL, ſome Years Poverty having made him approve of the Office of PRO-TECTOR. However, upon hearing of CHARLES's Approach, his Heart took ſuch a Yearning towards the lawful Prince, and indefeaſible hereditary Right flowed back upon him in ſuch a Tide of Loyalty, that he was one of the foremoſt to transfer Allegiance from RICHARD to CHARLES; in Acknowledgment of which forward Zeal that good-humour'd, liberal Monarch created him a BARONET; intimating, at the ſame Time, a Deſign, when

Af-

Affairs were entirely settled, of extending his Royal Bounty in a Manner more worthy his great Deservings.

But, alas! how vain, transitory, and delusive are human Expectations? How speedily does the ever-gaping Grave swallow up the air-built Fabrics of Imagination? Some few Nights after his new Dignity had been conferred upon him, the BARONET, while his heart was expanding with Joy at his Country's Felicity, sacrificed so profusely at the Shrine of BACCHUS, and swallowed so many Bumpers for the PUBLIC GOOD, that, falling asleep among some as much intoxicated as himself, he was, as is supposed, stifled, being found dead in his Chair by a Waiter. Thus — oh fatal and irreparable Chance!—died that great Man, who expired, as he had lived, in the Cause of old ENGLAND, a real and uniform LUNATIC.

As

As Impartiality is the very Essence of History, it shall be most carefully preserved upon this Occasion; wherefore, tho' Nature may plead to draw a Veil over the Failings of Ancestors, yet our Author cannot help acknowledging that Sir WHIMSICAL's Successor deviated considerably from the Dignity of his Name and Family; for notwithstanding he had so bright an Example before him, to light him on his Way like another ARCADIAN STAR, and came to his Estate in a bustling Time, yet did he meanly betake himself to the Retirement of a Country Life, making the Improvement of his Fortune, the comfortable Settlement of his Tenants, a plentiful House, and half a Dozen sociable Neighbours, his chief Pleasure: However, this phlegmatic Cloud, as I may call him, upon the Glory of the LUNATICS, complaisantly retired in seven or eight Years, and made Way for Sir HUMPHREY, Father of the Author.

Here

Here Family-Splendor again began to break forth; the young BARONET firſt diſtinguiſhed himſelf eminently upon the famous Bill of Excluſion ſo boldly framed againſt JAMES Duke of YORK, afterwards King. During the ſhort Reign of that obſtinate Prince, he alternately ſupported Royal Prerogative and popular Liberty; ſo, being of both Sides, reaped Advantage from neither. He was not in the Aſſociation for inviting the Prince of ORANGE, yet joined him ſoon after his Arrival; notwithſtanding which he was always one of the foremoſt to cramp that Monarch in the Operations of Government. The War of Queen ANNE he vehemently declared againſt; and, when the War was ended, was as vehement againſt the Peace of UTRECHT; juſt after which he died, expiring with this Wiſh, that the Authors of *ſuch* a Peace might never enjoy *Peace*. In ſhort, he was deeply concerned in the political Occurrences of

five-

five-and-thirty Years, fully inheriting the glorious Spirit of Oppofition, and exerting it with fuch Effect, that he was the main Caufe of removing a Dozen Minifters of State, moft of whom he thought honeft till in Office; but became convinced at laft, by repeated Experience, that if at any Time PLACE-HUNTERS do act upon juft Principles and are uncorrupt, their Virtue can only be compared to that of thofe Women, who are chafte for want of Temptation or Opportunity.

Our AUTHOR was, at the Time of his Father's Deceafe, but twelve Years old; and, by his Will, put under the Guardianfhip of a Perfon, who had ftrict Charge to infpire him with the Love of fome occult Science which might render him famous: Accordingly, his Genius being confulted, Aftronomy was fixed upon, in which he made an aftonifhing Progrefs; but as he is ftill alive, and an Actor on this great Stage

of

of Life, we fhall leave his Character and
Portrait to a future Day, that we may not
incur the Charge of Flattery or Malice,
by pointing out Beauties or Defects.

Be it fufficient then to remark, that
the prefent Sir Humphrey, tho' intimately acquainted with all Political Concerns, tho' a faithful Reprefentative of
his Conftituents, yet has taken a different
Method to the immortalizing his Name,
and embalming it for Pofterity; viewing
terreftrial Concerns, where fcarce any
Thing but Self-Love, and its Train of
fordid Confequences, prevails, but as fe-
condary Points of Care to a wife Man.
He has ftudioufly traverfed the whole
Planetary Syftem; and tho' fome worldly
Grubs may look on him as a mere Star-
gazer, the following Account of his
Trip to the Moon will fhow that he
deferves as exalted a Place in the Rolls
of Fame, as any Lunatic that ever
made

made a Figure in Life; having this Advantage over his Predeceſſors of conſpicuous Memory, that his Fame is, in the humbleſt View, founded upon innocent, not deſtructive Principles; upon univerſal, wondrous Philoſophical Harmony; not violent, deſtructive Political Diſſenſion.

In this Senſe he has conſented to ſubmit himſelf and the following Journal to public Opinion; perſuaded that however peculiar the Things he is to relate may appear, daily Experience proves they are not leſs true for being ſtrange; and he even flatters himſelf that they may not be leſs entertaining becauſe derived from a Country and People ſeldom mentioned in our World; for it is a Country much to be admired, and a People, in many Points, highly deſerving Imitation.

C H A P.

C H A P. II.

Sir HUMPHREY's *Translation to the* MOON; *his Reception in the Island of* NOIBLA; *Ceremony at the* NOTLAM; *and his Entry into the City of* NODNOL.

HAving always attentively busied myself in the Contemplation of those innumerable and wonderful Bodies, which catching Light from the Sun, when he descends below our Hemisphere, adorn the Firmament with golden Specks, for such they seem to unassisted mortal Eyes; and being always extremely curious to examine whatever related to those Bodies, I form'd great Expectations from a Piece which once fell into my Hands, called BERGERAC's VOYAGE to the MOON; the Title indeed gave me particular Pleasure, as I hoped to find somewhat very extraordinary in the Contents; yet was I vastly deceived, for tho'

there

there are ſtrong Marks of Genius in that
Production, upon the whole I could diſcover nothing very intereſting; however
the Thought of a Journey to the LUNAR
WORLD ſtruck very deep, and all my
Calculations, all my Wiſhes, were ever
after aſſiduouſly employed on the effect-
ing ſuch a Jaunt; till at laſt, without any
apparent Merit of mine, it happened in
the following Manner.

The latter End of laſt MAY, taking a
nightly Walk of Contemplation, I aſcended a green Hill of conſiderable Height,
whoſe Top was ſhaded with Trees, from
whence, in awful Silence, broke only by
lulling Notes from the plaintive Nightin-
gale, I beheld, below me, a ſpacious Vale,
interſected by the ſlow and ſtately Stream
of a well-known River, ſkirted by a
venerable Grove, whoſe Branches, as
SHAKESPEAR has it, were ſilvered by the
MOONSHINE's *watry Beams*; that Planet
having

having then filled its Orb with moſt un-
uſual Luſtre, wrapped up in pleaſing
Melancholy, Slumber inſenſibly fell upon me, and from thence I dropp'd into a
profound Sleep.

How long this ſoft Semblance of Death
remained upon me I cannot ſay; but imagine, Reader, if thou canſt, my Surprize,
and let me add ſome Terror alſo, when,
upon waking, I found myſelf ſeated in
a Kind of Triumphal Car, ſurrounded
by a great Number of human Figures,
not one of which I had the leaſt Idea of;
yet all ſhewing many Marks of Reſpect,
and murmuring out an extraordinary
Kind of Joy. My Aſtoniſhment being
too viſible for Diſguiſe, a Perſon of venerable Aſpect addreſſed me as follows,
moſt profound Attention being given by
the ſurrounding Crowd, who ſeemed
to have much more Pleaſure in the Prac-

B   tice

tice of good Manners, than many of our
polite Affemblies:

Son of Earth, faid he, fear not, thou
art in the Regions of Safety: Tendernefs
and Hofpitality ever fmile here: Envy
never fhewed her fnaky Locks, nor Slander her envenom'd Tongue, nor Cruelty
her blood-ftain'd Sword, in thefe Realms
of foft Repofe; rejoice therefore that thou
art fo highly favoured as to have an Opportunity of gratifying that Curiofity
which has fo long poffeffed thee; it was
laudably ambitious, and ftirred up to
raife thee above the common Race of
Men. Receive from me, in Behalf of all
prefent, and of a much greater Number
whom we reprefent, a zealous and unaf-
fected Welcome; may every Thing thou
meet'ft, during thy Stay amongft us, contribute to thy Information and Pleafure;
it fhall be our Care to confult and to
promote

promote both: May our Endeavours be
fuccefsful to thy Approbation.

Here, turning round, and repeating to
the Multitude a few Words which I did
not underftand, they again made Obei-
fance. Having by this Time collected
Confidence, I replied,

VENERABLE SAGE, whom yet I know
not either in Perfon or Dignity, how fhall
I fitly acknowledge this moft ho'pitable
Salutation? How pay the due Refpect to
fuch unmerited Kindnefs? Yet let it not
ftand as a Doubt of that Cordiality you
profefs, to afk where I am, and by what
Means I came hither, both being utterly
unknown to me. You, Sir, by your Language and Appearance, are ENGLISH; yet
many I fee around you fo different from
what I have ever feen before, that I am
almoft perfuaded to believe fome fuper-
natural Means have removed me fron

B 2   my

my native Land; besides, however conspicuous BRITAIN may be in the Rolls of Fame, the Character you give of this untainted Region far surpasses her proudest Boast; wherefore, good Sir, you cannot be displeased if I inquire where, and among whom I am at present placed.

Thy Desire, my Son, returns he, is natural, and that thou may'st not be kept longer in Suspence, know that what thou hast so long earnestly wished, is at length come to pass; thou art now within the Limits of the LUNAR WORLD; the imperceptible Method of thy Conveyance I cannot explain to thy Comprehension; let it suffice to say that some Rays of Attraction, sent down from the Mount of Observation, a Spot which from Earth appears to be the Nose of the MAN in the MOON, drew thee from the Place where thou lay'st asleep; which powerful

Ope-

Operation was not a little facilitated by
some sympathetic Pamphlets thou hadst
in thy Pockets, Pieces originally planned
in a certain Province of this LUNAR
WORLD, and thence inspired into the
moon-struck Authors of them. Upon this
Information examining my Pockets, I
found three of WHITEFIELD's Sermons,
half a Dozen NORTH-BRITONS, and as
many Schemes for paying off the National Debt, by JACOB HENRIQUES.

At this Point of Time my HOST, as I
may call my sage Welcomer, directed a
Kind of Procession, which tho' not grand,
nor very regular, appeared to be calculated as a high Compliment to me; my
Car of State was drawn by six Animals,
two of a Sort, with a Youth of about fif-
teen leading each; they were ELEPHANTS,
HORSES, and LIONS, all remarkable in
their Kinds; the ELEPHANTS were of
those which so remarkably contributed to

Victory

Victory in a Battle between the ROMANS and PYRRHUS; the Horses were BUCE-PHALUS, and that on which CURTIUS leap'd into the gaping Gulph for the Good of his Country; and as to the LIONS, one of those that let DANIEL pass unmolested, was paired with him that gratefully remembered the Slave who freed his Foot from a tormenting Thorn: These, as well as many extraordinary Creatures of the Human Species, had been translated to the MOON, and are there held in great Regard.

I was shaded by a thin silken Canopy, held over me with great Exactness by six EAGLES of the SUN, their Plumes shining like his Beams, whose Wings kept Pace with the Car, and fanned the Breezes very agreeably around me. A Band of Music preceded the Car, not much unlike that Kind of rude Harmony with which we are told the Antients saluted the

MOON

Moon in an Eclipse, suppofing her to be at that Time in Labour.

As we approached a Gate, which I perceived led into the City, we ftopped before a beautiful Arbor, formed by a Circle of moft pleafing correfpondent Trees; within this Arbor ftood a fmall neat Building, which inclofed a Well called the NOTLAM, or SPRING of PURIFICATION : I was led towards it, being told that I was to undergo a Ceremony necef-fary to every *Sublunary* Being before his Admiffion into the City.

On each Side the Well ftood fix beautiful Virgins in flowing Robes of Azure, each holding in her Hand fomething like a Cenfer of tranfparent Chryftal : On my Entrance one of them, with the moft courteous Solemnity, flowly approached me, and, according to my Conductor's Interpretation, fpoke thus :

May'ft

May'ft thou, earth-born Mortal, by drinking of this holy Spring, become as cold to Paffion, and as pure to Virtue, as its deep and lucid Stream. Having ended, and prefented me the Water, fhe retired; when a fecond came forward, and fprinkling my Hands, faid, *May thefe be the Inftruments of Induftry, and not of Violence.* A third, my Breaft being bared, fprinkled it, with thefe Words: *May Content ever dwell here, and focial Hoppinefs be the reigning Principle.* A fourth bedewed my Head, faying, *As Heaven's kindly Rain raifes and cherifhes the vegetable World, fo may thefe confecrated Drops here bring forth the Fruits of Wifdom and Virtue.*

So much of the Ceremony being over, the Twelve Virgins circling round me, dancing all the Time with very odd Geftures, and finging a Hymn of Exultation, gave me fo plentiful an Ablution, that I began to be weary. Having finifh-
ed

ed thefe Rites, they all proftrated themfelves before me, and then retired to their
Places on each Side the WELL.

Senfible of the Pains they had taken,
and forgetting where I was, I intended to
have made a pecuniary Acknowledgement; but my HOST perceiving the Defign, Hold, SON of EARTH, fays he, the
Works of Religion and Hofpitality are
not fold here; nor have we any Coin but
focial Intercourfe and mutual Regard;
did I not tell thee we had no Envy or Dif-
cord among us, and after that could'ft
thou imagine any Regard would be paid
to fuch Drofs as Gold? Did we want to
introduce Flames among our Fields,
Dearth among our Cattle, Diffenfions
among our Families, Bloodfhed into our
Cities, Difeafes into our Bodies, and pe-
ftilential Paffions into our Minds, that
inflammatory Trafh would foon effect our
irrational and vicious Purpofes. Yet,
                                        hold,

hold, one pleafing and ufeful Purpofe the Sight of it may ferve; lend me what thou haft, that, difplaying it to public View, and briefly explaining its pernicious Effects, I may render it, if poffible, ftill more contemptible and hateful to my Brethren of this World.

Here I gave him my Purfe, from whence taking fome Pieces of Gold, he held them in each Hand, and addreffed the Multitude in the following Manner, as he afterwards explained it to me:

Behold, my Friends and Brothers of the ISLAND of NOIBLA, the moft favoured Spot of all this LUNAR WORLD, behold, ye Sons of natural and untainted Liberty, the Fiend who, having got Footing on the Terreftrial Globe, rules every Government, and every Individual, of all Sexes, Ages, and Degrees; for the Sake of Bits like thefe, dug, *by half-fed Slaves*, out

out of the Bowels of the Earth, to pamper Pride and Luxury; thousands and ten Thousands march into the bloody Field of War, hung round with the most destructive Weapons of Cruelty, to mutilate and butcher their Fellow-Creatures; for these their Clergy pray; their Lawyers wrangle; their Physicians kill: For these Fathers and their Sons, Mothers and their Daughters, Brethren and Sisters, run into the most uncharitable Dissensions: Gilded with these, Vice claims Respect, while thread-bare Virtue stands shiv'ring and helpless at the unhospitable Doors of Luxury and Pride.

For these Parents match their Children without the least Regard to mutual Affection; hence splendid Misery glares in so many Places, while calm Content flies their mercenary Dwellings.—Would you persuade; here lies the most powerful Eloquence:—Would you prove the

Stea-

Steadineſs of a profeſſing Patriot; here
is the Touch-ſtone of intrinſic Worth:—
Would you ſmooth the Wrinkles of Age,
or proportion and harmonize Deformity;
here is the necromantic Beautifier that
can work ſuch Miracles; and that too
amongſt Animals which boaſt themſelves
of Rationality, and yet are ſo wrapp'd up
in Infatuation, that, while they moſt cau-
tiouſly avoid whatever might be hurtful
to the Body, devour, with inſatiable and
voratious Appetites, this more dangerous
Poiſon of the Mind.—Oh Reaſon, where
is thy Power? Mount, mount for Shame
thy Throne, nor longer abdicate thy
Judgment-Seat, leſt uſurping Paſſions
create univerſal and incurable Confuſion.

How, how ſhould we rejoice, my Brethren, that, free from the fatal Influence
of this Bane to ſocial Happineſs, no Blood
ſtains our Fields; no Fears ſhake our
Peace; that Religion is Gratitude, not
In-

Intereſt; that Inclination, moderated by Prudence, joins every Couple here; that Sons, when arrived to Diſcretion, enjoy equal Advantages with their Fathers, whom therefore they never wiſh to bury; that ſuch Failings as we have amongſt us cannot either be hid or rendered leſs ſhameful by ſuch Tinſel Covering; that here no Tongue will move, no Virgin yield her Honour for mercenary Bribes! Is not this, my Friends, a copious Field for Exultation? A beautiful and ſolid Baſis for juſt Self-eſteem and Congratulation? Let Avarice glote upon its ſhining Heaps; let Glory nod under her blood-ſtained Plumage; let Ambition ſwell with fading Honours, while we, oh Noiblans! wiſh no greater Happineſs than an uninterrupted Poſſeſſion of our virtuous Mediocrity; which we do, and ever muſt, eſteem an inexhauſtible Source of real and invariable Felicity.

This

This Oration, pronounced with great Senſibility of Expreſſion, harmonious Cadence of Voice, and much Grace of Action, gained univerſal Applauſe from the Crowd: Nor could it fail, for tho' delivered to them in a Language which I did not underſtand, yet the Manner of it ſtruck *my* Attention deeply. Being ended, we again moved on, and in a few Minutes entered the City Gate.

CHAP. III.

Is conducted to the REQUECEX. *The* NOIBLAN *Laws; their Chief Magiſtrate, the Manner of his Election, and his executive Power deſcribed; their Marriages; the Management and Education of their Youth,* &c.

HAVING entered the City, we were met by a conſiderable Number of Perſons who joined our Proceſſion, which moved onwards to a ſpacious Square, .wherein

wherein ftood a very large Building of or-
bicular Form, into which I was conducted.
My Host was the only one who entered
the Great Hall with me; when, defiring
me to recline myfelf on a Couch while he
took Place on another, he proceeded
thus: I doubt not, Son of Earth, but
many Circumftances you will meet with
in this Aresal, or City of Nodnol, the
Capital of Noibla, will appear pecu-
liarly ftrange, perhaps inconfiftent; but I
will endeavour to explain and reconcile
the moft material as they occur.

This Building we are now in is call'd
the Requecex, or House of Justice,
where Law is difpenfed, and all Matters
of Debate, which may arife in this City,
or the Diftrict under its Jurifdiction, are
decided; but, that you may better underftand this Part of the political Conftitution, I muft fketch out a general View of
the whole.

Know

Know then that this Ifland of NOIBLA
is divided into one hundred SEITNUOCS,
or Diftricts, each under a City, and each
City under the Guidance of one Magiftrate, called the NAMREDAL, who fits one
day every TOIRTA, or Week, for adjufting fuch Complaints as may come before
him. His Direction is the Body of Laws,
drawn up in a plain concife Stile, without the Intricacy and Incumbrance of
multiplied Claufes, which ferve only to
explain away the Senfe, and diminifh the
Force of the original Defign. If at any
Time he fhould be in Doubt, he has
Power to fummon a Council of Citizens,
not exceeding twenty in Number, to affift him with their Opinions, and, from a
Decree founded on fuch Precaution, there
is no Appeal; but in Cafe the NAMREDAL
gives Judgment of himfelf, to the Dif-
fatisfaction of any Party, that Party may
claim a frefh Trial, and then Arbitrators
are fixed on in the following Manner:

The

The Appellant chufes ten Citizens, and the Judge as many; thefe vote fix, three on each Side, to determine the Caufe; if they reverfe the former Decree, and impute it to a mere Error in Judgement, the NAMREDAL is difplaced as incapable; but, if they impute it to Partiality, he is then deprived of all his Rights as a CITIZEN, and banifhed to the dreary Mountains of NEROMA. This Check upon Magifterial Authority does not abridge the Power, tho' it prevents Oppreffion; for the Magiftrate is not obliged to give his Opinion fingly, but may fhelter himfelf under the Advice of a Council, if he is in Doubt.

Once every RAYAMON, or Year, all the NAMREDALS of the ISLAND meet in this REQUECEX, and confider the general State of the Inhabitants; whatever Defects appear are regulated by them; after which fix CITIZENS from each Diftrict

C   enter

enter into a minute Inquiry of every NAMREDAL's Administration during his Year, and as they determine give him an honorary Certificate, or render him incapable of that Dignity ever after; which indeed is the only Office of Pre-eminence thro' the ISLAND, all other CITIZENS being upon an equal Footing. Nor is the Post of NAMREDAL in any Shape lucrative, Honour and Respect being the only Reward of his Labour;—he hears without Pension, and before him each Individual pleads his own Cause without Passion or Malice; his Judgments are put in Force, if any Opposition should be made, which seldom happens, by any Citizen he fixes on, who thinks himself honoured, not lessened, by giving Efficacy to Law. Hence you see his Court is not scandalized by such blood-sucking Vultures as those in your World, who, under the Appellation of Officers of Justice, commit the most violent Depredations

and

and unheard-of Cruelties upon thofe unhappy Delinquents, who are committed
to their mercilefs Talons.

Juft when my fage Inftructor had gone
thus far, I was alarmed with the tolling
of a very large Bell, which he told me
was the ELKNITAN, or BELL of NOON;
and then defired me to look into the
Square on every Side, where I perceived
a confiderable Number of young Perfons
fetting out a Kind of Tables. Expref-
fing a Curiofity to know what could be
the Meaning of this Preparation, he told
me that the City of NODNOL was divided
into twelve SENIRATS, or Wards, in
each of which was a RUVENAL, or Square,
wherein all the Inhabitants took their
SELBATAZA, or Noon-tide Meal together, without Precedence or Diftinction:
This, continues he, creates a general Intercourfe, as they alternately go from
one SENIRAT to the other; and as each

Perfon

Perfon contributes proportionably to the general Stock, conftitutional Equality and a Sufficiency are thus daily renewed and fupported.

By this Time, again looking into the RUVENAL, I faw a prodigious Number of Perfons, Men on one Side and Women on the other, fet down to a pleafing Variety of Fruits and Herbage, difpofed with much Tafte and Neatnefs; behind ftood Boys and Girls all cloathed in Green, (a Colour which the Youth wear till they are married) with fmall Veffels of Liquid, and fome other Materials, which I could not diftinguifh; thefe he told me were the Children of thofe who fat at the Tables, who, from the Age of twelve to twenty, act as public Servitors, not only to create Refpect for their Parents, but for all thofe of fuperior Years.

Here I inquired, if all prefent were married, what became of thofe who were

fingle;

single; to which he answered, That Persons in a State of Celibacy were not allowed the Honour of sitting in the Ruvenal, but remained in their own Habitations, as do also those married Couples who are not blessed with any Children.

You observe, says he, no superfluous Luxury in that Repast; no Food for Sickness; every third Day Flesh-Meat is allowed, but in a small, limited Quantity; nor are there any high Sauces to flatter palled Appetites; all plain nutritious Aliment; hence, among Noiblans, no Fevers send the Blood boiling thro' their Veins; no Palsies shake their Nerves; no Rheumatisms cramp their Bones; but, free from Disorder, by the gradual and inevitable Decays of Age alone, they drop into the Grave spontaneously, as it were, like mellow Fruit, without Fear and without Pain. Nor is this Regularity, this healthful Simplicity, all; stated Times

C 3

of

of going to Bed and rising, which are sig-
nified by Toll of Bell thro' the Island,
largely contribute to thefe falutary Effects.

How different this from the Practice
in your World, where Nature's Profufions
are exhaufted to pamper Luxury under
the fallacious Title of *Tafte*; where every
Seafon, every Climate, every Stream,
and every Ocean, is ranfacked for the
endlefs Cravings of reftlefs Mortals;
where one Half reft by Day, the other by
Night; where Multitudes fcarce ever
fee that glorious Luminary the Sun, but
deftroy their Time and Conftitutions by
the Light of artificial Glimmerings, fit
only to delude Moths and Birds of Night.

Exercife and Labour alfo contribute
much to preferve and invigorate the Noiblans; no Perfon is exempt from either;
and the Mafter of every Family is obliged

to

to give in a weekly Account how the feveral Members of it have been employed; if not to the greateſt public Advantage, he is cenſured as having failed in his Duty, and an additional Taſk is allotted for the enſuing Week; nor can a fallacious Account be rendered, as all Tranſactions here are ſo open, that the leaſt Miſreprefentation muſt be detected, than which nothing can be more ſhameful.

To all this, continues he, I doubt not you would ſay that there is pretty Speculation, ſomething well imagined in ſuch a Plan of Policy; but then how can it be reduced to Practice, without more forcible, nay, more terrifying Reſtrictions than any yet mentioned?

The Reply to this plauſible Objection, which I have ſtated in order to your further Satisfaction and Information, is obvious, conciſe, clear, and concluſive; our

Method.

Method of treating Children here is so different from that in your World, that the
Paſſions, tho' the ſame in Nature, are ſo
corrected as to become Sparks to animate
Virtue, not Flames to deſtroy it.

To effect this moſt deſirable Purpoſe,
every Child, a few Days after its Birth,
is taken from the Mother, and given to
the Care of ſome other Woman, who
may, by corrective, conſtitutional Qualifications, alter the Child's natural Defects; if he is born of a Mother cold and
phlegmatic in her Diſpoſition, he is put
to one of a ſanguine Habit; and thus the
Contraſt is obſerved in other Caſes, ſo
that a due Temparament is formed from
the earlieſt.

The next Point of Care is not to indulge any perverſe Humours, but, from
the Moment an Infant is capable of Diſtinction, to check, by Means propor-
tioned

tioned to its Feelings, every irregular, superfluous Craving; hence that Untowardness of Temper so common amongst Youth, is timely suppressed; hence are they relieved from the innumerable Cares, the endless self-created Wants, which misapplied Indulgence gives Birth to.—How grosly then are they mistaken, who call it Cruelty to curb tender Years? when nothing is more certain than that one Desire granted creates another, till the unhappy Favourite grows thoroughly miserable either by having no more to ask, or by wishing for somewhat beyond his Reach. From this Error in Parents or Guardians, arises the disagreeable Necessity of corporal Punishment, which is so oddly administered by some, that thro' Passion, not Judgment, they correct, and thro' foolish Tenderness, not prudential Regard, the very next Moment they caress and sooth the Child into a Forgetfulness of its own Fault and their Corrrection.

tion. The Abfurdity of fuch Conduct needs
no Comment; be it enough then to remark, that, to thofe who are ufed to obey
a Word, a Word will ferve; and how eafy,
how natural muft it be for them whofe
Appetites are kept within Bounds, even
without the Affiftance of Reafon, to temper their Paffions when they have not
only that fafe Guide, but Experience alfo
to affift them?

At ftated Times Youth are fent to the
SNOISSAPANS, or PUBLIC SCHOOLS;
which, like all other Employments, are
filled up without Reward, except in Exemption from other Offices and Avocations, which is a Privilege every Profeffion alfo enjoys, fo that each Perfon
knows the Sphere he is to move in, and is
folely anfwerable for his Conduct in it.

At thefe SNOISSAPANS the NOIC-
TOCS, or Mafters, inftruct their Pupils in
the Principles of Morality, the Tenets of
Religion,

Religion, social Duties, and the Laws of the ISLAND: By the three first Branches each Individual learns how to conduct himself in a private and social, and, by the last, in a political Capacity; from this Method he becomes his own Divine, his own Lawyer, his own Magistrate. Having no Commerce with any other Country, or amongst ourselves, the Arts of Trade, and consequently Fraud, are unknown with us; as to what are called in your World polite Accomplishments, they are looked upon to be useless, or rather pernicious Superfluities, since they not only engross much Time, but also afford great Occasion to Vanity.

Our Females are also sent to public Seminaries, and early taught to know and practise those Branches of Employment which suit their tender Sex; they are carefully informed of the several Duties which will be expected from them

when

when they enter the Marriage State; they are instructed to despise Spirit without Conduct, Wit without Prudence, and Beauty without Virtue; they are also taught to believe that Complaisance, Affection, and Industry, are essential to her that would obtain the amiable and exalted Character of a GOOD WIFE; they are taught, for the PUBLIC GOOD, to resign their Children to the Care of others without Reluctance, and to treat those which are committed to their Charge with all fit Attention and Tenderness; for every Woman here, when her Condition answers and Occasion requires, is, by the Law, a Nurse to the Public; by which Institution there is a Kind of relative Fondness diffused thro' Society; for, as it often happens, one Woman may nurse for a Dozen or more Families, which unites her intimately to them; at the same Time that those, who do the same endearing Office for her, are joined in the

Knot

Knot of Friendſhip: Thus a Kind of connective Chain unites all the Inhabitants of Noibla.

Here I thanked my very kind Inſtructor for explaining to me, in ſo conciſe and clear a Manner, Points of ſuch Novelty and good Senſe; at the ſame Time requeſting that, ſince we had gone thus far, he would inform me how their Marriages were negotiated, which Deſire he obligingly complied with.

No Male, ſays he, is married till he is full twenty-one Years of Age, nor Female till ſhe is nineteen; from thoſe Periods till the former reaches *thirty-ſix*, and the latter *thirty*, they unite themſelves as proves agreeable; but, if they exceed the ſtated Time in Celibacy, they are baniſhed as unworthy and unprofitable Members of Society, the Men to the Mountains of Neroma, and the Women

men to the Country of OMYRCHAL, or
the VALLEY of WEEPING.

When a Man looks upon a Female,
who muſt be at leaſt five and not more
than ten Years under his Age, he is,
when the firſt Opportunity offers, to
make his Regard known with plain
unadorned Sincerity; he is not, by any
Degree of Flattery ever ſo diſtant or delicate, to warp her Judgment, nor, by
any Preſents, to bribe her Inclination:
If ſhe is free from the Sollicitation of any
other, ſhe may give him all modeſt En-
couragement; or, on the contrary, if ſhe
happens to be engaged in any previous
Treaty, ſhe is, without Reſerve, to let
him know it, in which Caſe he muſt immediately deſiſt; but if ſhe ſhould endeavour to keep him in Suſpence, and
extend her Converſation to others at the
ſame Time, when it comes to be known
all the Parties ſhe has encouraged have
an

an equal Right to demand her; nor can she be married to any one, unless all the rest renounce their Claim.

This makes Females cautious how they commence Coquettes, and frees disinterested Love from the painful Anxieties of Suspence. On the other Side, if a Man addresses a Female, and afterwards declines to marry her, he is banished; and any Couple who chance to be convicted of cohabiting before Marriage, are not only rendered incapable of ever marrying, but are also publickly stigmatized, which prevents ill-designing Men from making, or weak Women from believing, any Promises tending to the Disgrace of one, and the Ruin of the other.

If a Couple are agreeable to each other, and none of the above-mentioned Impediments keep them asunder, the Man first, in Point of Respect, mentions it to his

own

own Parents, and then to the Woman's;
both Sides, as mutual confent is all that
is required, meet and give their Approbation; at which Time they reciprocally
queftion each other concerning the Difpofitions of their Children, conjuring
that no Failing of Body or Mind, which
they have any Knowledge of, may be
concealed. The Declaration being made
before the young Couple, they are feve-
rally afked if any Objection arifes from
what they have heard; if not, the Bride's
Father appoints the Day of Solemniza-
tion, upon the Morning of which the
Parties repair to the Notlam, where
they are queftioned by the Virgins, whether they come there actuated by a pure
and undefiled Love, not thro' the im-
pulfe of irregular Paffions: If a fincere Defire of invariable Conftancy, if a
Defign to promote each other's Happinefs, and a Refolution jointly to cultivate
the Public Good, be their real Motives
for

for coming thither; which Queſtiòns being anſwered by them in the Affirmative,
they are placed on their Knees, are each
ſprinkled thrice, and vow by the Waters
of that HOLY SPRING, to keep the cordial Affection they have profeſſed inviolate; then the BRIDE preſents a tranſ-
parent Stone, cut in Form of a Heart, to
one of the VIRGINS, that ſhe may deliver it to the Bridegroom, who returns a
counter Part, and then, laying his Hand
upon the BRIDE's Head, ſays,—*In Judge-
ment let me rule*;—ſhe, preſſing her Hand
upon his Left Breaſt, replies,—*And in
Love let me prevail.*——Here a VIRGIN,
again ſprinkling them, ſays,—*May Ferti-
lity make you honourable, and pious Children
make you glad Parents.*

So ends the Ceremony; they are then
conducted back to the Bridegroom's Father's, where a neat moderate Entertainment is provided; after which they retire

D

to a lonely but moſt pleaſant rural Spot, called Zamela, or the Plain of Modesty, about ten Silcars, or Miles, from the City, and there live two Reapans, or Months, in Privacy; it being deemed inconſiſtent, with juſt Reſerve, for a Female to appear publickly in leſs Time after ſo ſerious and important a Change of Condition.

As Intereſt and the Influence of Parents have no Concern in theſe Marriages, it is no Matter of Surprize to find them happy; beſides, as it would be impoſſible, from the Method of living all over Noibla, to conceal any Coldneſs or Diſagreement, either of which renders the Parties highly contemptible to Society, if Love, by any extraordinary Chance, ſhould fail, the Fear of Reproach keeps up at leaſt an apparent Cordiality and Decency, which prevents the bad Influence of their Example, and reſtrains them from ſuch irrational

rational and unnatural Extremities of domestic Warfare, as you have seen among many Couples in your World.

Struck with the Ease, Simplicity, and Propriety of these Customs, I could not help breaking out into a Kind of extatic Approbation; happy, thrice happy NOI-BLANS, said I, on whom Happiness sheds her kindest Influence, how must I feel, in a comparative View, for my Brothers of the Terrestrial Globe, whose Inclinations, Devices, and Pursuits, are almost at continual Variance with Content; who live as if they were merely framed to torment themselves, or could find their own Repose only in disturbing Society; born with perplexing Appetites, nursed into tyrannical Passions, and ripening by confirmed Years in Disquiet; while Reason, dethron'd and enslav'd, becomes a base Procurer to the debauch'd Imagination, and servilely ministers where it should command.

D 2   Here

Here the great Bell again tolling interrupted my Reflection, and a Train of Remarks we fhould poffibly have made on this Subject.

C H A P. IV.

The NAMREDAL'*s Manner of dining; his Account of himfelf, and many other remarkable Perfonages tranflated from Earth; with their feveral Deftinations in the* LUNAR WORLD.

THE NAMREDAL, for fuch I found my kind Inftructor to be, here remarked that I fhould fhortly fee the higheft Mark of Diftinction that is ever paid in NOIBLA; for, fays he, the Chief Magiftrate, to fupport Dignity and gain Influence, dines alone in this Hall, and is attended by a certain Number of Citizens, who pay the Compliment in fuch

Ro-

Rotation, that each appears in that Station once a Year.

Here, being informed that Dinner was approaching, we retir'd into a neighbouring Chamber till the Provision was disposed according to Custom; which done, we return'd, and found a large Table supplied with very elegant Simplicity; a Number of respectable Persons appeared in Waiting on each Side, who all, tho' personally and intimately acquainted with the Chief Magistrate, paid as distant and humble a Respect, as if they had been no more than hired Servants. Not being used to a Circumstance of this Kind, I was in some Degree of Confusion at the extraordinary Honour offered me of sitting at the Table; which the NAMREDAL perceiving, he gently rebuked my Diffidence, and placed me near himself. Immediately after this a venerable Person, cloathed in a long flame-colour'd Gar-

D 3   ment,

ment, whom I found to be an AVOZEN,
or Prieft, with very awful and emphatic
Deliberation, fpoke thefe Words :

Fountain of Life, great and incomprehen-
fible Difpenfer of all Things effential to Hap-
pinefs here and hereafter, give to thefe Vi-
ands fuch falutary Effects, that they may che-
rifh and invigorate, not corrupt and impair,
the humble Receivers, who gladly praife thy
Name, and confidently reft every Hope in
thee.

Perceiving fome Difhes prepared in our
Manner, and juftly imagining they were
defigned for me, I help'd myfelf without
Referve, while the NAMREDAL confined
himfelf to a Sort of Pulfe and Vegetables,
mingled fomewhat in the Manner of our
Sallads, and moiftened with an aromatic
Liquid, called AZONIA. During the
Time of Dinner not a Word was uttered,
it being held indecent by the NOIBLANS
to

to converſe at Meal-Times, till Thanks
are rendered, and they have rinſed their
Mouths thrice with Water from the Not-
LAM.

Having given a Sign that our Appetites were ſatisfied, the Table was uncovered with the greateſt Regularity and
Expedition imaginable; when a Deſert of
various Fruits appeared, ſeveral of which
I taſted, and found them to the Palate as
much ſuperior in Richneſs and Flavour,
as to the Sight they appeared more
tempting than any which grow in our ſublunary Sphere. At the ſame Time there
was placed before us two Chryſtal Veſſels,
in Form of wreathed Snakes, containing
a Fluid of the pureſt Green I ever ſaw,
and fermenting with yellow Sparkles,
which appeared at firſt ſo like the ſhining
of a Serpent's ſcaly Skin, that I was rather ſtartled; but ſeeing the NAMREDAL
put his own Mouth to his, placing his
Hand

Hand to his Breaſt, and bowing reſpect-
fully round, I did the ſame; at which all
in Waiting ſet their Left Knees on the
Ground, and, leaning their Foreheads on
their folded Hands, remained ſo till the
NAMREDAL had finiſhed his Draught;
when inſtantly a numerous Band of Muſic gave Voice to their Inſtruments, and
play'd about five Minutes, during which
the AVOZEN preſented us·with Water;
and, having purified ourſelves, he with
his Right Hand on the NAMREDAL's
Head, and his Left upon mine, ſpoke to
the following Effect:

Moſt venerable Father of NODNOL, *Dele-*
gate of our univerſal Parent, and thou
highly-favoured Terreſtrial, be thankful for
paſt Bleſſings, and piouſly induſtrious to de-
ſerve future; nor hold ſuch Indulgences in
leſs Eſtimation and Gratitude, becauſe they
are daily conferred, than if they were admi-
niſter'd with a more ſparing Hand; ſtill re-
member

*member that, without the conſtant Support
and Direction of an unſeen Almighty Arm,
thoſe nor we; this Iſland, the lower Globe,
nor that great Maſs of Fire which cheriſhes
the whole with animating Heat; nor the
reſt of the celeſtial Orbs; nor that immenſe
Firmament thro' which they roll, could exiſt;
but, ruſhing into Anarchy and elemental War,
muſt crumble into nothing.——Remember alſo that the external Purification of Limbs is
no farther uſeful than as an emblematical
Remembrance of that Purification which
your Hearts hourly require.*

This Ceremony being concluded, the
Avozen and all the attending Citizens
retired. Being once more by ourſelves,
the Namredal reſumed Converſation
as follows :

Brother of the nether Globe, it is now
Time I ſhould let you know ſome Particulars, which have at leaſt Novelty to recommend

commend them to your Attention: Know
then that I was once an Inhabitant of
Earth, of that Part of it too which you
come from, and I doubt not but my
Name is familiar to you, few Perfons having made a greater Noife in the Field of
Speculation than Bifhop WILKINS:
Roufed by the Name, I begged Leave,
if not inconfiftent with his prefent Dignity, to embrace him as a near Relation
of the LUNATIC Family; which Requeft
he moft kindly admitted, and declared
himfelf doubly happy in finding not only
a Countryman in me but a Kinfman alfo.

Tho' to all Appearance I died, continued he, and was laid in Earth with the
ufual Solemnity, yet the ftrict, unwearied Attention I had paid to the LUNAR
WORLD, obtained me a Tranflation to
this happy Spot, where I have continued
ever fince in Eafe and Refpect, without
a Wifh to gratify, a Fear to perplex, or
any

any visible Decay. How long I may be
permitted to remain, is just as doubtful
as my Existence in the other World was,
because it is self-evident that all Beings
are in a continual State of Rotation, till
a general Consummation of the vast and
impenetrable Scheme of Creation dis-
solves all perishable Matter, and unites
the whole in one wide Field of incorrup-
tible Felicity.

Here my Curiosity led me to inquire
if there were any more earthly Inhabitants, or if he alone was thus highly favoured: To which he replied, that there
were great Numbers scatter'd thro' the
Moon, and that NOIBLA had a considerable Share. Most Men, says he, remarkable for either GOOD or EVIL, are translated to some Part of the LUNAR REGIONS,
as Natives of this World also are, in Return, occasionally transferred to yours.

I

I fhall mention a few of thofe at prefent in NODNOL, beginning with ALEXANDER and DARIUS; who, barring fome occafional Debates upon their former Quarrels, now live in a State of the moft perfect Friendfhip. CÆSAR and POMPEY alfo live together here upon much the fame Terms; CATO too appears amongft us, but retains fo much of felfifh Pride and Stoicifm, that he has very little Communion with others; like them, however, he is obliged to comply with the Laws of Equality prefcribed here, where there is no Diftinction, and only indulges his Pride in private.

Thofe Perfonages, you will allow, who fought after unreasonable Pre-eminence over their Fellow-Creatures in a State of former Exiftence, are juftly excluded from Naturalization and the Dignity of Magiftracy in NOIBLA. BRUTUS, but for his Ingratitude to his warmeft Friend

and

and reputed Father, would have been here, and well received; however, as that is deemed the deepeft Stain upon the human heart, he was excluded from this mild Region, and doom'd to the poor and turbulent Country of ERISHNOVER, or MOUNTAINS of BLOOD, where his gentle, humane, philofophic Difpofition renders him contemptible to others, and painful to himfelf.

We have PETER the GREAT of MUScovy, and the TWELFTH CHARLES of SWEDEN; HENRY the EIGHTH, Queen ELIZABETH, OLIVER CROMWELL, and CHARLES the SECOND of ENGLAND: LEWIS the FOURTEENTH of FRANCE, Cardinal WOLSEY, CECIL Lord BURLEIGH, and many others which it would be too tedious to mention.

Taking Occafion to remark that, among the Perfonages named, there was

a

a great Variety of Characters, and defiring
to know with what Propriety they could
be fent to the fame Spot, the NAMREDAL
fatisfied me as follows.:

The feveral Perfons fpoken of, fays
he, retain a confiderable Share of thofe
Paffions which prevailed in them on
Earth; and, according as they were
meritorious or culpable, are punifhed or
rewarded here; not by corporal or external Recompences, but by the Pleafures
and Pains of the Mind, which they experience in a moft fenfible Degree; a Perfection which I take to be in great Mea-
fure derived, on the one Hand, from a
comparative View of that unchanging Serenity they fee conftantly around them,
yet cannot themfelves enjoy; or, on the
other Hand, from a confcious Rectitude,
which makes them Partakers in that
Tranquillity.

That

That you may the better underftand me, and more clearly conceive how generally and impartially Juftice is adminifter'd thro' the Univerfe, I will fketch out the feveral Characters.

Alexander the Great, and Charles the Twelfth, his mad Admirer, were, as Hiftory has informed you, rapacious and unbounded in their Ambition; an enthufiaftic Devotion to the Phantom or Shade of Glory, for the Subftance can never be gained by lawlefs Principles, had extinguifhed every Spark of general Humanity in the Breafts of thefe Royal Plunderers; like Peftilence and Famine they waked but to deftroy; like Earthquakes they fhook and fwallowed up whole Nations; pale Defolation, with the red Right Arm of War, bore their Standards; infatiate Death nodded in grim Smiles upon their Helmets; and the devouring Grave yawned wide in all their Councils; in vain
the

the Groans of Widows, the Cries of Orphans, and the Wreck of Kingdoms, ſtruck their Eyes and Ears; fortified, the one by his Ambition, the other by his Cruelty, againſt all humane and tender Sentiments, they ran the Race of Deſtruction, till at laſt they themſelves fell Sacrifices to the Violence and Inconſiſtency of their Natures; at which Period they were tranſlated hither, with what Fitneſs you ſhall judge.

As a Thirſt of unlimited Power was the ruling Principle of their Lives; as Turbulence and the Diſtreſſes of Multitudes were their chief Enjoyments, they have been ſentenced to this Region of Peace; wherein, retaining their former rapacious Inclinations, they are tormented with a conſtant Deſire of Rule and Precedency, which they can by no Means obtain; and labour under hourly Diſappointments of thoſe Plans they are con-

ſtantly

ſtantly framing to kindle Diſcord and create Confuſion: Beſides which, ALEX-ANDER's Pride has the Mortification of being obliged, once each Week, to attend upon DARIUS as a menial Servitor; however, on Account of his generous and delicate Behaviour to the Females of that Monarch's Family, this Part of his painful Situation is rendered as eaſy as poſſible, while the hot-brained CHARLES is doomed to a daily unremitted Attendance upon the Czar PETER; which magnanimous Monarch, in return of his unwearied Attention and patriot Care to the Improvement of ſo great and uncultivated an Empire as he reigned over, not only enjoys every Privilege of a natural-born NOIBLAN, but, ſince his Arrival here, has alſo been three Times choſen NAMREDAL of this City by general Suffrage, and has as often been rewarded, for his worthy Exerciſe of that Office, with the moſt unlimited Approbation.

E   CÆSAR,

CÆSAR, as a generous, humane Conqueror, of an open, confident, and unsuspicious Nature, who being above Treachery himself saw it not in others, is held in considerable Esteem; but as he was the chief Cause of reducing his Country first under dictatorial and afterwards under imperial Power, he is not allowed to rank as a CITIZEN; yet his first Steps proceeding rather from the Principle of Self-defence than of Ambition, he is as much indulged as possible; while his Antagonist POMPEY, whose selfish, stubborn Pride was the Cause of subverting that LIBERTY he pretended to support, is placed in a much inferior Station, entirely dependent upon CÆSAR's Interposition for any Advantge he may desire: As to CATO, he passes his Time in a Kind of contemptible Solitude, branded with the indelible Stigma of having fled like a Coward from his Country when she most needed his Help, by

an

an unjuftifiable and ignominious Suicide ;
a Step fo mean and culpable, that, were
it not for the Counterbalance of many
private Virtues he poffeffed, his Doom
would have been much more fevere. I
had almoft forgot to tell you that MARC
ANTONY is here, as fond of Gaiety as
ever; but labours under the Inconvenience of being obliged to wear a Moppet
hung round his Neck, as a Mark of his
Folly in lofing the World for a worthlefs
Woman.

HENRY the EIGHTH has brought
with him hither all his Spirit of RELI-
GIOUS REFORMATION; it ftill remains fo
active and impetuous, that he never lets
our AVOZENS alone; who hear him indeed, but as often laugh at the vain Efforts of Innovation, to the no fmall Mortification of his Pride : He is alfo equally
amorous, without being able to gain the
Efteem of any one Female, or any Reply
to his Addreffes, except the Recapitula-

E 2

tion

tion of his Behaviour to thofe Wives whom he treated with fo much Cruelty on Earth : Befides which, that he may be the better known and more defpifed, he is once a Month carried thro' the City, at certain Parts whereof the following No-tification is fet forth :

Behold, ye NOIBLANS, *a* MONSTER, *who, while in Power, the Father of a gene-rous, brave, and free People, facrificed every Confideration, all nobler Principles, to Luft and Pride, making even Religion a Party in his abominable Schemes, whom neither hallowed Shrines, nor the tender and melting Tye of Beauty, could reftrain from Depre-dations and Cruelties.*

His Daughter ELIZABETH, for many great and eminent Qualities, is allowed Precedence of all Females in NODNOL, and would have been once chofen to the Magiftracy ; but the Caprice of having
facrificed

facrificed a Favourite to ill-grounded Rè-
fentment or Jealoufy, and the Cruelty of
having even agreed to the Execution of
fo amiable a Princefs as her Sifter of
SCOTLAND, were univerfally allowed to
be fuch Blemifhes in Charaƈter as rendered her unfit for the Dignity fhe follicited.
This Difappointment fo rankles in her
Breaft, that fhe is often heard to figh
deeply, and to exclaim, *Ob* ESSEX! *Ob*
MARY! *not content with having fix'd a
dead and painful Load upon my Heart while
in the lower World, do you purfue and haunt
me here to imbitter the Happinefs, difturb
the Peace, and prevent the Honour I might
enjoy? Muft your Blood ftain and cloud my
Charaƈter? Muft your Groans filence the
Voice of Fame?* Thus does fhe often be-
wail herfelf: So deep, fo lafting, and fo
powerful are the Stings of Confcience;
which, far outftretching the Wounds of
human Weapons, prolong their Pains to
Immortality.

E 3   OLIVER.

OLIVER CROMWELL, who next appears in View, ever since his Arrival had been endeavouring to obtain the Naturalization and Government of the City; full of the same Hypocrify which led him to the PROTECTORSHIP of ENGLAND; Master of the same infinuating Arts of Popularity, he had endeavour'd to recommend himfelf as an implicit, ftrict, and zealous Admirer of the Laws, both Religious and Political. Under this agreeable Semblance many began to look on him with a favourable Eye, efpecially as he had in a moft plaufible Manner painted himfelf as the Affertor of LIBERTY; and to the Charge of having been a Regicide, offered the following Vindication :

" I ftand before you, Oh NOIBLANS, to claim the Privileges of a CITIZEN; one only Objection you feem to make, the Fate of an unhappy Monarch, which has been chiefly attributed to me; but let me affert,

affert, and that with the ſtricteſt Truth, that CHARLES, thro' Obſtinacy and the Advice of evil Counſellors, fell a Sacrifice to the ungovernable Rage of a Nation highly and juſtly incenſed ; not, as Heaven is my Witneſs, thro' any ambitious Views or ſiniſter Influence of mine. Make the Caſe your own, Oh NOIBLANS ; ſuppoſe this ISLAND of the ſame political Conſtitution as ENGLAND ; that you had ſeen every Right infringed ; that you had traced Royal Prerogative advancing with gigantic Strides, and cruſhing LIBERTY on every Side ; would you not have felt? Would you not have ſpoke ? And, finding Remonſtances fail, would you not have rouſed Force to vindicate yourſelves? Does Reaſon or Law exempt any Man from Examination, or ſecure him in Oppreſſion, becauſe Chance makes him Heir to Regal Dignity ? Would you, like paſſive and defenceleſs Lambs, tamely wait till the ravening Wolf leap'd the Fold

and

and revelled in your deareſt Blood ? Your
happy Frame of Government knows not
ſuch Convulſions, and may it never know
them ; yet Imagination may awake your
Feelings and inform your Judgment. If
Self-defence be the firſt great Law of
Nature, is it not full as juſtifiable in a
Nation as in an Individual? And if ſo,
muſt there not be ſome Conductors, who,
like Sinews in the human Body, may brace
and give Strength to the Body Politic ?
In this Capacity it pleaſed Providence to
place me ; and, for many Years, much
againſt my natural Diſpoſition, I toiled
thro' Fatigues and Blood, not only en-
countering the Hazards of War, but alſo
the greater and more ſure working Danger of numberleſs Snares laid for my
Life, both by declared and ſecret Enemies ; who, not having Ability or Fortune to ſerve their Country ſo effectually,
wiſhed to remove me as the chief Ob-
ſtacle in the Way of their Pride.

Thro'

"Thro' all this I ſtruggled with unaba-
ting Conſtancy: Was it for me ſingly to
ſtand againſt Juſtice and popular Rage,
nay, againſt my own Conſcience too, in
Favour of CHARLES? I know it has been
ſaid that his Exile or Impriſonment would
have been more eligible than his Death;
yet to me either Alternative ſeems cruel
or wretched: Admitting he was a GOOD
MAN, but a BAD KING, which his moſt
ſanguine Friends have allowed; was it
not more humane, and more conſiſtent
with his Dignity, to remove him from the
Turbulence of this Life by momentary
Pain, than to keep him in a lingering
State of Captivity, or force him into foreign Climates, a poor and miſerable Dependent? But why, it may be ſaid, if a
GOOD MAN, ſhould he be removed at all?
Nothing can be more obvious than that
public and private Virtues are widely
different; the narrow Sphere of one can
never be extended to the wide Expanſion of
the

the other. Intention may be good, Execution bad; and as, in the natural Body, Reason directs us to part with the dearest Limb, however valuable and essential, if it threatens Corruption to the whole; so, in the political one, any Member, whose Life must inevitably be the Source of Contentions should be cut off: This being an indispensible Necessity, why should those who effect the Separation be more blamed than a Surgeon is for an Amputation? In this Light only my Adherence to the common Cause is to be considered; and surely my Administration, which was crowned not only with Respect, but Terror abroad, and national Happiness at home, must sufficiently prove that I acted upon such Principles, and such only; but arduous and precarious is every public Undertaking, however disinterested, however perilous, Envy lies in wait with her invenomed Tooth, and Slander with her poison-dropping Tongue; however

here,

here, where neither the one nor the other has any Exiſtence, I preſume this plain, unadorned, and unſtudied Apology for the ſole Objection that is urged againſt me, will be ſufficient to ſet your Suffrages at Liberty; which, if I did not mean to deſerve, I never would ſollicit."

Already prepared as they were, this Harangue conſiderably prejudiced the CITIZENS in his Favour, when CHARLES the SECOND produced a Paper, which CROMWELL could not deny to be his Hand-Writing, containing a Scheme for bringing the ISLAND of NOIBLA under monarchical Government. This raiſed ſo much Indignation againſt him, that he was immediately appointed to the ſervile Office of SOLARMAN, or COMMON CRYER, which he fills up with infinite Diſguſt.

The

The SECOND CHARLES, who, in his terreſtrial State, was remarkable for nothing but Libertiniſm, and a Diſregard of Religion, is, in Return, chained, as I may ſay, to the painful Office of RANEVER in one of our TEMPLES, a Place ſomewhat ſimilar to that of a VERGER; by which he is obliged to attend Devotion at leaſt four Times each Day, and is alſo totally debarred from the Converſe of Women, for whom he has as great a Paſſion as formerly when he was King.

There is not a Perſonage in NOIBLA that is in a more painful or ridiculous Situation than LEWIS the FOURTEENTH of FRANCE; Oſtentation having been his Idol, he is reduced to a more obſcure and penurious Appearance than any other in NOIBLA, under which he labours to maintain all his former Dignity; but having no Sycophants near to blazon his Praiſe, he writes miſerable Sonnets upon himſelf;

goes

goes about building Things he calls triumphal Arches, and Memorials of Victories; while CÆSAR, in PARTICULAR, laughs at his Folly, and ALEXANDER following, kicks down the frail Baby-houses of his Pride as fast as he raises them; but his heaviest Grievance is, that among the numberless Relations he makes of his own and the *French* Greatness, not one meets with Credit; it being well known that while a King, Truth and Faith were two Points he never regarded, when Pride and Ambition came into the opposite Scale.

WOLSEY, that puffed-up Mushroom of Fortune, in Return of his most exorbitant Insolence, is here reduced to the Office of keeping the RUVENAL; that is, sweeping it every Day, and tolling the ELKNITAN before the Citizens dine.

BURLEIGH,

BURLEIGH, as a faithful Minister, who consulted and held an exact Equilibrium between the Dignity of his Royal Mistress and the Liberty of his Countrymen, is naturalized, and generally makes one of the Council that are chosen to assist the NAMREDAL, upon dubious or intricate Occasions.

Thus I have sketched out some of the many remarkable Personages which are in this Capital; and I am persuaded their several Destinations will be thought just.

Here I expressed great Pleasure and Gratitude to the NAMREDAL upon this Relation, and begged Leave to ask him concerning some Persons who occured to my Recollection; he kindly desiring me to give full Scope to my Curiosity, I proceeded, and he replied, as will be found in the following Chapter.

C H A P.

CHAP. V.

Containing Strictures upon the Freedom of
AUTHORS *and the* PRESS; *a prevailing*
Sect in Religion considered; the Stations
of several of the Literati transferred from
EARTH *to the* MOON *considered.*

YOU ask me, says the NAMREDAL,
if none of the Tribe of AUTHORS
have gained Admittance here?—Yes.—
Many. For Genius is highly admired,
Laudatur et Alget is not the Case in NOI-
BLA; their Possessions are equal to any
CITIZEN's; wherefore, not having Poverty to chill, nor Perplexity to trammel it,
Fancy takes a full, unbounded Scope;
and as all write for Praise, none for Hire,
the Quality, and not the Quantity of
Things written is regarded; this prevents
the Subject from being soon thread-bare,
and relieves the AUTHOR from the disagreeable Necessity of being, like a Post-
Horse,

Horfe, obliged to drudge to a particular
Spot, wearied or not.

Every Writer being at full Liberty to
chufe his Subject, and not at all depend-
ing upon the Sale of his Book, is free
from any Obligation of flattering popular
Paffions; he thinks according to his Judgment, and honeftly writes as he thinks;
he need not, for the Support of Nature,
fcatter infectious Sentiments among the
People, to the great Prejudice of Morality, as was remarkably the Cafe upon
Earth when I was there. Anfwer me,
Have you not ftill the Vermin amongft
you who produce, and worfe Vermin who
love to feaft upon, fuch poifonous Materials?

Yes, venerable Sir, fays I, we certainly
have, tho', to the Praife of ENGLAND be
it fpoken, VIRTUE was never more feldom put to the Blufh than at prefent.
Our

Our Authors, for the moſt Part, want
Fancy, but their Sentiments are chaſte;
nor do I think this Merit owing to their
Integrity, ſo much as to the Public Opinion, which happily rejects and ſeverely
condemns licentious Productions, I mean
In the Works of mere Entertainment:
Indeed, as to Religion and Politics,
tho' we have leſs to complain of, and
more to admire in both than any other
Nation, yet they are in general treated
with great Freedom, and ſometimes with
much Scurrility, under the ſpecious Veil
of Liberty; a Word more admired,
more uſed, and more abuſed in Britain,
than in any Part of the Globe beſides:
However, as thoſe Convulſions which
ſometimes take Place in the general Conſtitution of Nature, ſuch as Tempeſts,
Earthquakes, &c. ſtrengthen and preſerve the whole, tho' they create Fear
and ſpread Deſtruction in particular
Spots; ſo watchful and turbulent Spirits

F

are

are effential to a Free State, to intimidate
and detect bad Statefmen, who may be
crawling, with the flow and fubtle Steps
of Snake-like Policy, to unwarrantable
Lengths. But it may be faid thofe loud-
tongued Guardians of Freedom are for
the moft Part defigning Men, of venal
Difpofitions; no Matter what their Views
may be, if they fet forth feafonable
Truths;—as to the Inconvenience real
Patriots may labour under from ground-
lefs and malicious Cenfure; it is an unavoidable Tax upon Office, yet of trifling
Importance; like the Babbling of an un-
ftaunch Hound, it may caufe the Pack
to open, but it cannot lead them far upon a falfe Scent; and however ftrong the
Web of Deceit may be wrought, Facts
are too ftubborn to be confined by it.
Hence the LIBERTY of the PRESS, however it may be abufed, (and no human Inftitution is perfect) ought to be moft carefully preferved, as an unreferved Monitor

to

to KING, STATESMEN, and PEOPLE:
Hence it is that BRITISH MONARCHS,
if they will but read, have an Advantage
above all others in regard of popular
Grievances; and hence is it also that
STATESMEN may be corrected in their
Blunders, or chastised for their Villany.
Conscious Honesty, founded on a Rock,
can weather the fiercest Gales of Faction; and I believe it is an irrefragable
Truth, that of all the Revolutions which
have taken Place among civilized Go-
vernments, there is scarce one to be produced, however wantonly it might be
carried on, but what was originally founded on Right. If an Administration, thro'
Obstinacy or ill Designs, will not hear and
redress the Grievances of a People, 'tis
not at all surprizing that the many-head-
ed Monster, once enraged and broken
loose, should subvert all Order, tread upon all Law, and mark its ruinous Steps
with Blood.

F 2   Most

Moſt Nations, Free ones eſpecially, ſhould be dealt with like a ſpirited Horſe, whom a judicious Rider will keep ſteady, by maintaining an exact Balance in his Seat, ſhewing neither Fear nor Cruelty, occaſionally giving and checking the Rein, while he prudently and reſolutely corrects with the Spur, or kindly blandiſhes with his Hand.

Your Obſervations, my dear Countryman, ſays the NAMREDAL, are perfectly juſt, and may the great Barrier of Freedom you have mentioned guard BRITAIN to the End of Time; may no Pretext of inſulted Dignity, no Artifice of Power, ever circumſcribe its Liberties.—How do I rejoice to hear that Modeſty finds public Protection; this is indeed a glorious and eſſential Limitation; but what am I to think of thoſe Attacks, ſometimes groſs ones you ſay, which are made upon Religion? Do they not appear

pear of a moſt irrational, pernicious, and criminal Nature? Does not the Breath of Infidelity go forth like a two-edged Sword to deſtroy? Does it not, like peſtilential Air, blaſt the rich Harveſt of future Hopes? Does it not intoxicate with chimerical Reaſonings and ſophiſtical Diſtinctions, which, like an *Ignis fatuus* in the Night, ſhoot forth deluſive Beams to miſlead the unwary Follower?

Such Effects, ſage NAMREDAL, ſays I, may undoubtedly be feared; and the more, as ſome Perſons of eminent Abilities have aſſiduouſly laboured in theſe Works of Perverſion; yet ſtill I comfort myſelf with Hope that the grand, uniform, and beautiful Fabric of RELIGION, framed by an Almighty Founder, can never be endangered by the Blaſts of Envy: Indeed its external Charms may be ſomewhat obſcured, its Purity defiled by occaſional Filth, with which its Ene-

F 3 mies

mies befpatter it; but, felf-exiftent, it ftands above the vain Efforts of Libertinifm, and, like the ERMIN, foon frees itfelf from all the Stains of Pollution.

If its Minifters were but half fo affiduous to fupport it as its Enemies are to pull it down, its Dignity would eafily be maintained: Neither Virtue, Courage, Wifdom, nor any Qualification, is known without Trial; almoft any one may fteer a Ship in a Calm, but Shoals, Rocks, and tempeftuous Seas prove the able Mariner; wherefore the Oppofers of RELIGION feem a Kind of providential Inftruments to aid and improve its Strength. From open Attacks it is in very little Danger; but there are unnatural Bofom-Foes, who, having got a Place in the TEMPLE, by the Flames of Enthufiafm endeavour to deftroy it; or, thro' the Incongruity of Zeal, heap difproportionate Additions upon the Edifice, till it becomes deformed

ed to the Sight, and ſo very tottering,
that the ſlighteſt Breath of rational Inquiry ſhakes it from the Foundation.

Here is the Danger to be feared and
lamented; yet ſo very gentle and paſſive are our PASTORS in general, that
they ſuffer Sheep-clothed Wolves to enter their Folds and devour their Flocks:
Nay, the Madneſs or Knavery has reached ſome of *themſelves*; ſeveral who ſhould
be its Guardians have joined this deſtructive Crew, and that not only with
Impunity from their Superiors, but with
the Character of Saints from the People.
I myſelf knew a Clergyman in that Part
of ENGLAND call'd YORKSHIRE, who,
while he uſed the common uniform Method of inſtructing his own Congregation, was no more thought of than any
neighbouring Gownſman; but being once
characterized as the Favourer of an en-
thuſiaſtic, and I fear hypocritical, Sect,
and

and purfuing their itinerant Method of preaching from Place to Place, his Influence fo far increafed, that he could draw People a Dozen or Twenty Miles to hear his *infpired* Doctrine.—Amazing Infatuation of the giddy Multitude! that a Man muft lofe his Senfes or his Honefty to pleafe them; that Madnefs or Hypocrify fhould prevail more than truly orthodox Principles, or clear and folid Reafon!

Aye, replies the Namredal! Is it even fo? You have then indeed rightly pointed out the real Danger, and I am particularly concerned at your Charge of Indolence againft fo many of the Holy Brotherhood; undoubtedly if they would fet ferioufly to work; if in their Preaching they would fpeak as much from the Heart, with as much Feeling as thofe Innovators *feem* to do; having found Doctrine, fit Morals, impartial Reafon, and eftablifh'd Authority, they muft foon root out,

out, by *Conviction*, such noxious Weeds as produce nothing but false Zeal, unintelligible Speculation, and rambling Exclamations, which extort, from Weakness and Ignorance, Astonishment, Tears, and Groans; while moral and social Virtues are swallowed up in a Chaos of ill-regulated Faith and uneffential Melancholy; the first of which audaciously prompts them to believe themselves Saints, and the latter, in a great Measure, renders them unfit for the reasonable and necessary Pursuit of their worldly Concerns.

Is it not wonderful, continues he, that in the most important as well as the most trifling Concerns of Life, Persons in the nether Globe are led by Ostentation? That notwithstanding multiplied Instances of pretending PATRIOTS making a snug Retreat under the Shelter of Places, Pensions, or Titles, and being as it were miraculously struck dumb, any Man, by the

the self-same Steps, shall become a popular Favourite, and be looked on as the Shield of LIBERTY, to ward off the Encroachments of Power? Is it not equally astonishing that in RELIGION also, tho' they are warned of false Teachers, every vociferous Fanatic or sanctified Hypocrite can mislead the Multitude? Who like him best who has the greatest Volubility of Tongue, whose Speech is the loudest and most impetuous, and finds most Fault with established Principles or Customs? But what surpasses all Imagination, is, how the most illiterate Upstarts can gain this Influence; Wretches who impudently boast of Ignorance as an Apostolic Recommendation. — Oh Hypocrisy!—Oh Novelty! How powerful are thy Charms! Before them Reason flies an Exile; or, turning Suicide, effects her own Destruction.

Here

Here, imagining that we had gone far enough upon this Subject, which, minutely confidered, would have led us into inextricable Prolixity, and that, after our utmoſt Endeavours, we could contribute little more than our Wiſhes to prevent or to amend, I returned to my Inquiry concerning Authors, and the Namredal proceeded to give me the following Account; confining himſelf, for Brevity's Sake, as he obſerved, to the moſt remarkable of the antient Claſſics, and the moſt diſtinguiſhed English Writers:

Homer, ſays he, preſides over Epic Poetry in Nodnol, aſſiſted by Virgil and Milton, who each conteſted Superiority with him; but, upon a fair Debate, were obliged to yield, he having made it plainly appear that his Plan and moſt of his Thoughts were original; that he had Recourſe only to his own Genius and Judgment, while his Competitors had

had the advantageous Example of his Labours; that tho' the MANTUAN was more correct and uniform, yet he excelled in Imagery and Characters; also that the BRITON's boasted ANGELS and DEVILS were but an Improvement upon his GODS and GODDESSES, drawn from a more copious, striking, and elevated Syſtem of Religion. Upon this approved Superiority he was, by univerſal Suffrage, allowed Precedence; of which however, in Compliment to the great Abilities of his two Brothers, he makes very little Uſe. Since his Arrival he has produced a Work of infinite Merit, call'd the ALEXANDRIAD, as a grateful Compliment to that Prince for the great Eſteem he ſhewed, while on Earth, for his Works and Memory.

HORACE, whom we have here alſo, and is reckoned a ſpirited ſocial Companion, is appointed to write an ODE to

each

each new NAMREDAL; wherein he muſt not, as is uſual in your BIRTH-DAY ODES, idolize the Magiſtrate, but point out and celebrate thoſe Virtues which may render him worthy of his Dignity.

JUVENAL, who poſſeſſes his former *Cacoethes ſcribendi*, with a Pen dipp'd in Gall, ſince we have no Vices amongſt us, cannot indulge his Spleen with brandiſhing the Iron Rod of Satire; but, as a Puniſhment for having uſed it unmercifully in the other World, he is obliged to write Panegyrics upon CÆSAR, who deſpiſes them; and is doomed to ſee Pleaſantry ſmile around, while he, unheeded, ſnarles and mumbles Diſcontent between his Teeth.

BACON, LOCKE, and NEWTON are veſted with the Superintendance of all Philoſophical Tranſactions, having ſucceeded as more general, and therefore more

more capable, to SOCRATES, PLATO, and SENECA. The STAGYRITE pleaded hard for Admittance, and his Abilities were complimented with eminent Approbation; but the irrational Action of drowning himself counterbalanced all Merit, and reduced him to the Necessity of being ASSELAN, or Usher, to NEWTON.——SHAFTESBURY also, with an Air of much Pertness and Importance, offered himself a Candidate; but was totally rejected for self-sufficient Peculiarity, and a restless Spirit of introducing his own chimerical Notions, to the Prejudice of established and well-grounded Opinions.

TACITUS and CLARENDON preside over History. My Brother Bishop BURNET would gladly have been their Co-adjutor; but being convicted of gross Misrepresentations and shameful Falsities in the *History of his own Times*, he was peremptorily refused, and obliged to

compound

compound for the Place of Amanuenfis
to CLARENDON; in which Capacity TA-
CITUS is ferved by QUINTUS CURTIUS,
who having been ufed to write nothing
but Romance and Flattery, feels infinite
Pain at being obliged to tranfcribe ufeful Maxims and Facts faithfully related,
without the Liberty to add one Flourifh
of his own exuberant Imagination.

Over the DRAMA SHAKESPEAR fits Supreme, and is dignified with the Title of
ANGAM ARUTAN, or Delineator of Nature. Here, as in his former State of
Exiftence, he furnifhes our ESTRALAM,
or THEATRE, with the moft celebrated
Pieces exhibited amongft us; while RY-
MER, and fome other carping Critics, who
fnarled at Beauties they could not comprehend, are obliged to clean his Shoes
alternately, as a Mark of their Subjection.

DRYDEN

DRYDEN, LEE, and OTWAY contribute also to the public Amufement, as well as feveral naturalized NOIBLANS. Thofe admitted to the Clafs of POETS are dignified by a Laurel Crown; but DRYDEN, as a Mark of his unfteady Principles, both in Religion and Politics, is obliged to wear a Weathercock alfo on his Head. LEE appears with a chained Maniac, Emblem of his Frenzy; and OTWAY is diftinguifhed by a Roll, pointing out his Fate on *Tower-Hill*, and ftanding as a Memorial of the Prodigality which brought him to that wretched End.

Not having heard any Mention of BEN JOHNSON or POPE, I afked the NAMREDAL if they were in NÓDNOL; the former, fays he, is not, but the latter is. Two Points, notwithftanding the Claim of a powerful Genius, which was admitted, excluded BEN : Firft, his abominable Principles bordering upon Atheifm;

theism; and next, his Ingratitude to
SHAKESPEAR, either of which was sufficient to shut him out; so that he is banished to ERISHNOVER; where, the very
Name of Genius being hated, he drags
on a tedious and despicable Existence. As
to POPE, on Account of his Abilities, his
filial Affection, and the particular Regard
HOMER expressed for him, he might have
been very happy; but, being charged by
poor DENNIS with most unmerciful
Cruelty to him, and a shameful Envy of
his Contemporaries, both which Accusa-
tions were fully proved, he was sentenced to wear a Laurel Wreath, mingled
with Sprigs of *Nightshade*, by which it is
not a little blasted; and, moreover, he is
almost continually tormented with the
Jests and Railery of COLLEY CIBBER,
BEAU NASH, and JOHN RICH, late Ma-
nager of *Covent-Garden* THEATRE, the
three MERRY ANDREWS of NODNOL.

G   AD-

ADDISON, who was rather admitted as a GOOD MAN than a GREAT POET, on Account of his Integrity, his Zeal for Morality and Religion while he was on Earth, has been naturalized a CITIZEN, and enjoys the Post of Secretary to the NAMREDAL, and thro' his Intercession, tho' not without much Difficulty, SWIFT has been admitted his Assistant; but, on Account of many Objections, he enjoys not any NOIBLAN Privileges, it being proved upon him that, while in the Ministerial Function, he paid more Attention to Politics than Divinity; that Ambition, not Piety, was his ruling Principle; that he ever took more Delight to censure than commend; that he anatomized Characters with as little Remorse as Surgeons do Bodies; and that he was guilty of unheard-of Cruelty in regard of VANESSA. However, as I have remark'd, ADDISON's Interest, enforced with the Argument that he had done many extensive and

well-

well-appropriated Charities, gained him
Admiffion; yet his Situation is but indifferent, for his Pride ill brooks fo fubor-
dinate a State, and his perverfe Nature is
mortified at the Tranquillity he fees a-
round him; fo that he never enjoys any
Satisfaction, unlefs he meets fome of his
Countrymen wearing Badges of their
Vice or Folly; and then, DIOGENES-like,
he gratifies his malicious Temper with
cynical Sneers and biting Sarcafms.

Inquiring whether there were any here
of other learned or honourable Profef-
fions, the NAMREDAL told me, Very few;
and the Reafon, fays he, may be given
without many Words: None of the
Clergy can be admitted, unlefs it evident-
ly appears that the firft great Motive for
taking *Orders* was, not the lucrative View
of a large Income, for the Indulgence of
an indolent luxurious Life, but a ferious
Refolution to propagate Religion and

G 2   Piety;

Piety; to form the Minds, correct the Paſſions, and cultivate the Virtues of their
Hearers; to be indefatigable in viſiting
and comforting the Sick; and, as far as
Circumſtances would admit, to be liberal
to the Poor; to be (that their Example
might enforce their Doctrine) tender Fathers, affectionate Huſbands, kind Pa-
ſtors, ſociable Friends, peaceful Neighbours, and loyal Subjects; moderate in
their Enjoyments, humble in their Deportment, and chaſte in their Converſation.

Under theſe Reſtrictions I have known
very few above the Degree of Curates
reach this Place; and, to confeſs the
Truth, Lawn Sleeves would have excluded me, but that ſeveral of my Deficiencies were over-looked, on Account of my
uncommon Attachment to the LUNAR
WORLD. As to Lawyers, they are generally excluded; for none are allowed Entrance

trance, unlefs they can prove that, to the
beft of their Knowledge, they have always been upon the Side of Juftice, and
never confidered the Fee before their
Client. PHYSICIANS, as fuch, are rejected; but extraordinary Qualifications
gain them Admittance; and all Military
Perfons, as turbulent, dangerous Animals,
incompatible with a Region of Peace, are
excluded without Exception.

Here a confufed Noife of feveral Perfons calling out in the Square interrupted our Converfation, the Meaning of
which will appear in the enfuing Chapter.

G ε   CHAP.

CHAP. VI.

The Manner of summoning the NOIBLANS
to the TEMPLE; *Ceremonies preparative
to entering the* TEMPLE; *and the Charge
given before Admission.*——*Some Account
of the* NOIBLAN RELIGION; *Observations upon Earthly Places of Worship;
the* NAMREDAL's *Plan for new modelling
the Ecclesiastics in* ENGLAND.

THOSE Persons, you hear, says the
NAMREDAL, are SNERRUNETS to
the SALMINA, Servitors to the TEMPLE;
they are now summoning the People to
the VESPERS, and the Words they Use
are NOIGLEVER GENVELA, be *grateful to
God.* Every one obeys this Call, and you
will immediately have an Opportunity of
seeing the NOIBLAN Method of Worship.
Come, go with me, the Citizens are in
waiting to conduct us.

As

As the Ceremonies muſt be new and ſomewhat unintelligible to you, your beſt Method will be to follow the Motions of others, do what you ſee done, and in your own Heart, after your own Manner and Ideas, pay Adoration to the Supreme Director of all Things; his Praiſe and Glory is the ultimate End of all that deſerves the Name of Religion. Sincerity of Intention is the firſt and principal Recommendation to Divine Acceptance, which it will certainly obtain: It is not the Splendor nor the worldly Value of an Offering, but the Affection and Duty of him who preſents it, that can pleaſe an Omnipotent Receiver.

Paſſing thro' a conſiderable Number of attending Citizens, we went forward to the Temple; in our Way I could not but admire the extremely neat Regularity of the Streets, and the uniform Compactneſs of the Houſes, which will be ſpoken of

more

more at large hereafter. Coming near
the Place of Worſhip, I perceived it to
be a moſt ſpacious ſexagonal Building,
riſing into a magnificent Dome; it ſtood
upon a green Eminence of conſiderable
Height, over the Sides of which flowed
ſeveral ſportive Rills of Water, ſo tranſ-
parent, that its Sparkles out-ſhone the
Luſtre of our higheſt-poliſh'd Diamonds.

The TEMPLE was conſtructed of a
Stone reſembling EMERALD, united with
Cement of a Gold Colour; the Dome
appeared to be of Chryſtal, ſupported by
a vaſt Number of Pillars of the AME-
THIST Hue, with Capitals and Baſis of
the pureſt White; the Order of Architecture appeared very different from any
I had ever ſeen, and exhibited to View
ſomewhat elegantly ſingular, preſerving
a Chaſtneſs of Grandeur not to be found
in the groſſer Materials of terreſtrial
Magnificence.

Having

Having entered the AREA of the TEM-
PLE, the NAMREDAL, and all who attended him, went to several Basons of
transparent, Saffron-coloured Stone, dip-
ped their Heads into Water, washed their
Hands, and dried both with Cloths offered them by Servants of the Church: I
did so likewise; when straight we entered
a most beautiful and spacious ISLE, where
we were no sooner placed, than instanta-
neously such a thick impenetrable Darkness wrapped us round, that I could by
no Means see those Persons who stood
close by: At the same Time, from above,
below, and every Side, the most dismal
Sounds, undulating thro' the Building,
struck my astonished Ears, and, I may
add, intimidated me not a little. On
one Side Torment screamed hideously,
and on another Despair vented her lamentable Groans. This lasted between
five and ten Minutes; when, as quick as
Thought, the inner Part of the TEMPLE
opening,

opening, such a Flood of Light burst
upon us, from many Thousands of Chry-
stal Lamps, that my Eyes could hardly
bear so powerful a Contrast: The doleful
Howlings were changed into Melody that
might almost be called Celestial. This
odd and striking Ceremony I found to
mean, that as all created Beings are imperfect in some Degree by Nature, and
more by Practice, Justice would condemn
them to the Seat of Mourning, but infinite Mercy, satisfied with temporary Pu-
nishments for temporary Crimes, opens
the Gates of Bliss and takes them in.——
This ECARUOCNE, or Ceremony of Remembrance, is performed once a Week,
to impress a deeper Sense of Duty and
Devotion; to deter the Worshippers from
Vice, as they wish not to continue in the
Gloom of Misery; and to urge them to
Virtue, as they hope for a speedy Admission into the Sun-shine of Joy.

Three

Three Avozens, habited in graceful
and awful Robes, now approached from
the inner Temple, at which all the Congregation bowed to the Earth; the elder
of the three, supported by the other two,
spoke, as I was informed afterwards, in
the following Manner:

*Children of God, I charge ye in his holy
and tremendous Name, (and remember that
before him you cannot dissemble) if any corrupt Thoughts at present taint your Breasts;
if there be any one among you who is not in
the most unlimited and perfect Peace with all
his Fellow-Citizens; if there be any Parents
who are not tender of their Children; any
Children who fail in Respect and Duty to
their Parents; if there be here a tyrannical
Husband, or abandoned Wife, begone; presume not to defile this holy Place with your
unhallowed Steps; but hide your Heads in
Darkness, veil your Eyes with Tears, clothe
your Hearts with Mourning, and gird your*

Loins

*Loins with Penitence, till you become pure
in his Sight, whose Eye beareth not a Stain.
This, in the Name of our Almighty Sire, I
command; but if you be free from these criminal Pollutions, by the same Authority I admit you to present yourselves before him in
this sacred Place, with joyful Humiliation,
an Offering fit for Heaven.*

Having thus spoke he retired, and the
Congregation followed, again prostrating
themselves upon entering the inner TEM-
PLE. How pleasing would it be, thought
I, to see such a Number of Persons upon
Earth daring to approach their CREATOR,
upon the same Principles, and under the
same Restrictions? How could our FA-
SHION-MONGERS, who go to criticise upon Dress, bear such a Test? How could
the Sons and Daughters of Gallantry,
who go to Church to worship one another, endure such a Trial?——O uncourtly
NOIBLANS, who banish Compliments,
ogling

ogling Smiles, and all Politeneſs out of RELIGION.

DIVINE SERVICE now began, and continued with ſtriking Solemnity near an Hour, the Congregation ſometimes proſtrated, at others kneeling, and then ſtanding.—Sitting is not allowed, it being obſerved, that if the NAMREDAL has ſo much Reſpect paid him, as that none preſume to ſit in his Preſence, it muſt be deemed a moſt unbecoming Inſtance of Impiety to take that Freedom before HIM who is UNIVERSAL LORD and FATHER of ALL.

The SENIOR AVOZEN having concluded with a very pathetic Benediction, we departed. The SNERRUNETS, as we paſſed thro' the Iſle of the TEMPLE, calling out,——*Maginleb Nalſina, yurne yelveren, phazaz wal Sezived :*——*Remember the Mediator*

*Mediator is in your Houfes, and fees all your
Thoughts as well as Actions.*

From VESPERS we went to the NAM-
REDAL's Houfe, and, being feated in a
Kind of Saloon, I entered into an Inquiry
concerning the Principles of the NOIBLAN
RELIGION.

The chief Points of it, fays he, are,
That they believe a fingle undivided
DIVINITY, indefcribable, incomprehen-
fible, to whofe Appearance they adapt
no Form, to whofe Attributes they pre-
fcribe no Bounds: They never confider
him as an angry, vindictive BEING; for
That, according to their Notions, would
be to fuppofe him fubject to Paffions,
and confequently imperfect: They fay
he beftows from BENEVOLENCE, pardons
from MERCY, and corrects from the fame
amiable Principles: That as by infinite
WISDOM he knows all created Beings to
be

be fallible, he will try them according to their Capacities and Opportunities: That he will not punish the Failings of real Weakness, nor reward untempted Rectitude. To design well, and to resist Temptation constitutes VIRTUE, as to act under Self-conviction, and to indulge pernicious Passions is of the Essence of VICE.

In this ISLAND it appears a most strange and partial Notion to fix one Place of Abode, one Degree of Punishment, and that eternal, for all Sinners. They believe in and worship a NALSINA, or MEDIATOR, whom they suppose to be formed and appointed by GOD for the Sake of erring Creatures; that he is coeval with the Universe, for which, however, they do not fix an Æra, taking such a Disquisition to be both unprofitable and presumptuous: That he has the Perfections of a DEITY, except that he is liable

to

to the Paffions of Grief and Joy; the one caufed by obftinate Sinners, the other by contrite ones. The Reafon they affign for the Exiftence and Belief of fuch a Mediator is, that the pure undefiled Effence of DIVINITY being incompatible with the corrupt Breath of Sin, this Medium has been formed, that the NALSINA may more particularly fuperintend the Actions of Mortals, receive their Petitions, and fupplicate for them to the Throne of Grace.

Once each Day at leaft every Perfon is obliged to attend public Worfhip, and no fchifmatical Notions are allowed to be propagated; tho' every Man is at Liberty to judge for himfelf, if he decently complies with eftablifhed Cuftoms; nor do they think that any Variation from their Syftem, if grounded upon pious Principles, will injure future Happinefs. All thofe, moreover, tranflated from Earth, who

who are not naturalized, are indulged in pursuing the Modes they practised in their former Existence, if it be agreeable to themselves.

I observed, continued he, that the Grandeur of our TEMPLE struck you; nor is it surprizing in a Place where every other Building, except the HOUSE of JUSTICE, bears a simple, unadorned, humble Equality; but the NOIBLANS think it serves to create a greater and more awful Respect to the DIVINITY to whom it is dedicated; it is to influence themselves, not to gratify their GOD; for they are persuaded that Works of Piety are as fragrant, and of as much Estimation from the lowly Cottage as the most towering Edifice.—How different is this Principle and Practice of the NOIBLANS from what I remember to have observ'd in *England*, where most of the Noblemen's Stables are Buildings superior to many of the Churches?

H

This

This laſt Remark I could not help acknowledging to be as much adapted to the preſent as to any preceding Times, and expreſſed my Concern that it ſhould be ſo, when, among innumerable other public Extravagancies, between Eight and Ten Thouſand Pounds yearly, beſides Matches, are given and ſubſcribed for Horſes to run one another to Death, and to impoveriſh the Breed of thoſe uſeful Creatures, who, for Sake of Speed, are reduced to meer Baubles : That ſo juſt a Complaint ſhould have Place, when, at a random Gueſs, Two Hundred Thouſand Pounds annually are laviſh'd in *over-grown* Salaries, or Stipends, to Churchmen who never officiate ; while ſeveral of thoſe, who toil and labour inceſſantly in the Paſtoral Office, as well as many of the Places of Worſhip, are pitiable Objects of Poverty.

True, ſays he, it is a Point of moſt juſt and rational Concern ; as to thoſe Bounties

which

which only promote the Spirit of Gaming, or, in plainer Terms, the Spirit of picking one another's Pockets, they are, instead of Praise, highly deserving of Censure; yet even they, considering some Advantages to Trade accruing from the Money that circulates at public Meetings, are not so heavy nor unjustifiable a Tax upon Society as the other Evil that was complained of.

What the Reason, what the Motive may be for making and continuing so many exorbitant Church Livings, no Man can tell, unless they be designed to make the MINISTERS of RELIGION mercenary Tools of Government. Why should any Man, by any Evasion whatever, be enabled to hold Pluralities? Why is not one Living deemed sufficient for one Teacher? Why not one PARISH, if small, served by one MINISTER, at One hundred and fifty Pounds a Year? Or, if large, by two,

H 2   each

each having fo much? Why might not
Bishops (for fuch Fathers or Infpectors
I think neceffary) officiate for One thou-
fand, and their immediate Affiftants,
Deans, at Five hundred? Why fhould
thofe, who ought to be intirely devoted
to Spiritual Matters, fit among Temporal
Lords, and, bufying themfelves about a
prefent State, entering into the Cabals
and Factions of Policy, lofe Thoughts of
a future? Why fhould fo many Preben-
daries and Dignitaries, who are otherwife well provided for, crufh Velvet Cu-
fhions in the Stalls of Cathedral Churches,
and annually fweep away fuch monftrous
Sums? Why fhould a Man, the higher
he goes in Church Preferment, be the
lefs affiduous?

Surely thefe Points well deferve to be
confidered, and loudly call for Reformation.—'Tis true *the Labourer is worthy of
his Hire,* but not of Superfluity; and certainly

tainly that Man in common Life would
be deemed very weak, who gave extraordinary Wages to a Parcel of idle Fellows, merely to ftand as Lookers-on;
while he half-ftarved the induftrious Part,
that carefully and laborioufly fulfilled
their Duty. Befides, continues he, there
is, in the Election of a BISHOP, fomething
fo farcical, that, were it not a Jeft upon
Religion, it muft excite Laughter: To
enter upon Choice, when the Choice is
abfolutely fixed before-hand, makes it
one of HOPSON's Kind; and what we may
deem yet more ridiculous, is the Negative three Times pronounced to a Dignity which the *humble* Creature, by himfelf
and his Friends, has poffibly, for many
Years together, been labouring to gain.

The NAMREDAL's Sentiments moft
perfectly coinciding with mine, I told him
it would be a great Service to Religion,
and a diftinguifhed Honour to the Policy

H 3   of

of Government, if such Complaints could
be redressed, and these Affairs settled upon a permanent and equitable Footing.

I think, replies he, after long and se-
rious Consideration, that they might; and
I shall briefly sketch out the Scheme by
which so desirable a Purpose might be
brought about. You will, no Doubt,
find me fallible in some Points; but I
hope not in many, nor material ones.

Observe then, first, That I would have
the KING act merely as Defender of the
Church; by his Magisterial Authority to
protect it from naturalized Foes, and by
the Force of his Arms to shield it from
foreign Attacks; by no Means to interfere in the Choice of Pastors, as his numerous Avocations to other Matters cannot afford him Time to examine into the
Characters and Abilities of those he is to
appoint; for which Reason he is under
the

the Neceſſity of taking Recommendations from the Tribe of Courtiers, who at all Events puſh on their own Relations and Dependents. This would poſſibly be deemed a Circumſcription of Royal Prerogative ; but nothing ſure that tends to promote Religion and Virtue can take from real Dignity; it muſt rather give additional Luſtre, and verify a Maxim which ſays, *That Limitation often ſtrengthens Power.*

I would recommend a total Annihilation of all Right to Preſentations, either in BISHOPS, CHAPTERS, COLLEGES, or private Perſons: This might be called an Attack upon private Property ;—but I aſk, What Property ? Do ſome Hundreds or Thouſands a Year enable a Man to chuſe out a proper Guide for his Fellow-Creatures ? Few People, I believe, would chuſe a blind Friend to fix on the Perſon of a Wife, or the Situation of a Houſe :

Houfe: Why then in the much more material Concern of being wedded to Futurity, or in the Choice of an eternal Dwelling, fhould Men, blind with Ignorance or Avarice, which is too often the Cafe, claim any Right to chufe? If they fell their Election to a Living, it is a mean and fcandalous Infult upon RELIGION, and therefore ought to be abolifhed; if they have no lucrative View, they may eafily give up the Privilege to more competent Judges.

To prevent Murmurings, as Men are apt to think what they have once enjoyed is their indifputable Right, the prefent Sons of the CHURCH, I mean fuch as have a fufficient Provifion, fhould enjoy their feveral Stipends for Life; but as they fell off, the proportionate Divifion I have mentioned fhould take Place, with all convenient Speed, among their Succeffors.

The

The CLERGY of each DIOCESE, in Convocation assembled, should, upon a Vacancy, chuse from among themselves the BISHOP or DEAN of the said DIOCESE, being first sworn that no previous Application from any Person, no partial Regard of Consanguinity or Friendship, but the unbiassed Opinion of real Deservings, swayed their Choice. Indeed, as the BISHOP and DEAN would have no Power of increasing their Incomes, there would be but little Chance of Partiality.

As to all other MINISTERS; upon the Death of an Incumbent Application should be made to the COLLEGES for a STUDENT in DIVINITY to fill up the Place; who, being recommended by them to the BISHOP, should be examined by him, the DEAN, and six other CLERGY-MEN, and, if approved by them, *ordained* and instituted. This Method of granting no *Orders* till a Vacancy happened,
would

would prevent such Shoals from seeking Shelter and Subsistence in the Gown, where too often they find Indigence.

The above Scheme, which you may ripen in your Thoughts, diminish, enlarge, or reject as you see fit, would be productive of several great and desirable Advantages, if carried into Execution: First, it would cut off all Adulation, Cringing, and mean Dependence from the Ministerial Function; Men of Morals and Learning would be the sole Judges of Persons fit for their Brotherhood, not the ignorant mercenary Fools of Fortune. If the Robes of Divinity then ever entered the Chambers of Great Men, it would be with a proper independent Respect; they would then, as MINISTERS, be only Servants of their Heavenly Master, having nothing to wish or fear of this World's Circumstances, their Thoughts might and would be more devoted to a future;

future; their Tongues might then, with honeſt and unprejudicial Openneſs, tell eſſential Truths, however uncourtly. In ſhort, being in a Manner ſelf-exiſtent, in Compariſon of their preſent Condition, Obedience to National Laws excepted, and being totally debarred of all political Reflections and Remarks in their Preaching, they would become a much more reſpectable Part of the Conſtitution, and more properly fulfil the ſacred Title of *Miniſters of God's Word*. As they are now ſituated, 'tis very much to be fear'd that too many are rather Retailers of the Words, and Flatterers of the Vanities of Men.

Another great Advantage from the Equality propoſed, would be the ſaving a great Sum annually from the preſent Church Revenues; which, being applied to the building or rebuilding of Churches, would furniſh what might be called decent Places of Worſhip in every

Spot,

Spot, and would alſo contribute much to
eaſe the Poor's Rates. No ſlight Conſideration, where ſuch weighty and multi-
tudinous Taxes prevail as in ENGLAND;
Taxes which, tho' framed by a National
Council, are, generally ſpeaking, more
unequally levied there than in any other
known State.

CHAP. VII.

Meets two Females; queſtioned by them con-
cerning the ENGLISH LADIES; *Remarks*
upon FASHION; DRAMATIC WRITERS;
the preſent ones, and THEATRES *conſi-*
dered.

I Know not to what Length of Converſation our Zeal, in regard of Churches
and Churchmen, would have carried us,
had not a blooming Youth of about Fif-
teen acquainted us that Supper was ready; when the NAMREDAL ſaid, Now
you

you shall see our private Method of Living, which is the same in all Houses,
my Office of Magistrate only confines me
to the Fatigue of Ceremony at Dinner,
at other Times I am in the Family-Way.

Here I was conducted into another
Apartment, where was set a small Table
and a very moderate Repast of Fruits and
Vegetables; soon after us two Females,
of very pleasing and respectable Forms,
came in, quite plain, but extremely neat
in Dress: The NAMREDAL presenting
me to the first, said, This is the Great
ELIZABETH of ENGLAND; I would have
paid Obeisance on my Knee, but she remarked, with most delicate Affability,
that her present State of Existence happily claimed no such Respect; said she
was highly pleased at seeing a Countryman, and that after Supper she had many
Questions to ask. Being introduced to
the other Female, I found she was the
NAM-

Namredal's Wife.—Take Notice that
Perſons tranſlated from Earth are not,
like the Noiblans, limited to a particular Age for Marriage; but, if naturalized,
may chuſe when and whom, as may be
moſt agreeable.

Conſcious of being unacquainted with
the Cuſtoms of Salutation, I pauſed for
ſome Time in a State of diffident Confuſion; which my kind Inſtructor perceiving—Bluſh not, ſays he, at being ignorant of what, before now, you could not
poſſibly be acquainted with; Ridicule
is a bitter Weed that rarely ſhoots up in
Noibla; we do not, like the Malevolent
in your World, wound Modeſty with
cruel unſeaſonable Sneers and Laughter;
on the contrary, we give with Pleaſure
all poſſible Information to thoſe who may
inadvertently do wrong.

How ignorantly inhuman is it to dart
the Stings of Ridicule at a Perſon for
taking

taking Steps too long or too short; turning Toes in instead of out; drooping the Head instead of holding it erect; or dangling the Arms instead of disposing them according to Art! Why should a volatile Frenchman laugh at the more temperate Briton for Gravity, or the Briton vent his Spleen at a Spaniard for Formality, and at a Dutchman for his wide Breeches? Indeed if any one of those Articles made a Man better or worse, they would deserve Remark; but as every Nation has its Virtues, and I believe the same may also be said of every Individual, some few Oddities, or what seem so, should be overlooked, or corrected with Tenderness.

But, continues he, I am going too far; know that our Method of Salutation between the different Sexes is, the Man holds his Hand over the Female's Head, without touching, and says, *May Virtue*
and

and Constancy ever flourish:—To which she replies, her Right Hand pointing to her Left Breast, *With Love and Obedience.*—This is the whole of Ceremony, and only used once each Day, let them meet ever so often.

Here we sat down to Supper, the NAM-REDAL having invoked a Blessing. During the whole we sat silent as at Dinner, and, having finished, performed the same Ablution. We were attended by two Boys and two Girls, Children of the NAM-REDAL; who, after Thanks returned, removed every Thing with a pleasing Dexterity; when my kind Host broke Silence in the following Manner:

As we are all acquainted with ENGLISH, says he, we will converse in that Language; I know that, were it not for Custom, whose arbitrary Power renders every Thing more bearable, the Ceremony of
Silence

Silence at Meal-Times would be deemed
as great a Hardſhip by the Females of
NOIBLA, as it muſt be to the Females of
the nether World; even now, Ladies, I
know your Tongues are itching for Liberty, ſo e'en let them looſe.

Upon my Word, Sir NAMREDAL, replies ELIZABETH, you ſhall be called to
Account if you are ſo tart upon our Sex;
don't you know that Talking is our Privilege here as well as on Earth; nay, let
me tell you, if once rouſed up, we can
think and act too; but you Lordly Creatures, called Men, would make Cyphers
of us; that was the Reaſon I always ſtood
by myſelf, and made ſome of my Brother
MONARCHS know that the Policy and
Reſolution of a Woman is as much to be
feared as thoſe of Men; come, Sir, ſays
ſhe, this is no Magiſtrate in his own
Houſe, ſo, for all his Gravity, we'll be as
prattling as we pleaſe.

I   With

With all my Heart, replies the NAM-REDAL, my Gravity can't have more a-greeable Relaxation, and, to prove it, I'll make one among you; so let us hear what you'll propose for our Entertainment.

Here, addressing herself to me, she said, I was so much fatigued with Politics while on Earth, that I shan't trouble you with many Questions that Way; yet I should be glad to know whether LIBERTY still flourishes as it did while I held the Reins of Government: To this replying in the Affirmative, and that an equal if not a superior Share of Military Fame attended the BRITISH Arms, she seemed parti-cularly pleased; and then asked me about her Countrywomen, what Virtues and Foi-bles at present prevailed amongst them.

This Interrogatory occasioned some Hesitation; Madam, says I, to speak the Truth will rather appear Severity, and I would

would not willingly enter into a Mifreprefentation by falfe Softening and mif-
applied Tendernefs; I fhall fketch out a
Picture as like the Originals as my Obfervation and Fancy will admit, in which
Light I hope you will candidly receive it.

Certainly, fays fhe; it is not the Cuftom to difguife Truth here in regard to
either Sex; it is told, contrary to the old
ENGLISH Proverb, at all Times and in
all Places, therefore you cannot oblige
us more than to adhere ftrictly to it; for
however we might wifh our Sifters thro'
the Univerfe to do as they ought, yet to
relate the Vices or Follies of any Part,
cannot poffibly give Offence.

Thus encouraged, I proceeded: The
LADIES of ENGLAND, Madam, as you
muft remember, taken in a general View
of natural Qualifications, Perfons, Features, and Underftandings, are excelled

I 2   by

by none; and I believe, did they not take extraordinary Pains to raise up Appearances against Reputation, they might justly claim an exalted Share of Virtue; but a strange, unaccountable Frenzy, called FASHION, so intoxicates their Brain, that almost every Consideration is sacrificed to the ridiculous Worship of that Idol; which has given such unlimited Sway, that if a Husband, Father, or Guardian, pretends to find Fault and advise, he is immediately silenced by that powerful Word; the extraordinary Effects of which you will more fully comprehend, by sketching the Outlines of a fine Lady's Life.

It has been justly observed, that a well-regulated Reserve and Modesty are the chief Points of Beauty in a Female Character; but this Opinion FASHION has totally overthrown, and stigmatiz'd them with the Terms of unbred Sheepishness;

while

while a shameless Front, staring Eyes,
wandering Limbs, and nonsensical Voci-
feration, usurp the Titles of Elegance,
Ease, and Wit; these admirable Qualifications are seen to a considerable Degree,
even in single Females, but arise to so
eminent a Pitch of Perfection in married
ones, that it would almost occasion an
Observer to believe they only considered
Matrimony as a Licence to free them
from every rational Restriction, as a Pass-
port to carry them thro' the Paths of Li-
centiousness; to such, all Men are alike
but their Husbands, they indeed find
Coldness and Reserve enough: But these
are general Remarks, I must come more
within the Bounds of a particular Character, which cannot be better struck out
than by giving you the daily Disposition
of Time.

In this Point, I know not well where,
or how to begin, as a fashionable Lady
has

has no Morning: Let it fuffice to fay fhe gets up at Noon, or after it; receives and reads Cards of Compliment during Breakfaft; takes her Chair or Chariot, and tires both the Men and Horfes in galloping from Street to Street, to pay what they call Morning Vifits; then returns and dines in the Evening, drinks Tea at Night, and plays Cards, Supper-Time excepted, till the next Day is advanced. This, with fome very inconfiderable Variations, is the continual Round of Tafte and Elegance.

I perceiv'd a Face of Aftonifhment poffefs Elizabeth at this Defcription, while the Namredal's Lady queftioned me, whether the Hufbands purfued the fame Courfe of Living: I told her many of them did; but took Care not to difgrace themfelves, or Wives, by appearing at the fame Places. Matrimony with them is fomewhat like a Country-Dance,

Dance, where, tho' you have a set Part-
ner, you as often dance up to those of
your Neighbours, and so change about.

Aye! says she, And pray what domestic
Happiness can such Couples enjoy? What
Cordiality, what mutual Satisfaction?
How can they possibly fulfill the Duty, or
feel the tender Sensations of Parents?
None of those Points, Madam, I replied,
are of the least Concern among Persons
of polite Taste; such mean Considerations
are referred to the vulgar, rusticated Part
of Mankind, never admitted amongst the
more polished Assemblies: Besides, they
are so infatuated with foreign Frippery,
that scarce any Thing which is not originally devised among our inveterate and
constant Foes will go down. Meat,
Clothes, and Manners, are so adulterated,
that I dare say this Lady, who once
swayed the *British* Sceptre with such illustrious Merit, were she to return, would
scarce

scarce be able to discover any one Circumstance that could bring her Countrywomen to Remembrance.

No truly, returns ELIZABETH, not by the Account you give of them; there was such a Thing as FASHION in my Reign, and it frequently varied, which, for Sake of Trade and Manufactures, should undoubtedly be encouraged in some Measure; but I do not recollect that ever it went to such a pernicious Length: It contributed to a reasonable Pleasure, but not an idolatrous Pride: Night and Day took their regular Turns among all Ranks of People, nor did any Degree of Quality exempt a Woman from due Attention to domestic Concerns. This did not prevent Hours of Relaxation and commendable Amusement; but, giving an Edge to Appetite, rendered them more pleasing, at the same Time that Regularity gave Spirit to the Features, Vivacity to the
Dis-

Difpofitions, and Health to the Conftitutions of my Countrywomen. Certainly, your fafhionable Ladies, as you ftile them, have very little of the healthful Bloom in their Countenances, and, while fubject to the Viciffitudes of GAMING, they muft frequently diftort their Features into very frightful Forms. I fhould think to prefent them with Mirrors, during a Run of very bad Luck, would deter them from fuch contemptible and pernicious Practices, unlefs indeed the Spirit of plundering themfelves and others happens to be more prevalent than the Confideration of their Beauty.

Well obferved, fays the NAMREDAL, I have liftened to the Remarks on every Side, and think them juft; but, furely, continues he, the Men muft be of a widely different Caft, elfe the Nation could never be in fuch Repute, nor crowned with fuch Military Fame as you have defcribed.

I

I anſwered, that, in general, they providentially were ſo, for the Defence and Support of LIBERTY; but that many of the Nobility in particular, and other Nurſelings of Fortune, aſpiring at the Character of FINE GENTLEMEN, act upon Principles diametrically oppoſite.

Aye there, replies he, lies the Partiality and diſgraceful Inconvenience of Hereditary Honours; by which the moſt contemptible Wretch, if he be born a Lord, continues ſo, and claims Precedence of many Thouſands better than himſelf; tho', uſurping the Poſt of a JOCKEY, with pitiful Ambition, he ſcampers over the Turf, or, in the Semblance of a GAMESTER, rattles the Dice, ſtill his Nobility of Blood conſecrates, as it were, ſuch Baſeneſs, and gives the Wretch an unmerited and dangerous Importance.——— Now, Shame upon it,—Did REASON ever authorize ſuch Principles? No, certainly, rather

rather Vice in the Garb of Reaſon, knowing her own Deformity, has run for Shel-
ther under the Glare of Political Honours,
which may render her true Shape leſs
perceptible, and conſequently leſs frightful. If Rank were to be the Reſult of approved Merit only, it would much more
juſtly and univerſally claim Reſpect. In
the preſent Diſpoſition of Things, tho'
it ſerves to awe the Vulgar, in the View
of ſenſible Men, it does but reflect Scandal upon the unworthy Poſſeſſors.

Several other Queſtions were aſked alternately by the NAMREDAL, his Wife,
and ELIZABETH; but as my Anſwers
were neceſſarily Deſcriptions of what the
Readers muſt be ſufficiently acquainted
with, as being intimately known to almoſt every Individual, I ſhall come to
the laſt Point of Inquiry, which was concerning the preſent State of DRAMATIC
Writing and our THEATRES.

Here

Here I confeffed that we have not at
prefent, nor have had for fome Years,
one AUTHOR for the STAGE, that, in any
Shape, deferves the Name of POET; the
TRAGEDIES are fuch cold, elaborate, un-
alarming Pieces of Declamation, that no
Action can give them Life, no Attention
purfue them thro' five dull Acts: Indeed
they boaft of ftrict critical Unities, and
fay that the Flowers of Poetry are defign-
edly rejected, as improper for Dialogue;
yet, were it not for fuch Pieces as abound
in thofe Flowers, and frequently break
thro' the Trammels of CRITICISM, from
which the THEATRES draw their chief
Support, our modern Scribes would not
have an Opportunity to crawl thro' nine
dull Nights in their Paffage to Oblivion:
Nay, I will do them the Juftice to fay,
I believe that their ftrict Attachment to
Criticifm proceeds from its being better
fuited to their barren Imaginations, which
want Force and Activity to get beyond
its

its infipid Limits. In regard of their COMIC Pieces, as the Duke of BUCKING-HAM faid, it was no eafy Matter to pen a Whifper, we find it now a mafterly Point to pen a Blank; befides, it is made almoft a conftant Rule for one of the Interlocutors to begin fpeaking before the other has done, which I always confidered as a Piece of ill Manners. In fhort, there is fuch Snipfnap, fuch Paufes, and Hefitation, that if Converfation in private was to take Example from what is exhibited on the STAGE, it would be reduced to a moft unmeaning, indelicate Stammering; a Labouring, like the Mountain, to bring forth a Moufe.

What, fays ELIZABETH, fuch a Depravity in a Country where SHAKESPEAR, DRYDEN, OTWAY, and CONGREVE have left fuch bright Examples! I am afham'd of my-native Soil, and wifh it had deferved

ved a better Character; but pray, Sir, have the Theatres declined equally?

To this I replied, That, to the beft of my Knowledge, they had never been more encouraged, nor ever were worfe fupported, than at prefent; the Incomes of Performers are immoderate, the Merit very confined. As to the former; why might not One hundred a-year, befides the Advantage of a Benefit, genteelly reward any Degree of Merit? By fuch a Regulation, fuch Savings might be made as would enable Managers to take more reafonable Prices for fo rational and effential an Entertainment as the Drama affords: In this I would by no Means leffen the Confequence or Credit of the Stage, for which no Perfon can have a greater Regard; but, by bringing it into lefs exceptionable Bounds, to guard it from the Envy and too juft Complaints which are now levelled againft it.

In

In regard of Performance; I have always thought that the general Courfe of Nature only can be a fit Standard of Example; every Character in private Life will be an unerring Original to copy for the Stage; only as Water-Colour Painting, which is feen at a Diftance, and by artificial Light, requires ftronger Strokes than the Oil-foften'd Tints; fo Action upon the Stage fhould enforce and render its Original more ftriking.——But how extremely different is the prefent Practice; inftead of Nature, ONE eminent Performer, who has certainly aftonifhing Abilities for his Profeffion, is fet up to View, and a fervile, unequal Imitation of him glides thro' the various Degrees. In the Play of *Richard* fcarce a Man but affects fome Peculiarity of the crooked Monarch; in *Lear* the whole Court is ftruck with a Kind of complaifant Debillity; or when this fame Idol of Imitation, with mafterly Tranfition, defcends into the meaner Scenes of low COMEDY,

COMEDY, his Grimaces, by a Kind of electrical Concussion, warp the Features of Characters widely different; so that almost in every Thing you may see his Starts, his Pauses, his Action, his Attitude, and his Variations of Countenance.——But ah! how changed! how misapplied! I have often thought this paltry ignorant Compliment to superior Merit, like a whole Town's taking Fancy to the Cloaths of a Connoisseur in TASTE; who, without regarding their own Size, taller or shorter, bigger or less, should make theirs exactly of the same Dimensions. In such a Case the Original may be pleasing and pretty, while the Copies must be utterly ridiculous.

Truly, says the NAMREDAL, at this Rate your Performances must lose much of the Energy that animates just and original Action, for no Qualification relative to human Nature can be more contemptible

tible or cruel than Mimicry, as it either
proceeds from a total Barrenneſs of Idea,
or an innate Malevolence, which catching at, and aggravating Defects, provides
Food for the inſatiate Appetite of Ridicule,——I am amazed, continues he, that
ſo much good Senſe, as muſt be poſſeſſed
by an *Engliſh* Audience, can digeſt ſuch
groſs Food, or be contented with the
Skeletons of Merit.

Nay, Sir, I replied, if good Senſe was
to prevail, the Caſe muſt ſoon take a different Turn; but there is a deluſive Mon-
ſter called Prejudice, which, leading
Judgment by the Noſe, decides: Scarce
one Auditor thinks for himſelf, but catch-
es from his Neighbour, and retales to a
third; nor is this confined to Performance,
it reaches Authors alſo; which may, in
ſome Meaſure, account for that Decline
of Genius I have mentioned: Scarce any
Piece can arrive at a Peruſal, unleſs recom-
K mended

mended by some RIGHT HONOURABLE
Personage; who, tho' he can hardly read,
is, from his Title, by the Courtesy of
England, a profound Judge of Wit, Sentiment, and Stile. A Sort of Necessity to
indulge this usurped Prerogative exculpates the MANAGERS from the Charge
of not regarding Merit. Whenever a
Penny is to be got, Nobility and Interest must put forth their monopolizing
Claws, and draw it all to the Dens of their
hungry Dependents, who are thus laid a
Tax upon the Public, and become Ido-
laters of those illustrious Patrons that
purchase the Immortality of DEDICA-
TION-FAME, at the Expence of others;
they cannot keep those more valuable
Appendages of Quality, MISTRESSES
and RUNNING-HORSES, so cheap.

At this Rate, cries ELIZABETH, I shall
lose all Patience, and begin to despise
my Country; I got out of it in Time,

and

and am happily come to a Region where
impartial Judgment is allowed its juſt
Influence; no Piece here is valued for
the Name of its AUTHOR, but only for
its intrinſic Merit: Even SHAKESPEAR,
tho' he has never failed yet, is as critically
examined as one who had never wrote before; indeed there is a precautionary Method which renders this Impartiality unavoidable; for every new Dramatic Performance is, without any Intimation of the
AUTHOR's Name, ſubmitted to twelve
CENSORS, who conſider it, and give the
Sanction of their Approbation, or condemn it as unfit. According to the Degrees of Merit they are performed; and
then, when ready for Exhibition, the AU-
THOR confeſſes himſelf: Such a Court of
Critical Inquiry would enlarge the Field of
Genius in BRITAIN. When you return
you may propoſe it if you chuſe; in the
mean Time, if you will accompany the

NAM-

Namredal, this Lady and me, to our
Estralam, you will have an Opportunity of feeing the Rules and Action of
our Noiblan Drama.

Well, fays the Namredal, fince the
Ladies have propofed you fo agreeable
an Entertainment, I requeft your Company in the Morning to the Requecex,
'tis the Day for adminiftering Juftice,
and I dare fay there will be fome Trials
worth your hearing: I had fcarce Time
to reply when the great Bell tolling interrupted our Converfation; the Ladies,
wifhing me a calm Repofe, immediately
withdrew; and the Namredal telling me
that was the public Signal for retiring to
Reft, conducted me in Perfon to a fmall
agreeable Apartment, where Neatnefs
fupplied the Place of Elegance; there,
after the moft kind and hofpitable Ex-
preffions, he left me to compofe my
Thoughts

Thoughts by Slumber, or to give them full Scope in the wide Field of Reflection upon what has been hitherto related.

When alone a vaſt Variety of Ideas crowded upon each other in my Imagination; firſt, my unaccountable Conveyance to the LUNAR WORLD, ſurprizing and inconceivable in its Nature; next, that peculiar and kind Reception I had met in it; the Novelty of thoſe Ceremonies I had gone thro'; the happy Situation, the tranquil Equality of the People I had, as it were, dropp'd among; with many other Circumſtances which do not now occur: Moreover, I felt ſome Degree of Uneaſineſs, that I knew not how I was to return, nor when, nor if at all; but Sleep, like a kind Friend, came to my Aſſiſtance, and, by its oblivious Influence cloſing up the Eye of Memory, relieved me from thoſe Anxieties which my

K 3   new

new and extraordinary Situation had oc-
cafioned.

C H A P. VIII.

Account of the GARDEN BIRDS; *breakfafts*
with the NAMREDAL'*s Lady*; *their Re-*
marks upon BEAUTY, LOVE, *and* MAR-
RIAGE; *goes to the* REQUECEX; *fome*
remarkable Trials.

NOtwithftanding the Hurry of Imagination which difturbed me when
I retir'd to Bed, I enjoyed all Night the
Refrefhment of compofed Sleep: Being
waked by the tolling of the Bell, which
I underftood to be the general Signal for
rifing, I got up; as there was no Window
but at the Top of the Room where I lay,
and that in Form of a Cupola, I afcended to it, and looking out perceived the
Sun to be an Hour high, or thereabouts,
beaming upon the moft compact and
beautiful Range of fmall Gardens that I
ever

ever faw, wherein an infinite Number of
Flowers, Herbs, Shrubs, and Trees were
delightfully variegated; feveral Birds,
about the Size of our common Hens,
were hovering round; their Plumage appeared charming beyond Defcription;
their Heads were covered with a fhining
Down of Golden Hue; their Wings exhibited the brighteft Scarlet; their Necks
vied with the Azure of the Firmament,
and their Bodies fhamed the pureft Snow:
Thefe I afterwards underftood to be called *Dofen Alopu*, *Garden Birds*, and that
they are highly reverenced in NOIBLA
for two Reafons; becaufe, firft, they deftroy all the Vermin and Infects that are
pernicious to the Fruits of the Earth;
and next, becaufe they are a Kind of natural Phyficians; for when any NOIBLAN
is indifpofed, as fometimes is the Cafe
flightly, he goes into his Garden, lies
down on his Back, when the firft of thefe

Birds

Birds that fees him will light directly upon his Breaft, put its Bill to his Mouth,
give him three or four Flaps with its
Wings, then rife and hover round him
till he ftands up, when it leads him to
whatever Herb may be falutary for his
Ailment, and this taken never fails to
give immediate Relief.

About half an Hour might have paffed
away in Obfervation before I heard any
Body come, when the NAMREDAL's Son
approached with fome Water in a Chryftal Veffel; which prefenting with a fine
Cloth, he told me that his Mother attended my coming to Breakfaft; this oc-
cafioned me to haften; and, having wafh-
ed, I followed the Lad, who conducted
me whither fhe was.

She received me with moft delicate
Affability, and kindly enquired whether
the

the Novelty of my Situation had not interfer'd with my Reſt: I replied, That tho' an, unavoidable Surprize poſſeſſed me, yet every Circumſtance I ſaw or heard was ſo exceedingly agreeable, that my Nature had never been more pleaſingly or more rationally gratified than ſince my Arrival in NODNOL. This Declaration ſeemed to give her ſenſible Satisfaction, and ſhe propoſed Breakfaſt in the moſt hoſpitable Manner; obſerving, at the ſame Time, that they had none of the Materials in NOIBLA which ſhe underſtood we uſed for Morning Meals in the lower World, yet hoped Novelty would not render them leſs agreeable.

Nay, Madam, ſaid I, my Taſte is rather plain and unpoliſhed, any Thing will do for me; but, were I one of the niceſt Sort, Novelty would be a ſtrong Recommendation. Oh, how would Perſons

sons of Quality and Fashion in ENGLAND
envy me a Breakfast in the MOON? How
would they pay, were there a Communi-
cation for Rarities from hence? Our
EAST-INDIA Trade would soon decline,
as this would be more impracticable and
full as useless; for tho' we have every
Thing in our Island that Nature can reasonably require, but *Content*; yet are we
so industrious to cultivate Trouble and
Expence, that immense Oceans are
ploughed, and the most furious Tempests
encounter'd, to bring home an Herb,
which (being fashionable) some Wretches,
who can hardly purchase Bread, must have
at any Rate.

Here, laughing at what she justly call'd
such artificial Necessity, she poured out a
Kind of Azure-colour'd Liquor. She told
me it was extracted from the *Maltra Enuthe*, or *Tree* of *Health*; and that the small
Cakes eaten with it were made of the
Bark

Bark, dried, powdered, and wrought into a Confiftence like our Bifcuits. On Trial I found the Liquid delicious to the Palate, and highly balfamic to the Stomach, which would have induced me to drink a good deal more than fell to my Share, for as I found afterwards the Quantity is limited; you take as little as you pleafe, but not as much as Appetite calls for. The Cakes relifhed but indifferently; however, upon the whole, I could not complain.

Before Breakfaft I afked for the NAM-REDAL, but was informed that, being to enter upon the Diftribution of JUSTICE, he would not be feen till he was going to the REQUECEX; that he eat nothing till the Trials were over, nor ever fuffered himfelf to be difturbed during the Time of preparatory Devotion. It will be near an Hour, Sir, fays his Wife, before he appears; if a weak Woman's Prattle can make that Space lefs tedious, I will rather

ther expose my own Deficiencies than
suffer you to want Amusement. I respectfully thanked her for such unmerited Condescension, wherein she so much
under-rated her own Merits; adding, that
nothing could be more agreeable than
her Conversation, were I not intimidated
by a Fear of discovering a Deficiency on
my Side.

Mighty well, replies she, I have often
heard that you Men of the LOWER
WORLD are vastly given to Flattery,
which you *always* bestow most plentifully
upon Females, and *sometimes* upon one
another; but, pray, is it not in both Cases
of a mean and pernicious Nature? It can
only serve to make Vanity flourish, and
predominate over such empty Idols as
are fond of this Incense, while you who
offer it, however it may answer particular
Purposes, must naturally have a poor
Opinion of that Feeling you labour so

in-

induftrioufly to create. We have luckily
no fuch Artifice, no fuch Parent of Folly
among us; all Approbation is limited to
Minds, not Perfons; to Conduct, not
Beauty; becaufe one is the Merit or Fault
of Nature, the other merely our own:.
But pray, Sir, that I may be the better
informed of the State of Love in your
Country, let me know whether all are
obliged to reinforce their Paffion with
this intoxicating Ingredient, or is it poffible to fucceed without its Aid.

Madam, fays I, to confefs the honeft
Truth, fuch Footing has infinuative Addrefs gained among all Sorts of People,
that Delufion is much more prevalent
than Honefty; all cry out againft Flattery, yet all take it down with great
Pleafure; but then it muft be varied in
its Shape according to the Patient it has
to work on; and tho' the Effect of it upon Women is certainly moft extenfive

and

and powerful, yet Men of all Denominations are liable to its Influence.

As to LOVE, it has been well affirm'd by many eminent Authors, that it is the nobleſt Feeling of the human Heart; noble when properly fix'd, and ſupported by a delicate Sincerity; dangerous when, at War with Reaſon, it captivates all our Intellects, and leads even our Senſes to their own Deluſion. I would endeavour to deſcribe the faireſt Side, and ſhew diſintereſted Affection in its pureſt Colours; but 'tis in vain to attempt a Deſcription of that which ſo rarely exiſts amongſt us; to find it in any Rank of People is almoſt a Miracle; Marriages indeed are negotiated, becauſe Nature and Cuſtom prompt the different Sexes to ſuch Connections; but then they are tranſacted like any other Branch of Trade, and Money appears the chief Match-Maker; beſides, as if we had not

been

been fufficiently fordid in our Way of
thinking, the LEGISLATURE took Care
to frame a legal Bar againft mutual Inclinations; a Law which ferves no one
End but to enlarge Church Revenues by
exorbitant Fees.

A very extraordinary Piece of Policy
indeed, replies fhe; thank Heaven we
have no fuch LEGISLATORS here. I
thought you told ELIZABETH laft Night
you had the fame LIBERTY as in her
Time; now I don't recollect to have
heard my Hufband, who was long after
her, mention any fuch Law as you have
juft fpoken of.

No, Madam, fays I, 'tis of very late
Date, and, as it did not affect me directly,
I had forgot it. And pray, returns fhe,
how came it ever to be thought of? I replied that I never heard nor could imagine how fuch an Abortion was concei-
ved;

ved; some People conjectured it to be the Fruits of a few Great Men's Apprepensions that their Daughters, to the Disgrace of Blood, might prefer hale, sensible, vulgar Fellows to emaciated, wornout Fools of Quality; so, in a Rage, they determined to make as many young People thro' the Kingdom unhappy as they could; and in numberless Instances I believe it has had the desired Effect, by occasioning otherwise well-disposed Couples to take imprudent Steps, rather than encounter parental Tyranny, (which shews itself too frequently) and the superfluous Forms required by Law.

Here she expressed great Surprize that a Nation, famed for Wisdom and a Love of Freedom, should suffer one of the tenderest Rights of Nature to be infringed, or incumbered with unreasonable partial Restrictions; then continued to question me about a Kind of Animals she had
heard

heard of, call'd PRUDES and COQUETTES; when I told her we had Plenty of them; the former being a Creature which declines all reasonable Freedoms for a forced Reserve, after sheltering the worst Principles under an aukward Semblance of strict Modesty; the latter, a Kind of wanton Butterfly, which flutters and expands its gaudy Wings as much as possible in the Sunshine of FASHION; fond of being admired, and never more happy than when it can make its Admirers miserable.

And are Men, says she, such arrant Dupes as to be imposed upon by mere Semblances? Or is it the extraordinary Beauty of your Women which gains them such an unlimited Influence over Reason?

I told her that it was beyond my Power to account for it; that Beauty was fre-

L quently

quently to be met with, and certainly had much Power; but that, among the polite World, one scarce knew what was Beauty, as the Fashions of Shapes and Features were so often altered; sometimes oval Faces are the Standard, then round ones; sometimes broad Waists, sometimes narrow; so that what is Beauty at one Time is Deformity at another; and Nature, who is not confined within the narrow Bounds of Rule, suffers frequent and undeserved Censure from the ignorant Caprice of prevailing Opinion.

Here she burst out into a loud Laugh, and repeated the Words FASHIONABLE BEAUTY several Times, till the NAMRE-DAL's Appearance terminated our Conversation.—He told me that, if I had a Mind to accept of his Invitation to the REQUECEX, he was just going thither, and would be glad of my Company; I
paid

paid my Compliments to his Lady, and went with him directly.

We were conducted by four-and-twenty Citizens, some of whom carried, as among us, the *Insignia* of Authority immediately before the Magistrate; the chief of which was three Figures in one Piece, most admirably cut from a brilliant Stone or Composition; the chief Figure was JUSTICE; on her Right Hand appeared WISDOM supporting her, and on the Left MERCY, (to whom she kindly extends her Hand) kneeling in a supplicative Posture. The Characters were set forth with much the same Emblems as we see on Earth.

Having reached the Court, the NAMREDAL placed me on the Left Hand of his own Seat, which I found to be a Mark of Distinction in NOIBLA. Two Citizens immediately approached, raised

a

a Canopy over the Magiftrate, and then
clofed him in, except on the Side where
I fat, with fomewhat like a Silk Curtain;
I wondered what the Meaning of this
could be, but was foon relieved from
Sufpence; for he told me that, as the
Eye was a Parent of Prejudice in almoft
every Point of View, and the beft Underftanding or foundeft Judgment might be
warped by it, the Cuftom of NOIBLA was
to veil the Magiftrate from Sight of thofe
who came to plead before him, till his
Arbitration was determined; it has alfo,
fays he, the good Effect of keeping Attention from being difturbed by furrounding Objects.

Juft as he had ended this Obfervation,
a Citizen, with much emphatic Deliberation, repeated thrice the following
Words:——*Bineda, Ob* NAMREDAL,
*Twanto Selben Twantaftez.--Temper, Ob Fa-
ther, Juftice with the Dew of Mercy.* This
was

was the whole Ceremony ufed in opening the Court; which being performed,
two Females came up, and one preferred her Complaint in the following Manner:

FATHER of NODNOL, I come before
you to feek Reparation for an Injury
done me by a Woman here prefent; an
Injury of the niceft Nature, and unpro-
voked by me in any Shape, as it has been
my conftant Endeavour to live in Harmony with my Fellow-Citizens; yet has
fhe, for what Caufe I know not, given
out fuch prejudicial Reports, that the
warm Cordiality which has fubfifted between my Hufband and me ever fince
we were married, is like to abate much;
at leaft if it does not, I fhall be more
obliged to *his* Love and Gentlenefs of
Difpofition, than to *her* Tendernefs in
talking; wherefore I humbly befeech Af-

L 3   fiftance

fiftance from your Authority to reftrain
her.

Is it not aftonifhing, fays the NAMRE-
DAL, that where Law is fo very precife
and plain, where alfo it is fo generally
known, that any can be found hardy
enough to tranfgrefs it? Is there any
Property we ftand poffeffed of fo valuable
as Character? Any Happinefs equal to
Peace of Mind, or any Weapons fo dangerous as bufy Tongues? How much
Cenfure do they deferve who with Slander taint the one, or embitter the other?
It is a Cruelty of the moft affecting
Kind, unprofitable, and ignominious;
you then who are charged with fuch uncharitable, fuch licentious Behaviour, and
to one of your own tender Sex, who are
as eafily blafted as Flowers in the Field,
fay how can you acquit yourfelf of the
Complainant's Accufation; or on what
Con-

Confideration can you plead a Mitigation
of that Punifhment, which, according to
Law, falls upon the Guilty?

Moft venerable Sir, replies the Defendant, in whom dwells impartial Juftice, to the Charge againft me I plead Innocence, which I hope to manifeft in few
Words; TRUTH can never be Slander;
our Laws, we all know, point out the
Duties of our feveral Stations : This
Woman, my Neighbour, who knows and
is well able to perform all that can be required of her, by an unufual Influence
gained over her pliant Hufband, has for
fome Time paft prevailed on him, together with his own Charge, to undertake
feveral Concerns which properly fall under her's; by which Means gaining more
vacant Time than any other Woman can
command, fhe has made it her Bufinefs to
run from Houfe to Houfe, promoting
Idlenefs by unprofitable Converfation,
and

and making induſtrious Women uneaſy
by ſneering at their commendable Application: Rouſed to Reſentment by ſuch
Behaviour, I own I have ſaid that her
Huſband ſhows himſelf weak to be ſo laviſh of Indulgence, and that ſhe proves
herſelf highly unworthy of it by ſuch
Miſapplication. This is the Extent of
my Crime, if ſuch it be, and to your Clemency I ſubmit.

This Caſe, ſays the NAMREDAL, conſidered both from the Accuſation and
Defence, pronounces each Party equally
guilty; you the ACCUSER, for ſhameful-
ly withdrawing from the Duties of a *good
Wife* under the Shelter of a Huſband's
Fondneſs; and you, the ACCUSED, for
being ſo very forward to publiſh your
Judgment upon an Affair which in no
Shape came under your Cognizance. By
what Authority are you the INSPECTOR
of your Neighbours? You ſhould be the
Friends,

Friends, the Advisers, and not the Censors of each other; rather studious to
conceal than forward to expose Failings
of this Nature; but, since you are come
here fraught with the Spirit of Contention, hear your several Sentences.

You who have been so ready to alarm
Justice by the Clamours of Complaint,
knowing yourself to be guilty of at least
as great a Crime, shall for three TOIR-
TAS lose your Seat in the RUVENAL, and
attend your Husband there publickly as
a Servitor during that Time, having the
Words *Retho ettibem Elbal*,—*An artful
Wife*,—labelled on your Breast in large
Letters; and you, who have been so alert
to proclaim a Neighbour's Failings, shall
be enjoined strict Silence for the same
Space, being stigmatized with the Words
Retho slintat Elbal,—*A tatling Wife*.——
Hence therefore, and from the Shame
you have both incurred, learn that social
Agree-

Agreement is preferable to Contention; that to correct our own Failings, to mind our own Buſineſs, and not to interfere with other People's Concerns, is the ſureſt Road to Quiet and Proſperity.

The Females being removed there appeared two Brothers, named EFFILAR and AITROTA; the former addreſſing himſelf, ſaid — AWFUL SIR, we are Brothers and Twins, not more intimately united by our Births than our Inclinations; yet as the Death of our Mother, as ſoon almoſt as we were born, has left the Elderſhip doubtful, and as, without fixing this, we cannot make any legal Settlement of our Affairs, we humbly preſent ourſelves before your Wiſdom, and ſupplicate Advice how we may ſurmount the Difficulty; which is ſtill rendered more diſagreeable as we both love the ſame Female, but cannot prevail with
her

her to declare in Favour of either till the Point in Debate is settled.

Before I proceed to determine, says the NAMREDAL, inform me, with the most undisguised Truth, whether you seek my Judgment from any View of Precedence arising from Eldership, and whether to decide in Favour of one will create any Uneasiness in the other? Or whether, united by the tender and natural Tie of brotherly Love, you seek it simply from the Motives you have mentioned?—They replied, solely from the Motives they had mentioned.

Well then, continus he, you shall have my Opinion; but some Space of Consideration will be requisite in so new a Case. In the mean Time, I must let you know that there is a poor Man, who, by Accident, is rendered incapable of contributing his Share to the common Stock, where-

wherefore he is in Danger of being removed from his Seat in the RUVENAL,
the thought of which wounds him deeply; he has follicited Help from feveral,
but found none; if you, or either of you,
can fpare Time to affift him, it will be an
Act of great Benevolence.

To this EFFILAR replied, VENERABLE
FATHER, I could wifh that I had the
Power of affifting him, but my Hours are
fo limited and fo fully employed, that the
kind Wifhes of Pity are all I can afford
him.

Alas, replies AITROTA, when Affliction
wounds, Wifhes are but a poor and painful Palliative, my Hours are limited and
engaged alfo; yet, if to fpare one Half of
what is allotted for my particular Ufe
can relieve him, I will moft gladly, Oh
Father, let him have it.

Aye,

Aye, says the NAMREDAL, then you have fully convinced me who is the elder; 'tis not a few Hours or a few Years that should place one Man before another; he who excells in Humanity, Benevolence, and social Duties, deserves the most worthy Precedence; That, AITROTA, do thou enjoy, and exert thyself in Pity to thy Brother; to enlarge his Heart, to soften his Feelings, and to create in him an Emulation of thy Goodness.—Here the Twins embraced, and he whom the NAMREDAL had set aside, seemed as well pleased as if the Decision had been on his Part; only a conscious Blush glow'd on his Cheek at the just and gentle Rebuke of the Magistrate.

As they were on the Point of departing, the NAMREDAL said, Hold, I remember you told me that one Female had engaged the Affection of both, but that the Doubt of Eldership prevented her from accepting either: This appears

to

to me a Proof that fhe is unworthy, and
that fhe feeks to gratify Pride more than
Love; therefore let me advife you to
bring her before me, and I'll negotiate,
if poffible, to your mutual Satisfaction;
but take Heed not to mention the Determination I have made. This Propofal
was joyfully accepted, and EFFILAR
went immediately to bring the Damfel;
with whom in a few Moments he return'd,
when the NAMREDAL fpoke thus to her:

Virtuous Maid, here are two Brothers,
both, I underftand, Suitors of yours;
they have agreed, before me, to abide by
your free and unbiaffed Choice; fay then,
whether you will become the Wife of
EFFILAR, now in Court confirmed the
Elder, or throw yourfelf into the Arms
of AITROTA, the Younger? (in faying of
which he reverfed them) the Girl, without any Hefitation, fixed upon EFFILAR;
when the Magiftrate, having made her
repeat

repeat the Choice three or four Times, and declare that Love only fwayed her, he informed her of the Deceit, and that in Reality fhe had chofen the youngeft; upon which her Colour went thro' a Variety of Changes, and fhe appeared in the moft painful Confufion; which the NAM-REDAL perceiving, for now the Curtain was drawn from before him, he cried out, with unufual Severity,—Thou Shame to the NOIBLAN Race; thou poor unhappy Slave of Pride, unworthy and ignorant of that pure æthereal Flame which difinterefted Love beams into the Heart; how couldft thou be fo blind to thy own Happinefs, and cruel to that of another, as to have thy choice directed by fo falfe a Meteor as Vanity? Fly, begone, worthlefs as thou art, from the Comforts and Pleafures of Society, that thou may'ft not again have the Opportunity to impofe a worthlefs Heart, through Recommendation of a lovely Form; I banifh thee for five

RA-

Rayamons to Omyrchal, at the End of which Time thou may'ſt return, but never to enter the honourable State of Marriage; bring forth, ſays he, the Garment and Veil of Mourning, in which that adventitious Merit, on which ſhe prides herſelf ſo much, may be immediately obſcured.

At this dreadful Sentence the ſelf-betray'd Female fainted away; the Brothers could not avoid aſſiſting her, nor even ſhedding Tears; yet, in ſuch Caſes, Sentence once paſſed is irrevocable, and however they might lament her Fate, all allowed it to be juſt.

Mercy deliver us, thought I, what a deal of Baniſhment we ſhould have in England if ſuch a Law was to take Place; whole Swarms of the pretty, ſprightly, fluttering Animals called Coquettes would be ſwept away, to the

no

no small Diminution and Prejudice of the *Beau Monde*: Harmless Beaus would then be deprived of Subjects for Eloquence; Winks, Nods, Leers, Becks, Smiles, and Ogles, the powerful Artillery of artificial Love, would be rendered useless, and the whole Œconomy of Intrigue totally annihilated.

This Reverie would, in all Probability, have extended itself to a considerable Length, but that I was roused by a confused Noise arising from the Approach of two Disputants, one of whom I recollected to be my old Friend BEAU NASH; the other, in Appearance, I knew nothing of. The BEAU, who still retained his Badge of Office, the white Beaver, spoke to the NAMREDAL, as we shall find in the next Chapter.

M   CHAP.

C H A P. IX.

Continuation of Trials in the REQUECEX.

MAY it please you, Sir, I was esteem-
ed upon Earth a very confiderable
Perfonage; 'tis true I am in the MOON
at prefent; but no Matter for that, I was
MASTER of the CEREMONIES at a Place
called BATH: Indeed they ufed to ftile
me KING of it; and, tho' I am no CITI-
ZEN here, I ruled all the CITIZENS there;
nay, fcolded Ladies, cut Jokes upon
Lords, directed Balls, befpoke Plays, and
did—in fhort I did what I pleafed: The
Corporation idolized, the Long-Rooms
reverenced, the Coffee-Houfes adored
me: I had my STATUE fet up in the
PUMP-ROOM, not a good Likenefs; but
no Matter for that,—I was always a
great Enemy to Quarrels, and therefore
never fuffer'd a Sword to be drawn in my
Territories; fo not knowing there would
be

be any Occasion for such Implements in
another World, I came hither quite un-
provided; which this grim old ROMAN
being acquainted with, took the Advantage of superior Strength, and Yesterday
pulled me by the Nose all round the
SALMINA RUVENAL, spurring me on
every six or eight Yards with a severe
Kick, which I think very Ungentleman-
like Treatment, and I hope you will think
so too, that he may be corrected for it.

The familiar Nothingness of this Speech
occasioned a general Smile thro' the Audience, and I observed that even the
NAMREDAL had some Difficulty to command his Muscles; however, Reason and
the Dignity of his Office checking other
Feelings, he took Occasion to remark,
that neither of the Parties being naturalized, nor any Law provided in NOIBLA
against such violent Proceedings, the Justice to be adapted in this Case must lie en-

M 2   tirely

tirely upon his Judgment, which he would adminifter with all poffible Impartiality: For this Purpofe he defired the Defendant to offer his Negative, or Palliation.

The Accufed, who was no lefs than the great CATO, delivered himfelf to the following Effect: SAGE SON OF JUSTICE AND LAW, to be Competitor or Difputant with fuch a Thing as now ftands before me, is Punifhment equal to the higheft Crime; yet unworthy, and far beneath my Notice as he is, I fhall enter into an Account of my Conduct, which has difcovered no Fault but that of too much Mildnefs.

This felf-blown Bubble has, in tracing himfelf, fufficiently fhewn his Emptinefs and Infignificance; nor will it avail much to fet the paltry Portrait in more glaring Colours than that he fpent a Life of Fourfcore Years in a motley Mixture of Vice, Idle-

Idleneſs, Foppery, and ridiculous Authority; the Jeſt of ſenſible Men, the Companion of Sharpers, and Terror of dancing Girls; laughed at in Youth, and de-
ſpiſed in Age.

How different from this the Race I
run? My early Years employed in the
Cultivation of my Mind; thoſe of ripen'd
Manhood worn, as I may ſay, in ſtem-
ming the Torrent of Faction;—there
view a ſkipping Child of Folly—here behold a diſintereſted Son of LIBERTY;—
and ſhall—Oh Heavens—this Inſect, not
two Degrees above mere Inſtinct, becauſe
we are met in a Region where juſt Diſtinctions ceaſe, dare to mate himſelf with
CATO unchaſtiſed? No, let it not be ſaid.
Rouſed by his biting Taunts, I own I did
treat him in the Manner he has ſet forth;
nor can I think unjuſtly; yet if Fortune,
which has purſued me even hither with
her Frowns, continues to torment me, I

M 3   cannot

cannot avoid her Malice, and therefore muſt endure it.

This Reply being concluded, in which may be diſcovered as much of Stoical Pride as the other ſhewed of Foppiſh Self-ſufficiency, the NAMREDAL diſcuſſed their Caſe in the following Manner:

It is amazing that, in this Region of Tranquillity, neither Example nor the Fear of Diſgrace, which is the moſt poignant Sting of all Puniſhment, can re-duce Sublunars from that turbulent Spirit ſo prevalent amongſt them.--You, NASH, continues he, who boaſt of having been ſo many Years Conductor of public Man-ners, ought to know better than to break untimely Jeſts upon a Man ſo much more eminent than you ever could pretend to be ; notwithſtanding thoſe who think themſelves Wits on Earth may indulge a ſuppoſed Privilege of caſting their Darts
in-

indiscriminately round, we never can suffer it here, unless in Form of legal Punishment, since it is repugnant both to
Reason and Humanity; I shall therefore
enjoin you to observe an absolute Silence
for one RAYAMON, never hereafter, on
any Pretence, to utter a Falsity, and to
be clothed all the while of your Silence
in a coarse Garment, the direct Contrast
to that you seem so fond of. ——Here the
BEAU groaned deeply, and begg'd for his
white Hat, but even that was denied
him, which seemed to have still a more
sensible Effect; while CATO confessed a
Kind of cynical Joy at so ridiculous a Di-
stress; but, as the Enjoyments of ill Nature ever should be, it was of very short
Continuance; for when he thought himself justified in his Antagonist's Sentence,
the NAMREDAL opened his Eyes, and
mortified his Pride thus:

Think

Think not, CATO, that the Conviction
of him exculpates you; though you did
receive some slight Offence, yet I know
not any rational System that unites the several Characters of Complainant, Judge,
and Executioner: Besides, there is in your
Defence somewhat as blameable as in
the former Part of your Conduct. Your
Accuser sets forth his own Character justly, without throwing any Sarcasms upon
yours; he betrayed Pride, but then it is
of the inoffensive Kind.———On the contrary, you have endeavoured to mount
yourself on his poor Ruins; you have
carefully diminished him, and oftenta-
tiously magnified yourself; tho' a Man of
your Reflection must know that the greatest Merit vanishes before Self-praise, like
Chaff before the Wind: Besides, you have
enviously suppressed one most amiable
Part of his Character, an industrious, unlimited Disposition to Charity, which must
have reached your Ears as well as other

Points

Points relating to him.—You boaſt of Philoſophy; how comes it that, ſo armed, you could not reſtrain yourſelf from Blows, and ſuffer his Inſignificance to paſs unheeded? But the Paſſion of ungovernable Pride which intoxicated you on Earth, ſtill viſibly prevails, tho' you have ſo often felt its bad Effects; in this Caſe I cannot avoid paſſing upon you the following Sentence: That, after NASH has performed his Pennance, you ſhall be obliged to keep him Company for two RAYAMONS; when, by my Authrity, he may talk as much, as loud, as faſt, and vent as keen a Ridicule as he pleaſes, being at Liberty once each TOIRTA to claim the Aſſiſtance of his Aſſociates CIBBER and RICH.

Theſe Names made the Stoic ſhudder; but knowing the Matter was unavoidable, he collected what Reſolution he could to carry off Appearances, and flounced

ced out of Court with a Look of ineffable Contempt, while Cæsar and Pompey, who had been liftening from a Corner to the whole Tranfaction, indulged their Mirth very freely on this Occafion.

The next Complaint was a Charge of Ingratitude preferred by one Man againft another, in which the Plaintiff fet forth, That he had, upon feveral Occafions, affifted the Defendant; that he had been induftrious to oblige him, notwithftanding which, continues he, forgetting the Feelings every honeft Man fhould have for Favours received, he has taken the firft Opportunity of fhewing himfelf my Enemy.

What, fays the Namredal, is it poffible? Can there in Noibla be fuch a Wretch? Ingratitude, the very Mention of a Temper fo difgraceful to the reafonable Nature, provokes our Indignation.

nation. Shall Beasts of the Field cast off their Wildness, and enter into a grateful kind Intimacy with their Keeper? Shall the winged Inhabitants of Air come tamely to the Hand that feeds them; and shall Man steel his Heart against all Impressions of Kindness, and all Sentiments of GRATITUDE? Oh Shame! Shame! Shame! Say thou who art complained against, how thou canst wipe off so deep a Stain; a Stain which, were it possible thou couldst have a thousand other Virtues, would fully and depreciate them all.

Sage and merciful ADMINISTRATOR of JUSTICE, says the Defendant, to describe the Anxiety I feel in being even supposed capable of such a Crime, requires more forcible Expression than I am possessed of; it pains me too that, in my Defence, I must cast some Censure upon a Man who, I acknowledge, has often done me Service; but his own precipitate

cipitate Temper forces the difagreeable
Talk upon me, and Self-defence requires
me to perform it; which, however, I
fhall do in as gentle and concife a Manner as poffible.

I have confeffed myfelf indebted for
Favours received; but how far the Obligation was diminifhed by my Benefactor's
public boafting of his Kindnefs to me, at
feveral different Times and Places, I fubmit, Oh NAMREDAL, to your impartial
Determination : Notwithftanding this,
my Feelings were not leffen'd, nor would
I have neglected any proper Teftimonies
of Thankfulnefs. This Complaint of his
arifes from my having reported fome Mif-
conduct I obferved in his Family while I
acted as one of the ELBIROS, weekly Infpectors; a Neceffity irkfome in itfelf,
yet at that Time unavoidable by me.

Moft

Moſt certainly, replies the NAMREDAL; are Acts of Friendſhip to take the Place of Bribes? Muſt Truth and Juſtice be ſacrificed to them? Shall the delegated Truſt of public Offices be betray'd to private Partialities? Beſides, continues he, applying to the Plaintiff, thy mean Proclamation of thy Bounty not only diminiſhes, but even annihilates all Obligation; hadſt thou exerted it merely to ſerve thy Friend, the ſilent delicate Pleaſure of doing it would have ſufficed thee; but Oſtentation was the Principle, and being deſtitute of Virtue, it is fit thou ſhou'dſt be deſtitute of Reward for theſe Reaſons; and more particularly for impeaching the Character of thy Fellow-Citizen, I conſider thee as a Criminal, and ſhall ſentence thee to act as his Servant three REAPANS, and once each TOIRTA to make a public Acknowledgement of thy Guilt in the RUVENAL, ſolliciting his Forgiveneſs.

Here

Here the Defendant earneſtly implo-
red a Remiſſion of the Sentence, remarking that it would be as painful to him as
to the condemn'd Perſon; and that he
was certain this public Repuſſe would
correct that Impatience of Diſpoſition
which led him into Error.————Well, ſays
the NAMREDAL, I yield to thy humane
and generous Sollicitation, which, for malicious Proſecution, returns the gentle
Balm of Mercy: Depart full of that Satisfaction a generous Heart muſt feel
from alleviating or averting Diſtreſs; and
thou, unworthy Object of this Goodneſs,
endeavour, by a zealous Reformation, to
deſerve ſo valuable a Friend.

The next Subject of Judicial Conſideration, which came before the NAMRE-
DAL, was an Accuſation againſt a young
Man for uttering ſome Expreſſions inconſiſtent with Modeſty before a Company of Females: As he acknowledged
the

the Circumſtances at large, and reſted his Cauſe on the Clemency of the Court, nothing more paſſed but the following Remarks made, and Sentence paſſed by the Magiſtrate.

Haſt thou not been taught — Oh inconſiderate Youth — that MODESTY ſhould be held ever ſacred? That it is the Shield of Virtue, and, if once penetrated by the Stings of Vice, ſcarce admits Repair? Like Snow it diſcovers the ſmalleſt Speck that chances to light upon it, and as that watry Conſiſtence melts away before the Sun, ſo MODESTY vaniſhes before the Heat of inordinate Paſſions, or even Words expreſſive of thoſe Paſſions.——Wouldſt thou preſerve Purity in Feeding, and yet defile thy Mouth with impure Language? Haſt thou no more Regard for Society than to vent ſuch pernicious Poiſon? Will it pleaſe thee to breathe Infection that may blaſt the Roſes

of

of Beauty? Art thou endowed with Reafon to make it an Inftrument of Good or Evil? If of Good, how canft thou employ it to wound the tender and delicate Ear of VIRTUE? If of Evil, like thofe venomous and naufeous Animals, which are equally dangerous and loathfome, thou fhouldft be fhunn'd and excluded from Society.

Thus much I have fpoke, if Shame be not dead in thee, to roufe it. What remains for me is to pafs the Sentence eftablifhed by Law for fuch Offences; which is, that barefooted, with thy Head uncovered, and the Words, *Retho efol na itfedom,*—*A Foe to Modefty,*—on thy Breaft; thou art to be publickly led thro' NODNOL fix Days fuccefively, and afterwards in the fame Manner thro' every ARESAL in the whole Ifland of NOIBLA; during which Space thou art difranchifed from all thy Rights and Privileges as a Citizen.

After

After this a grave Man and a young Female made their Appearance, and the Man spoke to this Effect: I am, VENERABLE NAMREDAL, Father of this young Woman now brought before you, and in that Relation have always exerted my tenderest Care, as well from natural Affection as from the Principle of parental Duty; I have not only studiously cultivated her Mind, which I have found most apt and teachable, but I have also, upon all Occasions, allowed her every prudent Indulgence; like a delicate and beauteous Flower she has flourished under my Care, yet it grieves me to add that, for some Time past, she has conducted herself in a Manner very contradictory to my Opinion, which I take to arise from an Intimacy she has contracted with a Female lately arrived from the nether World. By our Institutions all Women are dressed in the same Kind of

N   Ma-

Materials, therefore she cannot have Variety of Garments, yet has she an infinite Number of what she calls FASHIONS; sometimes long Sleeves, sometimes short; sometimes Wings as if she was going to fly, then bare as an unfeather'd Pinion; sometimes a Tail sweeping the Ground, then so much curtail'd that half her Legs may be seen; besides which, tho' I have often pointed out agreeable Partners for Marriage, she puts me off with saying she cannot give up her Liberty yet; that such a one is not handsome enough; that another is not witty; a third has no Spirits, and many other such-like trifling Evasions; notwithstanding which she is never easy but when flaunting with Men: This I have often remonstrated against, but to no Purpose; and of late she has had the Confidence to tell me that Men in Years were no Judges of what was fit for young Women; wherefore, Oh FA-

THER

THER of NODNOL, I have brought her hither for your Wisdom and Authority to influence.

Aye, replies the NAMREDAL, have we Disobedience and a Contempt of parental Power creeping in amongst us? If so, adieu to Order, Peace, Virtue, and social Happiness. — Pray, young Madam, how have you ventured to depart so far from the Obligations of Nature and the strict Laws of this Island? If you have any Apology, any Plea, make it, and I shall attend.

The poor Girl, covered with extreme Confusion, had scarce Power to utter the following broken Sentences; that she loved her Father very well, and had a great Pleasure in obeying him, but that the COUNTESS of ——, (her Title is omitted in Respect of some living) lately arrived from ENGLAND, told her, Fathers were

N 2   such

such chuff Fellows, who would not willingly allow their Children any Pleasures; that no Girl of Spirit should mind them; that if she married it would cut of all Admirers; that by keeping Company with different Men she would have a better Choice; and that making Cloaths in various FASHIONS would set her off to more Advantage.

A very hopeful Account, truly, says the Magistrate, and for all this sensible, kind Instruction you are indebted to the COUNTESS. Upon my Word it would be great Pity, and reflect upon us much Disgrace, if so public-spirited a Lady, who would reform our Manners, teach us Elegance for Simplicity, and Spirit for Prudence, should go unrewarded; wherefore, Oh ye Citizens, you who this Day give Force to Law, take Notice that I sentence the said COUNTESS, without Hope of Redemption, to the VALLEY of

WEEP-

WEEPING; there let her expatiate on Taſte; there let her diſplay faſhionable Knowledge; there ſet up the vain Idols of her frantic Brain.

As for you, young Daughter, continued the NAMREDAL, who have been led aſtray thro' Inexperience, I ſhall endeavour to inform you better, by remarking upon each Particular of what you have ſaid; this the Duty of the Magiſterial Office requires, and my Duty is enforced by thoſe tender and ſympathetic Feelings which urge us to guard or reſcue natural Innocence from artificial Guilt.

Firſt, then, as to the Love of your Father; I grant it may be affectionate, but it cannot be truly filial or perfect without an unlimited Obedience to his Authority, and an implicit Compliance with his Precepts; which, you may be ſatisfied, are both exerted to promote your Welfare

and

and Happinefs. I know that he and you
view Things in a very different Light, as
Age and Youth ever do; the Vivacity of
the latter, like an impatient Courfer,
ftruggles for the full and dangerous
Stretch of natural Liberty, while the former is making Ufe of the prudential
Check-Rein of Reftraint.——Confider,
Age fees Actions and Circumftances in
their true Shape, and difcerns what Confequences they lead on to; while Youth,
looking through Paffion-tainted Optics,
views them colour'd according to their
Fancy and their Wifh; hence therefore
the Opinions and Advice of experienced
Elders, of Parents efpecially, fhould be
allowed all due Influence.

Your Choice in Marriage is, by the
Laws of the Ifland, undoubtedly free,
and Reafon fanctifies thofe Laws, therefore in this Point you have no Compul-
fion to fear; but Freedom is not infringed

fringed by the cordial Advice of thofe
who have your Profperity at Heart. As
to the idle Notion of lofing Liberty and
Admirers by taking a Hufband, nothing
can be more abfurd; true Liberty does
not confift in a licentious Indulgence of
Follies and Proftitution of Time, but in
an uncontrouled, voluntary, prudent Purfuit of Virtue and domeftic Happinefs,
to which the very Name of Admirers is
a Bane, I mean Admirers of external
Charms only; for of thofe who admire the
unfading Beauties of the Mind, who can
gain more than fhe who diftinguifhes herfelf by the eminent and moft amiable
Title of *A good Wife?* She has number-
lefs Opportunities of commanding Praife,
which the fingle State affords not; in that
Character are comprized fuch invincible
Charms as brave the Attacks of Sorrow,
Pain, Sicknefs, and even Death itfelf; the
Matrimonial Union collects into a Train
of uniform, folid, and lafting Enjoyment,

that

that Happiness which in Celibacy is diffused variable and imperfect.

By associating with a Variety of Gallants you think Power and Choice enlarged; it may be so, but then it becomes dangerous, since nothing can be more prejudicial to the Character of a young Woman, nothing more repugnant to Prudence; and tho' it be not an absolute Violation of Virtue, yet is it a great Blemish in her Reputation, for even Appearances of what is wrong should be avoided; in the Eye of Reason the Prostitution of the Mind, which certainly leads to it, is little less offensive than the Prostitution of the Person.

As to the Variation of Fashion, which is in itself childish, it may possibly add somewhat to Attraction of Features; nor would there be any great Matter of Offence in it, but for the Time it must necessarily

ceſſarily engroſs, and the unprofitable
Emulation it muſt create of outvying
each other in Trifles, when all our Con-
teſt ſhould be to gain an honourable Diſtinction in the Race of public and private Virtues.——Dreſſing to draw Admirers
is one of the pooreſt Baits of Folly; Neat-
neſs is agreeable to Reaſon and Nature,
and equally eſſential to Maid and Wife;
more is at beſt but idle Superfluity.

Lock up theſe Remarks, fair Daughter, in your Heart; think not that, being
grave, they are ſevere; entertain a grateful Remembrance of your Father's kind
Attention to your Welfare; give Heed to
his Advice, Obedience to his Commands,
and on ſuch Conditions I will not only
free you from Puniſhment, but even from
Cenſure.

Having thus concluded, the Father re-
verently made Obeiſance to him, and the
Girl

Girl returned silent Thanks in Tears of penitent Joy. So terminated the Bufi-nefs of the Day; when the NAMREDAL, descending from his Judgment-Seat, con-ducted me, thro' the attending Citizens, to the Dining-Hall; when seated, he ask-ed me how I liked their Court of Judica-ture, which occasioned me to break out into a rapturous Exclamation: Happy! supremely happy NOIBLANS! among whom Justice appears in her own un-adorned, modeft, native Dignity, not ar-ray'd in the Fool's Coat of Tricks and Equivocation: Where the Magiftrate is indeed a Parent of the People; where un-incumber'd Reason takes its free Courfe without paffing through the Windings and inextricable Confufion of Sophiftry; where Innocence and Guilt are contrafted with judicious Impartiality; where Riches, Rank, or Power, never appear to influ-ence; but where the calm determined Voice of Equity, speaking with the Or-gans

gans of Truth, not only impreſſes Conviction, but even commands Approbation from thoſe who receive Cenſure or
Puniſhment.

I am much pleaſed, replies the NAM-
REDAL, that you conſider this Part of the
NOIBLAN Inſtitution in the ſame Light as
I do; other Peculiarities which you have
met with ſince your Arrival in theſe Regions, I know cannot ſo well ſuit the active
Spirit of a SUBLUNAR Being.—There is a
general and amiable Tranquillity here, but
then it is founded upon Principles which
entirely reſtrain progreſſive Knowledge;
all here think themſelves ſufficiently wiſe,
ſufficiently happy; they ſeek to know no
more than they are already acquainted
with, nor to poſſeſs any Thing better
than what their Fathers have enjoyed:
This will appear to you a mental Lethargy, and undoubtedly it is ſuch; but many
Ad-

Advantages accrue from such a Mode of thinking, which are in themselves so evident that I need not point them out, especially as you will next Week have an Opportunity of hearing somewhat more at large upon this Topic, when all the NAMREDALS of the Island come to their annual Conference at NODNOL.

The MOUNT of OBSERVATION, the VALLEY of WEEPING, the ESTRALAM, NEROMA, with other Subjects worthy of Observation, will afford you Matter of very agreeable and not unuseful Speculation.

Here the BELL of NOON gave Warning for Dinner, and interrupted a Conversation which would probably have extended itself to a considerable Length. Here also, kind Readers, after conversing and travelling so far together, I hope on friendly Terms, you will think it fit that,

for

for a while at leaſt, we ſhould part: If you are inclined to accompany me any farther in this extraordinary Progreſs, I ſhall attend your Call, and in the mean Time I bid you heartily farewell.

The END *of the* FIRST VOLUME.

A

TRIP to the MOON.

Containing an Account of the

ISLAND of NOIBLA.

Its INHABITANTS, RELIGIOUS and POLITICAL CUSTOMS, &c.

By Sir HUMPHREY LUNATIC, *Bart.*

---

*I am but mad North North-West; when the Wind
blows Southerly I know a Hawk from a Hernshaw.*
                                        SHAKESPEAR.

VOLUME II.

L O N D O N:

Printed for S. CROWDER, in *Pater-noster-Row*; W.
NICOLL, and W. BRISTOW, in St. *Paul's Church-
Yard*; and C. ETHERINGTON, in *York*, 1765.

THE Title of a GOOD MAN *being superior to all the Honours that a Monarch can bestow; whoever is so happy as to know his valuable Character, will approve the Patron to whom I recommend this Volume, and justify me in submitting it to the Protection of*

TINDAL THOMPSON, Esq;

NEW MALTON,
December 1764.

To *the* PUBLIC.

SIR *HUMPHREY* fhould think himfelf undeferving the particular Approbation beftowed upon his former Volume, by fo many *able* and *independent* Critics, not to acknowledge the Obligation; and takes the Liberty to obferve, That it is with Defign he makes his *Lunar* Journals attend to the *ufeful*, rather than the *miraculous*.

Speedily will be publifhed,

L I F E:

A N

E P I S T L E.

Addreffed to

SAMUEL DERRICK, *Efq*;
MASTER *of the* CEREMONIES *at* BATH.

A L S O

CHARACTERS,
In Three EPISTLES.

A TRIP to the MOON.

Prefatory Matter—Remarks on the Use and Abuse of Travel—The Ceremony of Banishment—Strictures upon public Executions, &c.

FELLOW-TRAVELLER, according to Promise I have again met you, in order to continue our *Tour*, and I doubt not but the same Degree of good Humour, the same Flow of Spirits, the same commendable Curiosity on your Side, and the same friendly Disposition to gratify it on mine, will render our farther Progress both pleasant and profitable.

Before we set off, however, let me express my Hope that you will not prove

like a learned and ingenious *Critic* upon
my *former* VOLUME, who declared a general Approbation of the Matter and
Conduct, were it not that he deemed the
Afcent of a Mortal to the MOON impracticable: How flender muft his Faith be!
How liable to Megrims, and incapable
of extraordinary Elevation, his Shuttle-
cock Pericranium! Let Animals of
this groveling Nature, who, formed
meerly of Clay, without one animating
Spark to lift them above the Sphere of
common Attraction, drudge upon their
Mother Earth; let them fneer at, or condemn, what they cannot underftand,
while we, difdaining, like ALEXANDER,
to own ourfelves pent within the penurious Limits of one World, range thro'
the whole Planetary Syftem: Let Men of
Titles and Fortune, without Heads, purfue one fafhionable Tract, while we afpire
to Climes, Speculations, and Curiofities
beyond their Reach.

The

The Advantages of TRAVEL in this nether World (a Branch of *Education* more followed for Parade than Improvement) have been induftrioufly blazon'd by fome, while the Dangers of it have been as partially difplay'd by others. Without entering upon tedious or intricate Difquifitions, we may reafonably conclude that much valuable and ornamental Knowledge may be deriv'd from vifiting various Countries, if the different Policy and Manners of the feveral States be properly confidered, and their conftitutional or artificial Virtues and Vices impartially furvey'd.

But if Attention, as is too frequently the Cafe, childifhly plays with Trifles, or, under the Influence of Novelty, it dwells upon fuch irrational Enjoyments as flatter unruly and dangerous Paffions; if a Man only learns exceffive Drinking in GERMANY; low Tricking in HOLLAND; Levity in FRANCE; dogmatical Pride in

A 2 SPAIN;

SPAIN; and lewd Intrigue in ITALY, then were it better to be confined within the narrow Boundaries of one Profpect; for home-bred Follies are lefs awkward and lefs pernicious than foreign Coxcombry: On the reverfe, if, properly prepared by Study and a competent Knowledge of our native Land, we collect Military Knowledge from the GERMANS; Œconomy and Affiduity in Bufinefs from the DUTCH; Spirit in Converfation, and Eafe in Deportment, from the FRENCH; nothing from the SPANIARDS; from the ITALIANS, a juft and delicate Tafte for MUSIC, PAINTING, and ARCHITECTURE, we give Nature all the Affiftance neceffary to make it fhine with confpicuous and falutary Luftre.

In our NOIBLAN Progrefs I dare promife you there is no Danger; for if you part from me no wifer nor better than when we met, you may at leaft depend
upon

upon it that you will leave me no worſe; for it is an invariable Maxim with me to appear rather dull and ſtoical, than pert at the Coſt of Decency, or wiſe at the Expence of Virtue and Religion: However, tho' bound within ſuch unfaſhionable Limits, tho' I am not ſo popular a LUNATIC as to employ my Pen in trifling Memoirs or political Scandal, I hope to produce ſuch Matter as will at leaſt keep you awake, unleſs you read in Bed, which, by the Bye, I would adviſe you againſt; and if I ſhould, as becomes my Name and Family, ſometimes ramble beyond the Sphere of general Comprehenſion, fear not, truſt me that I ſhall prove a faithful Guide, and conſult your ſafe Return with all imaginable Caution.

Thus agreed, Friend Reader, let us, like cordial Acquaintance, ſhake Hands. Hold! you ſay, not ſo free with a Fellow in Maſquerade, one whom neither I,

nor

nor perhaps any Body elſe knows.—He
calls himſelf a KNIGHT, but for ought we
can tell he is a KNIGHT of the *Poſt*.—You
have ſaid it: Now let me ſpeak, and, if it
muſt come to an Examination, inquire
whether you know all your Acquaintance:
Are none of them in Maſquerade? Are
they all exactly what they appear to be?
If there are *Lords* among them, have they
all real as well as titular Honour? If *Ladies*, are they diſtinguiſhed by domeſtic
Virtues as well as public Rank? If ſo,
you are a happy Mortal indeed; but let
me tell you, Hearts and Tongues, Looks
and Thoughts, Words and Actions, Dignity and Worth, Criticiſm and Knowledge, are, for the moſt Part, at Variance
in this very wiſe and very virtuous World
of ours.—Very wiſe and very virtuous!
why not, Sir HUMPHREY, you'll reply—
what, I ſuppoſe, in the common Place of
Satire, you would inſinuate ironically that
we are much worſe than our Anceſtors;
that

that all Merit muſt be ſought for amidſt
the Ruſt of Antiquity, and that our Age
is not only the moſt ignorant, but the
moſt corrupt alſo; or are you ſo enthu-
ſiaſtically fond of your favourite Planet,
your new-found World, as utterly to con-
temn the Inhabitants and Productions of
this ſublunary Sphere?

Soft, ſoft gentle Reader, you are rather too haſty, tho' kind, in explaining
my Ideas; for I take our Age to be adorned with as much Wiſdom, Virtue, and
Courage as any that ever preceded it, or
poſſibly any that may be to come; at
the ſame Time you will give me Leave
to ſay it is blemiſhed with an equal
Number of Imperfections, and thoſe ariſing from the ſame Materials, only in different Shapes, that produced ſimilar Imperfections a thouſand Years ago; our
Manners and Conduct, like our Cloaths,
only

only change Names and Fashions, yet are literally the same; as to the LUNAR REGIONS, you will hereafter find that I can look upon them with as impartial an Eye as I do upon the terrestrial ones.—But to return to my Inquiry: I have asked if you know all your Acquaintance; as I love to be free, let me extend the Question, and inquire whether you even *know* YOURSELF?—What, silent—no Answer? Why then I may reasonably suppose you do not as you ought—for Shame, look at home—turn your Eyes inwards, first examine your own Heart, then look into the Breasts of your Neighbours; and, from a comparative View of Merits or Failings, learn to value or commiserate your Fellow-Creatures, not according to their Riches or Poverty, but according to their commendable or unworthy Conduct in Life; judge of them not as *Solar*, *Lunar*, or *Terrestrial* Beings, but as CITI-

ZENS

ZENS of the UNIVERSE, whose expanded
Hearts reverence and embrace all the
Works of GOD.

What a tedious dull Moralist, cries
every *fashionable* Reader, is this Sir HUM-
PHREY? Probably it is so; but, that we
may be the more agreeable Company,
do, good new Acquaintance, only grant
me the Indulgence to think me as wise,
as witty, as honest, or, in the more popular Phrase, as clever a Fellow as yourself, and ten to one but you will read
with as much Pleasure as I write—thus
much to Male Readers. As for the
LADIES, I can only sollicit their Favour
and their Attention by declaring, that a
handsome Woman captivates my Eyes;
that a *sensible* Woman awes my Tongue;
and that a GOOD Woman (which three
Characters, I dare believe, are united in
you, Madam, who are now reading here)
ravishes my Heart.

Thus

Thus much we have talk'd upon Earth, and modifhly, fo far as Senfe and Fafhion can agree, having disjointed Connexion to give a Relifh of Spirit, now let the bold and rapid Wing of full-fledg'd Imagination bear us to the NOIBLAN REQUECEX, where, as I remember, we left the good NAMREDAL going to his Noontide Meal; which having paffed over with the ufual Ceremony, my Ears were ftruck with flow and folemn Sounds echoing drowfily thro' the RUVENAL; when looking out I faw a confiderable Number of Perfons approach in awful and deliberate Proceffion, which was led by twelve Men in long Purple-coloured Garments, marching four and four; then fucceeded a Band of Vocal Mufic, fuch as I had heard at the SALMINA, who, in the folemn Paufes of a dead March, chaunted a moft affecting Hymn of Sorrow: The Emblems of JUSTICE followed; and after them moved two Females cloathed from Head to Foot

Foot in flowing Sable Robes, their Hair dihevelled and covering their Faces; two Virgins dreſſed in White ſupported each; then a Train of near one hundred Matrons cloathed in White, and their Heads covered with long Purple Veils, cloſed the Proceſſion.

This Ceremony was very ſtriking; the moſt profound Silence was obſerved amidſt the attending Crowds, except at ſtated Places, when a reverend Citizen read the Crimes and Sentence of the Criminals, and thereby drew forth a general Sigh of Compaſſion from the Spectators. One of the Sufferers I found to be the *Engliſh* COUNTESS formerly mentioned; the other unhappy Victim remained quite ſpeechleſs, as if Conviction and Penitence had ſeized her Faculties, and lock'd up the Powers of Speech: But her Ladyſhip retaining the ungovernable, ſhameleſs Pride of Terreſtrial Quality,

Quality, every now and then exclaimed
vehemently—*Is this Ufage for a Woman
of Rank and Spirit?—O happy* ENGLAND,
*where every Thing is fanctified by Nobility!
No Diftinction paid here!—Mon* DIEU,
*what a miferable vulgar World have I got
into?—I have heard of* HOTTENTOTS, *and
fure I am among them.*

What incorrigible Affurance has that
Creature, cried the NAMREDAL, who,
after attacking the very Vitals of Female
Modefty and filial Piety, dares think her
Sentence hard? All thefe and her future
Sufferings are juftly due to the Life of
unprofitable and licentious Diffipation
that fhe led in her former State of Exiftence, exclufive of her infectious Maxims
and Example here. The other Criminal,
continues he, is fhe whom the TWINS
contended for; they are now, according to my Sentence, conveying to the
VALLEY of WEEPING, and this Proceffion

fion is the Ceremony ufed upon fuch Occafions; thofe Virgins who fuppor: the
Exiles are dreffed in White, as an Emblem
of their Innocence contrafted with Sable
Guilt; the Wives who follow are robed
in White alfo, as Daughters of Virtue,
but wear Purple Veils in Token of Sorrow for the difgraceful Fate of their unhappy Sifters.

I own the very decent, rational Solemnity attending this Act of Juftice impref-
fed me with a melancholy Pleafure, and
I could not help exclaiming to the NAM-
REDAL how much Approbation it extort-
ed from me, when compared with the
Circumftances that attend a public Punifhment in our World, where unhappy
Criminals are purfued and gazed at by
unfeeling Crowds, who feem more bent
to gratify an inhuman Curiofity, than difpofed to commiferate the unhappy Fate
of their Fellow-Creatures.   Among the
NOI-

NOIBLANS, who are happy enough to
know no Crime that reaches Life, a filent,
fenfible, fympathetic Concern attends
fuffering Guilt; among us even the terrifying Brow of Death cannot prevent a
bufy, buftling, indecent Noife; fome few,
perhaps, upon fuch awful Occafions, let
fall the kindly Dew-Drops of Compaffion,
and breathe forth the foft Sighs of Pity,
while a large Majority indulge the malevolent Spirit of Cenfure, in remarking,
that if People won't do right they muft
fuffer; that it is but fit Examples fhould
be made, tho' not at all affured but that
they themfelves, under the fame Impulfes
of Paffion, imperfect Education, bad
Example, Neceffities, or Temptations,
all which are Misfortunes rather than
Crimes, might be found capable of the
fame Delinquency they are fo ready to
condemn. Juftice, to maintain Property
and Order, fhould undoubtedly, among
every Rank, fupport her Dignity inviolate,

late, and therefore muſt let fall the Rod
of impartial Chaſtiſement upon convicted
Guilt, to terrify thoſe into Obedience
whom the Charms of conſcious Innocence
cannot keep within the Pale of Right.

The NAMREDAL having attended to
my Remarks, replied, Your Sentiments
are perfectly right; when I was on Earth
it gave me infinite Surprize and Concern
to ſee Pleaſure oftener expreſſed at the
Miſeries than at the Happineſs of Hu-
mankind; nor could I ever diſcover the
Riſe of ſo unſocial a Satisfaction, unleſs,
perhaps, it may proceed from a falſe Imagination, that, while we are anatomizing
and cenſuring the Characters of our
Neighbours, we exhibit our own to more
Advantage.

How pitiful, how impolitic a Species
of Ambition, which deſtroys what it ſeeks
for, and caſts an ÆTHIOP Veil over that
White-

Whiteneſs it would ſet forth as clear as the unſpotted Snow? If thoſe who poſſeſs this peſtilential Spirit, more blighting than the Eaſtern Blaſt, would but conſider the Conſequence of indulging it, that the Diſgrace or Ruin they meditate for others will moſt infallibly retort upon themſelves, perhaps that ruling Principle, SELF-LOVE, might create a Tenderneſs, which Charity and ſocial Obligations recommend in vain.

How fatal have undeſerved Aſperſions often proved, by urging weak, innocent Perſons into a Contempt of Reputation, than which nothing can be more dangerous to moral or ſocial Virtue; for what we deſpiſe we always neglect; and to give out Appearances which bear a ſtrong Reſemblance to Vice, is next to the actual Commiſſion of it. But come, continues he, we are dwelling too long upon a Subject more grave than entertaining, what

what think you if, by Way of Relaxation, we should take a general View of the City?

I gladly embraced the Proposal, and for that Purpose attended my kind Conductor to the SALMINA RUVENAL. As we passed along I could not but express my Surprize that we met so few People in the Streets; notwithstanding that, from the Numbers I had occasionally seen, the City appeared to be extremely populous.

Your Surprize, says the NAMREDAL, is natural enough, but it will soon cease, when you are informed that no Person here traverses the Streets upon an idle or superfluous Occasion; the unavoidable Concerns of mutual Intercourse alone call People forth here; no Visiting Cabals, to dissect and pry into the Concerns of neighbouring Families; Hours of

VOL. II.　　B　　healthful

healthful and innocent Recreation are allowed in proper Places adjacent to the City; the ſtated and well-known Buſineſs allotted for each Individual takes away thoſe ridiculous Pretences for rambling and purſuing each other, which are ſo induſtriouſly framed and propagated amongſt SUBLUNARS, to the unſpeakable Prejudice of their Minds and Circumſtances. Among the NOIBLANS the juſt Œconomy of TIME is a general and leading Conſideration.

C H A P. I.

A Deſcription of the City; its ſeveral Parts and Peculiarities—A Funeral—Preparatory Circumſtances—The Temples of TIME *and* DEATH——ROCHESTER *and* CHARLES II. *introduced.*

HAVING reached the TEMPLE, we aſcended to the Baſe of its DOME,

from

from whence a diftinct View of the City
prefented itfelf, wherein I perceived the
SALMINA and REQUECEX to be the two
principal RUVENALS, each of them about
half a Mile in Circumference, branching
out two Streets, of a Quarter of a Mile
in Length, from each Side of the Square;
Half-way in every Street appear'd a fmal-
ler Square: The Houfes are all uniform,
built of a bluifh Stone, and piazza'd with
white Pillars; no upper Stories, nor are
there any Windows, all Light defcending thro' flat Roofs; the Streets may be
about fixty Yards wide, with two fmall
Rivulets of a Yard broad in each; and in
the Center of every Square is a fuperb
Fountain of an EMERALD-colour'd Stone,
from whence thofe Rivulets receive a
conftant Supply of Water. Thefe, the
NAMREDAL obferved, were not fo much
for Ornament as Ufe; by Means of thofe
fmall Streams, fays he, the Streets are
eafily cleanfed from any noxious Matter

B 2   that

that might grow offensive, or taint the
Air; and upon an Accident of Fire,
which however rarely happens, so immediate and plentiful a Supply of its opposite Element enables us to restrain the
Mischief, and put a timely Stop to it.
Every House has exactly the same Portion
of Ground allotted to it for Gardening.
The MAGISTRATE, assisted by twenty-
four CITIZENS, determines regularly at
the Season what every Family must plant
or sow for the general Stock; and fixes
both the Quantity to be furnished, and
the Time when it is to be brought in.

This Institution may appear both singular and partial, since some Subjects of
Labour require more Assiduity, and are
attended with much more Trouble and Fatigue than others: In such Cases an equi-
valent Advantage is allowed; but to de-
scend into Particulars would be too tedious, and must divert your Attention from
what

what you will find more agreeable: Come,
let us afcend higher, that you may not
only command a better Profpect of the
City, but alfo of the adjoining Territory.
We afcended, and a moft enchanting
Profpect open'd on my View; extenfive
Lawns, beautified with vernal Smiles,
and interfected by the flow ftately Windings of a majeftic River; fkirting Woods
in different Forms and Situations, and
terminating Hills, delightfully irregular,
entertain'd the Eye with an inimitable
Scene of rural Elegance and Pleafure.
What you now behold, fays the NAMRE-
DAL, is a Miniature Sketch of the whole
Ifland, juft as we of NODNOL are a fmall
Sample of the Inhabitants, except thofe
of NEROMA and OMYRCHAL, both which
deferve a particular Defcription; but I in-
tend you fhall fee them.

Having fufficiently contemplated the
Beauties that furrounded us, we defcend-

ed,

ed, and I afked my Conductor whether
the Climate of NOIBLA was fteady as well
as ferene, or whether it admitted fuch frequent and violent Changes as certain Seafons produce among us: No, replied he,
the Elements here are an Emblem of that
Tranquillity which prevails among the
Inhabitants; we have no greater Altera-
tion than what you have feen; no Tem-
pefts ever whirl their Devaftation here;
we have no Thunder to alarm us; no
Lightning to blaft us; no Floods of Rain
to fweep away the Fruits of the Earth:
We know nothing of the Severities either
of Cold or Heat; temperate Breezes cool
and purify the Air, refrefhing Dews moi-
ften and fertilize the Soil, and we have
all the Bleffings of a perpetual Spring:
Whatever Induftry can procure, whatever Prudence would purfue, or Contentment can fupply, is found in this
mild and happy Region, where the natural-born NOIBLANS ufually enjoy about a
hundred

hundred Years of Life, free from all internal and external Pain, unlefs they bring it on themfelves by fome Inadvertence of their own. As to thofe who have been tranflated here from Earth, their Duration is uncertain—while they remain they appear in the fame matured Form they wore in the SUBLUNARY WORLD, without any perceptible Increafe of Years or Decline of Conftitution. Now that we have touched, continued he, upon Mortality, it may prove a ufeful Gratification of your Curiofity to fee a FUNERAL according to the Manner of this ISLAND, and the Circumftances preparatory to it, which, I dare believe, will appear fomewhat extraordinary to you.

Having acknowledged that nothing could be more worthy of my Attention, we proceeded to a Houfe from whence iffued loud Sounds of Mufic and triumphant Chorufes of Joy; many Perfons
dreffed

dreſſed in gay or rather antic Habits, and crowned with Garlands, ſtood before the Entrance, diſplaying magnificent Banners, ornamented with Variety of Hieroglyphics.

Behold, ſays my Guide, the Manſion of DEATH. Perceiving me to be ſurprized at the Appearance of ſuch Feſtivity, he told me it was intended as a Compliment to the dying Perſon, who is ſuppoſed thereby to have Spirits infuſed, to bear up againſt the Weakneſs of Nature, and to render the Satisfaction of being ſo near his Removal to a better State of Exiſtence more ſenſible. This Point being cleared up, I yet remained under another Difficulty; I could not account for it that a Number of People ſhould be aſſembled to attend the Funeral of a Perſon not yet dead; however, the NAMREDAL informed me that an Hour would clear up the whole Matter; for,

ſays

says he, the FINAL EXPERIMENT has been made, and the old Man, tho' not quite dead, is moſt certainly not far from breathing his laſt.

I here aſked what was meant by the FINAL EXPERIMENT, and was inſtructed, that when, from Age and Weakneſs, any Perſon is ſuppoſed to be upon his Death-Bed, one of the GARDEN-BIRDS is brought into the Room; if it tamely flies towards him, Death is not near; but if it flutters about with Noiſe and Screaming, then his End is inevitably at Hand.

I was by this Time conducted into a Chamber, where I ſaw the Victim half ſet, half laid on a rich Couch under an elegant Canopy, with the Muſicians ranged on each Side of him: Soon after our Entrance the feſtive Strains we had heard were gradually lull'd into Silence, when a young Man of noble Deportment, pro-
ſtrating

ſtrating himſelf before the dying Perſon, ſpoke as follows:

"Tender and benevolent Parent, kind and faithful Guardian of our younger Years, let not this unavoidable Separation from the immediate Society of your Children and Friends, totally deprive us of your paternal Care and Affection; when thy Spirit ſhakes off its material Fetters, Oh condeſcend to ſuperviſe our Conduct, and to direct our Courſe; whiſper into our Minds whatever may be needful to a blameleſs Exiſtence here; pour the Balm of temperate Deſire and calm Contentment into our Souls; be thou the kind Conveyance of the Bleſſings that are allotted for us by our UNIVERSAL FATHER, and when we ſtand upon the Verge of Time, bring us ſome Beams of heavenly Radiance to cheer our Way, and to light us thro' the gloomy Vale of Death."

This

This Addreſs was received with a Countenance full of the ſincereſt Reſpect and the tendereſt Affection, which immediately broke forth in the following Reply:

"Son of my Care, and you other Children of my deareſt Love, doubt not the Influence and Protection of my ſympathizing Spirit; the Pinions of the Morn ſhall bear me to aſſiſt you, and even on the ſable Wing of Night I'll hover to protect you: Yet place not too much Confidence in ſupernatural Aſſiſtance, exert your own Faculties to the moſt worthy Purpoſes, ſo ſhall my Guardian Care be the more effectual, and your Heavenly Father will be more diſpoſed to grant me the Power of protecting and of bleſſing you."

This I found was a Cuſtom among the NOIBLANS, ariſing from a traditional Opinion,

Opinion, that the Spirits of departed Perſons are inveſted with the Superintendance of their ſurviving Friends, and that, without ſuch Guardians, the immaterial Agents of Vice and Confuſion would deſtroy all Virtue and ſocial Order.

Soon after this Piece of Religious Ceremony, the old expiring Noiblan demanded of the Namredal who I was; when, being told that I came from the Sublunar World, he ſeemed much pleaſed, as ſuppoſing me to have undergone ſomewhat ſimilar to that great Change which he himſelf was about to experience; however, being ſet right in this Point, I was moved, by his hoſpitable Reception, to offer Condolance on his approaching Diſſolution, after the Manner uſual with us upon ſuch Occaſions.

"What, replied he, viewing me with an Eye of ſtern Regard, have I ever done to provoke

provoke thy Ill-will, that thou fhouldſt
mourn, like an Enemy, at the moſt fortu-
nate Period of my Life, my ſecond and
more glorious Birth? Nature, thou feeſt,
haſt accompliſhed her End, and is now
brought to the laſt Ebb: Time has dried
up the Springs of Action, and I have
nought remaining of my former Self, but
a Remembrance of the Faculties I once
poſſeſſed; which, like the Breath I have
drawn, are faded into nothing; and canſt
thou, unprovok'd, wiſh me to totter about
longer, wearifome to myfelf, and bur-
thenſome to others? I have heard, Son
of Earth, that the *Monſter* Envy is very
prevalent in thy World; does it reach even
to the Border of the Grave, and extend
ſo far as to deny the weary, worn-out
Traveller his hard-earn'd Reſt?"

" Venerable Sir, I replied, Death is
a Confummation, which, tho' eſſential to
Nature, and common to all, every Man,
wiſhes

wiſhes to his Neighbour before himſelf;
a Period the Aged ſhun, and tremble at
as much as Youth; however temporal
Poſſeſſions may be coveted, this deſirable
Change is induſtriouſly avoided by all;
the Pride of Beauty, Riches, Fame, and
Grandeur, ſhrinks before it; and the Im-
preſſion it makes is ſo awful, that Survi-
vors, not content to vent their Grief in
the natural Expreſſion of it, carry the
Semblance of their inward Sorrow for
their departed Friends even in their
Dreſs and whole outward Appearance."

"Oh Fools! Fools! Fools! returned he,
if they are ſo afraid to die, how comes it
they are not afraid to live, one being as
unavoidable as the other, and the natural
Conſequence of it? Far hence be removed ſuch irrational Timidity; while I at
this bliſsful Moment, with you my Children, Fellow CITIZENS and Friends, who
muſt all in due Time experience the
same

same eligible Separation, rejoice that I have been placed in a World whose Inhabitants live with Contentment and die with Compofure; where, without yielding to the unprofitable Weaknefs of childifh Grief, we take Leave of the Departing as fetting out upon a pleafant Journey; where we lie down in the cold Arms of Death with as much Tranquillity as in the nightly Repofe of Nature; lie down! nay, meet with Joy our kind Reliever; where that felf-tormenting Raven, a guilty Confcience, never preys upon the Heart, nor croaks Defpair unto the Dying:—But hold, my impatient Spirit fprings forward towards Liberty— thro' thefe failing Eyes I fee the NAL-SINA, attended by my venerable Anceftors, approach; his heavenly Voice charms my Ear—and lo—he fpreads the fnowy Wings of Mercy to bear me from Imperfection and Infirmity to immortal Blifs."

Here,

Here, fainting in a Kind of enthufiaftic
Extacy, the attending Avozen proceeded immediately to a ftrange, and, in my
Sight, inhuman Operation, no other than
that of feparating the old Man's Head
from his Body. The fmall Quantity of
Blood which iffued, was carefully receiv'd
by his eldeft Son into a Chryftal Recep-
tacle.

After this the Corpfe, having undergone a very ceremonious Ablution, and
being furnifhed with an artificial Head,
fo nicely formed and judicioufly colour'd,
as hardly to be diftinguifhed from the natural one, was arrayed in moft magnificent Attire, and, being feated in a Triumphal Carriage, was conducted, with
great Pomp and Joy, to the Nesova
Rennam, the Field of Death, about
two Miles from the City, a Place of much
rural Beauty, near four Miles in Circumference, fenced by a large Dyke ten Yards
wide,

wide, and ornamented by two elegant
Buildings placed on oppofite Hills at the
Extremities of a Grove, awfully delight-
ful; one of thofe Edifices is a TEMPLE
dedicated to TIME, called, in NOIBLA,
RINMETHOL, the ACCOMPLISHER; the
other to DEATH, ftiled LARDETHAC, the
DELIVERER.

At our Entrance into the Field, the
Corpfe was met by fome PRIESTS belong-
ing to the TEMPLE of TIME, and conducted thither by them; where, being
placed before a large Statue of a human
Figure, thick fet with Wings, and wearing a magnificent Crown, all who attended the Funeral proftrated themfelves,
while the ALMAZET fpoke as follows:

" Behold, Oh great ACCOMPLISHER, at
thy Shrine, the perifhable Part of a deceas'd Brother, who, during the Exiftence
of this material Body, profeffed himfelf
VOL. II.   C   thy

thy faithful Servant, nor ever vainly la-
vished any of the Moments appointed for
moral or social Purposes; by us, his Sur-
vivors, he sollicits that honourable Stamp
of Approbation upon his Memory, which
may encourage his Posterity perseveving-
ly to imitate his commendable Application; pronounce him a worthy Sacrifice
made to thee by the Great DELIVERER,
and fill our Hearts with Joy."

Here, as I presume, by a Kind of mechanical Influence, the Statue three
Times flapp'd all its Wings, and thrice
utter'd a Sound resembling that of a deep
howling Wind; upon which the Children
and Relations of the Deceas'd sung a
short Hymn of Rejoicing, and then
moved in a most extravagantly antic
Form of Dancing, which done, we passed
on to the other TEMPLE; at one End appeared a Skeleton of enormous Size,
seated on a Throne, with the Emblem of
Power

Power, proftrate, fupporting one Foot, and that of Grandeur the other.

At the Foot of the Throne was an Altar with Fire upon it, into which the Head and Blood of the deceas'd Perfon were thrown: I afked the Reafon of this, and was told that the NOIBLANS believed Fire to be the parental Element, and Origin of all created Matter; that they fuppofed the Spirit, during its temporal Exiftence, to refide in the Parts that were now devoted to the holy Flames; which, as they feparated and purified it from the groffer Particles with which it was connected, were deemed the propereft Conveyance to an undefiled State of Immortality.

After this, and a few fhort Thankfgivings, the Body was let down into a round Hole, three Feet Diameter and twelve or fourteen deep. A Hymn concluded

C 2   cluded

cluded the whole Ceremony; when, according to Custom, the artificial Head was, by the eldest Son, conveyed home with much Care and Reverence; such Memorials, or Semblances of the Dead, being held in high Veneration.

On our Return I asked the NAMRE-DAL if any other Use was made of the TEMPLE of TIME; to which he replied, that a LECTURE on the ŒCONOMY of that most useful and elusive Appendage of Mortality, was delivered there once a Month; when the Inhabitants of one SE-NIRAT, or WARD, that is a twelfth Part of the City, are obliged to attend; and if any have, since a former Meeting, knowingly omitted any Duty, or an Opportunity of doing Good, such Persons are obliged to make an open Acknowledgement of their Failure, with a solemn Promise that their Offence shall not be repeated under severe Penalties, which in such Cases certainly take Place.

In

In this Point there never was an In-
ftance known of Mifreprefentation; which
is not only owing to a general Deteſta-
tion of Falſhood, but alſo to the Belief
that TIME is an abſolute Agent, capable
of Perception; and that the Figure which
reprefents it in the TEMPLE, would by its
Influence be animated to point out Deceit. A Notion however extravagant,
like Prieſtcraft, not without Uſe.

You will poſſibly be ſurprized, continues he, to hear that the ALMEZAT,
or Father of the TEMPLE, is no other
than the famous JOHN Earl of ROCHE-
STER. That Station being vacant ſome
ſhort Time after his Tranſlation hither,
ſeveral Candidates appear'd for it; among
the reſt EPICTETUS, who ſeemed to command moſt Approbation, as having, even
in a toilſome and ſervile State of Dependence, ſcrupulouſly appropriated his few
Hours of Leiſure, or rather of needful
Reſt,

Reft, to the moft commendable Purfuits, thofe of Virtue and Knowledge: His Claim, modeftly preferred and fenfibly fupported, was on the Point of taking Place, when the prefent Poffeffor appeared an unexpected Candidate, and addreffed our Citizens to the following Purpofe:

" Encouraged—Oh Noiblans—by Candor and Impartiality, thofe lovely Characteriftics of this happy Island, I prefent myfelf before you; not as prefuming upon fuperior Abilities, but from a Defire of extenuating, by Strictnefs and Affiduity, the Errors of my former Exiftence.

" Here let me own — with Shame let me own, that, while on Earth, I had ample Means and frequent Opportunities to confer Happinefs on others, and Honour on myfelf; I had Fortune to command every

every Thing defirable but Content; Genius to furnifh Improvement and Delight; with Reafon to correct my Paffions, and hereditary Honours to enforce Refpect;—yet, alas! to what did I convert thefe fignal Advantages? My Abundance ferved only as a Float to bear me down the rapid and dangerous Stream of Pleafure; my Genius, like an alluring poifon-pregnant Flower, difplayed its Beauties only to infect thofe who admir'd it; my Reafon poorly turned a Pandar to my Vices; and debafed Nobility funk me into Pity, or Contempt, with all the Senfible and Judicious.

"Such, SAGE CITIZENS, was your Suppliant, till a providential Vifitation called his Senfes to their juft Order, and fhowed in a true, but agonizing, Light, the perilous Path he had trod. Full of that powerful Conviction, even now with the dark and terrifying Retrofpect ever in my View,

View, my Feelings of the Mifapplication of TIME muſt be ſtronger, and my Senfe of the lamentable Confequences of it more forcible than theirs, whom Prudence and natural Inclinations have made Œconomiſts of Time; if any Objection ſhould arife from my Youth, ſince I have ſcarce paſſed the Meridian of terreſtrial Exiſtence, let it be noted that tho' I did with great Rapidity run thro' an Age of vicious Diffipation, yet I have ſince moſt painfully experienced a long and bitter Age of Repentance; and EXPERIENCE, not Years, teaches WISDOM. For the reſt, I ſhall gladly ſubmit to your Determination, with one ſhort Remark for my Concluſion, That comparative Knowledge and eſtabliſh'd Penitence, are rather more to be relied on, than philoſophical Speculation and yet untainted Virtue."

This Addreſs ſeemed to have confiderable Influence; yet I believe it would not have

have prevailed but for the voluntary, modeſt Reſignation of EPICTETUS in his Favour. He has ſince gained great Credit in his Station; on all Occaſions he diſplays the moſt eminent Ability; one Inſtance out of many I ſhall give you.

When CHARLES the SECOND of ENGLAND reſigned his terreſtrial Crown, he brought with him a full Flow of his former Spirits and Inclinations; which, for ſome Space, ran him into Difficulties and Diſgrace: Upon his firſt Examination at the SALMINA RINMETHOL, his Account of himſelf appeared moſt trifling and unſatisfactory; however, being fortified with a Confidence uſually attending ſuch Characters, and recognizing his former gay, diſſolute Companion and Subject, he ſhook off all Concern, and addreſſed himſelf to the ALMEZAT, with a ſprightly Negligence, to the following Effect:

" Who

" Who, in the Name of common Senfe, JACK ROCHESTER, would have thought to find you in fuch a Character? What, make a Prieft of one who hated Priefts as much as I did! and fet *him* up to preach of TIME, who never thought of any but the Time prefent! a mighty odd World we have got into this, where a Man muft tell all he does; nay, not only Man, but Woman alfo. Heavens! my Friend, what would fuch an Inftitution have done upon Earth when we were there? What a gloomy Cloud would it have caft over the Sunfhine of Wit and Gallantry, in which bright Region I was myfelf the leading Star? But why need I repeat what muft fo ftrongly dwell upon your Recollection; be it enough to fay, that having you, my Friend, for a Judge, I muft ftand ac-quitted of all Error, in regard of fome little amorous Sallies, and fome other Steps towards Politenefs; fince a Perfon of the high Rank I held, cannot in Rea-

fon

fon be expected to enter into fo low and
mechanical a Difpofition of Hours as the
vulgar Cuftoms of this unpolifh'd ISLAND
feem to enjoin."

"How ftrange—Oh CHARLES—replied the ALMEZAT, have been thy Notions,
how irregular thy Practices? Not the immediate Hand of Heaven vifiting thy
unfortunate Father in Blood; not feveral
imminent Dangers and Hair-breadth
Efcapes of thy own Perfon; not Obfcu-
rity, Exile, nor the fevereft Rod of Ad-
verfity, could teach thee to make a commendable Ufe of that Power to which
thou waft fo providentially reftored:
Placed in the confpicuous and flippery
Station of political Parent to a brave, free
People, what engroffed thy Attention?
Didft thou felect, not regarding Men but
their Capacities, able and faithful Coun-
fellors? No—thy Minifters were, in general, a Set of Knaves or Fools; weak,
or

or wicked Tools themselves, who made a Tool of thee. Didst thou plan patriot Schemes, or patronize them? No—all thy Schemes and Devices were to obtain Sums sufficient for the Support of Prodigality and Passions, not only below a King, but even below the meanest Rank of human Nature. Wast thou a commendable Example in domestic Life? No—thy numerous Concubines, those Leeches of the State, to countenance their own splendid Infamy, turned *Modesty* out of Doors, and rendered *Vice* fashionable. From these, and similar Circumstances, thy Term of Government became a Scene of Perturbation at home, and Contempt abroad. A Tide of Infection flowed from thy Court to corrupt the Manners of thy People; bloated *Debauch* stalked uncontrouled and blushless in the broad Eye of Day, while Religion and Virtue retir'd desponding in unfrequented Shades. An unhappy Proselyte to thee,

how,

how, alas! did I abuse my Station and
Nature? Actuated by a polite Delirium,
I made TIME a Slave to Irregularity;
but must Folly triumph ever? Will not
Change of Existence work a Change in
thee? Hence, and know that, till thou
hast renounced thy former Self, I shall
disclaim all Knowledge of thee; and, as
Father of this TEMPLE, if at the next Examination thou art not better prepared,
if thou dost not learn and practise those
Golden Precepts, to *know* and *rule Thyself*, I shall sentence thee to a Punishment
suited to such irrational Obstinacy."

This severe, yet just Reproof, which
met with general Applause from the NOI-
BLANS, seemed to have no other Effect
upon CHARLES than to raise some Sneers
of Ridicule; for which, and his obstinate
Perseverance in his Irregularities, he was
sentenced to the Office he now fills, of
RANEVER, or VERGER in the TEMPLE.

Here

Here I could not avoid expressing a warm Approbation of the Institution the NAMREDAL had been explaining——Oh that such a Temple and such a periodical Examination, exclaimed I, were established on EARTH, then would not *Scandal* find Leisure to prey, Vulture-like, upon defenceless Characters, nor *Gaming* Opportunities to fasten its unrelenting Talons upon the Vitals of suffering Families; *Indolence* and *Procrastination* would be roused from their *Lethean* Slumbers; *Fraud* and *Envy* would be chained in their unhallowed Cells; *Oppression's* Iron Hand would be unnerved; *Shame* and *Guilt* would hide themselves in the thick Gloom of Night; while the rose-lipp'd Cherub *Innocence* smiled Peace upon the World.

These and such-like Observations employed us till we reached the NAMREDAL's House; at the usual Hour we retired to our several Chambers. This Night

Night again Reflection preceded, and for
some Time prevented Slumber; however,
I became suddenly so naturalized to my
new Residence, that I could almost have
given up all Desire of re-visiting the
EARTH, which had ever appeared to me
in the Light of a perilous Seat of Perturbation, imperfect Enjoyments, and mul-
tiplying Cares; but much more so when
I now compared it with the mild, unruf-
fled Region I had reached: However,
when I considered this unvarying State of
Existence, I found it very ill calculated
for the active Spirit of a Sublunar, and
determined within myself, that Tranquillity among the NOIBLANS was little
more than mental Indolence; that their
Philosophy consisted in a total, and therefore prejudicial, Suppression of the Passions, which are the sole Springs of Action in the Soul; and that their Virtue
consisted not so much in resisting, as in
preventing Temptation. With these Sen-
.timents

timents came the drowſy Power that *knits up the ravelled Sleeve of Care*, and lock'd up my Senſes in Repoſe; Reader, if you be thus diſpoſed yourſelf; if, from Wearineſs of Spirits, or the Tediouſneſs of this Narration, he has touched thy Eyelids with his *Leaden Wand*; or if, for any other Reaſon, thou may'ſt be inclined to pauſe, I ſhall gratify thee with a convenient Opportunity by concluding the CHAPTER.

CHAP. II.

Some Account of the NOIBLAN *Opinion concerning* DREAMS, SPIRIT, MATTER, &c. *carried to the* TOIRTAZAN *of the* SUBLUNARS—HELIOGABALUS, THE. CIBBER, JAMES I. JOE MILLER, *and many other remarkable Characters exhibited.*

AT Breakfaſt, next Morning, the NAMREDAL inquired concerning my Reſt, and being informed that viſionary fionary, romantic Dreams had fomewhat difturbed me; then, fays he, your Spirit, according to the Opinion of Noibla, has taken Flight on the Wing of occafional Liberty. Requefting to be a little better informed of this Notion, he proceeded thus:

" You muft know that the Soul of Man is here believed to be an Emanation of *Divinity*; that tho' it acts in Conjunction with the Body, yet it is totally independent of it; that it is immortal and unceafing in its Operations; fo fubtle of Effence, as to elude the Power of human Perception or Defcription; that, like the Sun-Beams, it pervades and enlightens furrounding Matter: The Body is confidered as a beautiful harmonious Piece of Mechanifm, miraculoufly compofed of grofs Materials, and utterly perifhable in its Nature; that it is but a paffive Machine, calculated for the Reception and Influence of those amazing Faculties which are annexed to human Ntaure; and that all Sensation absolutely resides in the Spirit, not the Limbs of Man.

" This Opinion they defend by remarking, that tho' the Body of a deceas'd Person retains materially the same external Appearance, no Impression can give it either Pleasure or Pain; that tho', from particular Accidents, as a Wound or Fracture, the corporal Parts seem to cause disagreeable or tormenting Ideas, yet the original Sensation is in the Mind, which becomes disturbed and agitated according to the Degree of Violence offered to its Residence, or any Part thereof.——— Many Circumstances, which wound the Mind, leave the Limbs unhurt; but there is no Impression, external or internal, which does not affect the Spirit.

" Pof-

" Poſſeſſed by theſe Notions, they believe Sleep to be an unavoidable and
neceſſary Relaxation for the periſhable
Parts; but deny the Spirit to have any
the leaſt Share in that death-like Semblance; and affirm that, while the Body
continues in this Condition, the Soul, enlarged from its mortal Incumbrance, flies
abroad upon the Wings of Thought, en-
countering, viewing, and diſcuſſing various Points as at other Seaſons. This un-
connected State of Action is called REN-
MULZABA, or DREAMING; and Dreams,
ſay they, are ſometimes recollected and
ſometimes blotted from the Table of Memory, according to the ſympathetic Im-
preſſions they make. As to any progno-
ſticative Inferences deriv'd from theſe Ex-
travaganzas of the Soul, they are held in
utter Contempt, except by ſome credulous SUBLUNARS, who, having dreamed
away their former State of Exiſtence,
chuſe to ſtick by their favourite Notions,

D 2   and

and derive from Shadows, imaginary Bleffings or Misfortunes.

" Obferve, continues he, that in making you acquainted with the NOIBLANS,
I do not at all mean to impofe their Manners and Opinions in general upon you;
they are only candidly fubmitted to your
own Choice and Determination, to be
communicated by you with the fame
Freedom on EARTH, fhould they feem
either ufeful or entertaining."

I thanked my kind Inftructor, and replied, That his Condefcenfion was more
than I could expect; that I had yet perceived nothing of evil Tendency; and
that I fhould have been particularly glad
to enter into a more enlarged Difquifition
of the Connexion fubfifting between *Spirit*, or *Effence*, and *Matter*; but that fo
much had been already faid without any
tolerable Illuftration of the Subject, unmeaning

meaning Diſtinctions, and indeterminate
Refinements, had been ſo voluminouſly
multip!ied, all ending in a Chaos of
Metaphyſical Confuſion, that I would
not attempt to prolong Diſcourſe upon a
Theme ſo inextricable, and perhaps, if
clearly unravelled, profitleſs.

" I am perfectly of your Opinion, ſays
the NAMREDAL; there is a great and ſufficient Variety of uſeful, comprehenſible
Speculations to employ the Mind; who
then, uncompelled by Madneſs, would
wander in the Perils of Darkneſs, when he
might have the Safe-Conduct of Light;
or truſt himſelf to the Horrors of tempe-
ſtuous Seas and faithleſs Shores without
a Compaſs, when ſo certain a Guide as
RELIGION lies within his Power? But a
Truce with this ſententious Matter: You
have had ſince your Arrival in the ISLAND
very little but Subjects of grave Reflection, it may not be amiſs to offer you ſome

Scenes

Scenes of a fprightlier, tho' not lefs ufeful, Nature, for this Purpofe I'll introduce
you to a TOIRTAZAN, or *weekly Meeting*,
with which all the SUBLUNARS in NOD-
NOL are indulged; and, as no natural-
born NOIBLAN is admitted, they may
talk of what Subject, and with what Freedom, they pleafe. In this, as in all terreftrial mix'd Societies, you will perceive
an odd, incongruous Medley of good
Senfe, Pertnefs, Contradiction, Vanity,
Envy, Emulation, and Abfurdity."

Being conducted to the ARESMA, or
HALL of the SUBLUNARS, the NAMRE-
DAL, for the Convenience of hearing and
feeing unperceived, led me into a private
Gallery, where I was confiderably ftruck,
not only with the real Dignity which appeared in many Characters, but that extraordinary Variety which ran thro' the
whole; a Variety of which nothing can
give fo juft an Idea of as our Mafque-
rades

rades; the Revolutions of Fashion in several Climes and Ages were here displayed at large; some sweeping with long Robes, like *Peacocks* in their Pride; others skipping in short Doublets, like *trimm'd Fighting-Cocks*; some with cropp'd Hair, others with voluminous Wigs; some with whisking Beards, others with smooth Chins. Among the Females, of whom there appear'd a considerable Number, the Distinctions of Dress appear'd more numerous and fantastical than those of the Men. The Hour of Conversation not being come, I filled up the Time, after taking a strict Review of the Figures, with inquiring of the NAMREDAL after some Particulars that struck me, and had my Curiosity thus gratified:

" That Person, says he, who sits among the Men, though dressed in Women's Cloaths, is our FIRST CHARLES, who bears the Disgrace of those Female Garments,

ments, for having tamely given up the
Prerogatives both of KING and MAN to
the fhallow and pernicious Influence of
his QUEEN: A Piece of Weaknefs which
multiplied his Cares while alive, ftained
his Fame when tranflated from Earth,
and now fubjects him to the Ridicule of
all his Brother Monarchs here. The Figure next to him, on his Right Hand, is
that very odd Mixture of a Man, his Father, who is condemn'd to wear the Habit
of a Jack Pudding, with the Figure of a
Witch on a Broom hung round his Neck,
in Difgrace of his defcending fo far beneath the Royal Character, as to countenance low Jefting, mean Quibbles, infig-
nificant Puns, and the moft inconfiftent
Notions of Witchcraft: That grave-
looking Woman on the oppofite Side"—
here a Signal being given for opening the
Affembly, my Inftructor was interrupted
by a Debate between HELIOGABALUS,
the ROMAN EMPEROR, and THEOPHI-
LUS

lus Cibber, the English Comedian,
both of luxurious Memory.

The latter of thefe two moft *valuable*
Perfonages, adjufting himfelf with a true
Lord Foppington Air, and all that fro-
thy Pertnefs which fo remarkably diftinguifhed him on Earth, addreffed the vo-
racious Monarch in Manner following:

" It is odd, very odd, my dear Sir, that,
notwithftanding the *Tendre* I have always
had for you, we can never be intimately acquainted; it was ever my Rule to
like an honeft Fellow, fplit me; befides,
you know, my dear Sir, whatever we
were in the other World, we are all upon
a Footing here; and though, *entre nous*,
I hate this Place as much as you can do,
I fhall enter into a Comparifon of our *former* State of Exiftence.—To begin then:
In Rome, for a fhort Time, you played
the Part of a real Emperor, hated by
Mil-

Millions; in ENGLAND I have often exhibited a mimic one, loved by all——
but my Creditors.————You admired fine
Cloaths, fo did I—good Eating, fo did I—
handfome Wenches, ftap my Vitals, fo
did I—You was thrown into the TIBER
by the PRÆTORIAN Band, I into the
Sea by a Storm, and here, at length,
we have met in *ftatu quo*—there's a fair
Parallel, fplit me."—"A Parallel! replies
the *Imperial Cormorant*, with a Sneer of
Contempt; what, a Tinfel Mimic, a paltry Shadow, compare himfelf with HE-
LIOGABALUS, whofe Magnificence and
Tafte ftretched both Art and Nature to
their utmoft Bent! Poor, vulgar Reptile,
formed but of common Clay, haft thou
not heard of my Purple Robes adorned
with Gems? my *Arabian* Balms, my Golden Veffels, my Rooms ftrewed with Saf-
fron; fix hundred Oftriches at a Supper;
the Tongues of Peacocks, Singing-Birds,
and innumerable other fumptuous Articles

ticles, to the Amount of more in one
Meal than fuftained the whole Expence
of thy paltry Life from Beginning to
End; and, after this, dareft thou prefume
to mate with me, vile Plebeian?"

" Hold, hold, replies the Son of THE-
SPIS, if we muft come to a clofe Comparifon, pray, who did moft according to
our Capacities? We had both the fame
Game in View; who moft warmly purfued the Chace? You, my dear Sir, had
the whole ROMAN EMPIRE to live on, I
my Wits alone—You never wore Cloaths
twice, I could not change fo often, yet
fome *Englifh Taylors* found me ready
enough that Way—You had no Bailiffs to
fear, I often felt their griping Paws, yet
ftill kept on my Courfe, and obey'd Fafhion as critically as any of my Contemporaries; nor did I fall fhort in the delicate Science of refined Eating, witnefs,
Oh glorious Remembrance! the many
Turtles

Turtles I have helped to demolish; the *Haunches* of *Venison*, *Westphalia Hams con-suma*, *Beef Marinate*, *Mutton a la Mer-corance*, *Lamb a la Conte*, *Tongues Espag-nole*, *Pullets a la Royale*, *Chickens a la Reine*, *Ortolans*, *Mushrooms au Blanc*, *Cardons a la Bejamel*, *Blomanges*, *Mar-brays*, &c. &c. &c." During this Rhap-sody of Dainties I could perceive the Difputants alternately lick their Lips with much Eagernefs; for the ROMAN, tho' he knew not the *frenchified* Viands men-tioned, yet, like BONIFACE in regard of *Latin*, he thought they muft be good by the Sound, from whence a friendly Sym-pathy touched his Breaft; and, upon the HISTRIONIC Hero's adding, as a conclu-five Proof of his own fpirited Appetite, that once, not having a fingle Shilling in his Pocket, he went into a Coffee-Houfe, pufh'd a bold Front, there with fome Difficulty borrowed a Guinea, and imme-diately laid the whole out upon a Pint of

green.

green Peas, a Duck, and a Bottle of Cla-
ret. HELIOGABALUS warmly embraced
him, declared future Friendſhip, and
promiſed that, if any Change ſhould make
him an EMPEROR again, THEOPHILUS
ſhould certainly be appointed PRIME
MINISTER : But this Poſt, from a Knowledge of it in ENGLAND, the new Favourite declined, and propoſed himſelf for
the more peaceable Employ of STEWARD
of the HOUSHOLD, having, as he ſaid,
more Liking to Cooks than Politicians,
and was accordingly nominated to that
moſt noble Poſt.

Here a thin, cogitative Figure riſing
up, ſaid, That if Philoſophy could at any
Time give up Patience, it muſt be to
hear ſuch irrational and inſignificant Contentions; behold a Couple of Creatures,
cries he, in the human Form, taking all
imaginable Pains to render one another
contemptible; nay, warmly emulating
each

each other in the Race of Infamy: One
glories in guzzling the Revenues of an
Empire that was curfed with his Sway,
the other boafts of fwallowing whole Families of honeft Tradefmen, who were
credulous enough to truft him. Wretched Infatuation, to take that for Merit
which *Reafon* totally condemns; *Reafon*,
which points out Moderation and Competence as the *Summum Bonum* of Life,
juftly towering above the tranfitory Grandeur and fuperfluous Luxuriance of the
nether World; which, ripened into Wifdom, confiders no Treafure as of equal
Value with the Riches of the Mind, and
declares that every Man poffeffes ample
Means of Happinefs within himfelf.

Here a jovial Figure, blooming with
focial Eafe and Pleafantry of Countenance, feated at fome Diftance, interrupted the *Moralift*, crying out, " Who tries
Patience now, Mafter SENECA? Are not
you

you a pretty Fellow, of all Men, to talk
at this Rate? I won't contradict your
Principles in general, because I begin to
think something that Way myself; but,
Compliments apart, why should *you* be so
severe? Of the two, an Eating Fool is
more pardonable than an Hypocritical
Knave; the first shews himself, and meets
double Punishment, hurting both Constitution and Character; the latter, like
a gilded Snake, carries Poison under an
alluring Appearance: Those Persons you
so severely tax have Strength of Passion
and Weakness of Judgment to plead
in their Excuse; while you, well knowing what was right, wrote indeed according to that Knowledge, yet acted upon
Principles diametrically opposite: You
recommended Competence and Moderation, with Plausibility and Zeal; yet,
with the Spirit of an Usurer, you accu-
mulated the most enormous Sums. Who
raised more sumptuous *Villas* than the
humble

humble SENECA? Who lent out Money upon more exorbitant Interest than this very Moralist? Who, to feed the devouring Jaws of Avarice, ever bred such a Plague for the human Race as you did in your Pupil NERO? Vicious as that Monster might have been by Nature, honester Instruction would have made him much better; however the Temper, which your Thirst of Gain and Fear of losing Favour caused you to indulge in him, at length grew outrageous, and, like an ill-tam'd wild Beast, fell on its Keeper, emptying your Bags of their Money, and your Veins too of their Blood.——That such may be the Fate of every sycophantic Preceptor of Royalty, who, to ingratiate or aggrandize himself, sacrifices the future Happiness of a Nation, is the sanguine Wish of EPICURUS."

At this Period the antic Monarch JAMES rose up, and expressed himself thus: " Well, well, Master Philosopher,

say

fay what you like, Œconomy is a very
good Thing; not becaufe the Word is of
Greek Derivation, but becaufe *A Penny
faved is a Penny gained.* Though I know
this Proverb can't found well to fuch a
Ventriculator, a Belly-Man and Wine-
Bibber, from the *Latin* Verb *bibo*, to
drink, as you were; now, that you may
give the greater Credit to what I fay, you
muft know when I was KING of GREAT-
BRITAIN—(a Name of my own Invention for SCOTLAND and ENGLAND) they
ufed to fay I was a wife one—a fecond So-
LOMON—tho' I am told, when they could
no longer get any Thing by me, they
changed their Tune—for among them,
as the Proverb fays—*No longer pipe, no
longer dance.*—But I fuppofe the Reafon
of their finding Fault is, becaufe I was
too good a Chriftian to quarrel, and, if I
had received a Slap upon one Cheek,
would have turn'd the other rather than
fhed Blood: Nor was this for Want of

Courage, for tho' I was not so mad-headed as to draw my Sword in Defence of what some Fools call National Glory, yet I did a bolder Thing with my Pen, when I tickled off those Imps of the Devil, *Witches* and *Warlocks*—many an evil-ey'd old Wife was singed between the Fingers with Brimstone Matches in my Reign—but *Tempora mutantur*—I'm only laugh'd at here.—Poor BUCKINGHAM, as handsome a Fellow as ever was made a Lord—if I had him with me—tho' he led my Son CHARLEY a Wild-Goose Chace into SPAIN, and caused all EUROPE to make a Jest of us, it would be some Comfort; even that poor Rogue SHAKESPEAR, who used to pun so curiously for whole Pages together in my Taste, and introduced the Weiard Sisters into his MAC-BETH to please me, now barbarously confines himself to common Sense, and says he never believed a Syllable in *Witches*; so that I have not a Companion
worth

worth a Bodle but honeſt JOE MILLER, who would have been created a Peer had he lived in my Reign. Here, JOE — what aſleep, Man? Rouſe up, and ſpeak for yourſelf." Here he wakened a ludicrous Figure who ſat by him, and reproved Drowſineſs as unbecoming a Wit; " Troth, JEMMY, replies the *Jeſter*, when there's nothing worth waking for, a Man cannot do better than ſleep. I have been ſo often tired with laughing at the Diſputes of PHILOSOPHERS, Fellows as thickheaded as a Parcel of DUTCH *Burgomaſters*, that I can't be diverted with their formal Nonſenſe any longer; beſides, to hear a Couple of Blockheads debate about good Eating and Drinking in ſuch a ſcurvy Country as this, where there is neither, is juſt as ridiculous as for a FRENCHMAN to talk of Liberty; a SPANIARD, of Humility; or a GERMAN, of Temperance. I remember, continues he, when I was on Earth, one of your grave, wiſe Fellows

E 2 plagued

plagued me over a Pot of *Porter* so long, that he obliged me to give him a wicked Wipe; and what do you think I said, JEMMY? What, says his Royal Friend, chuckling with Expectation—why, Faith, I e'en told him that his Babble was like a *Scots Fiddle*, well enough at first, but damn'd troublesome at last." This unfortunate Simile drew poor MILLER into a Scrape; for JAMES, tho' he had enjoy'd the general Reflections upon other Countries, no sooner heard this Slight upon his own, than, throwing aside his peaceable Disposition, and encouraged by the known Timidity of JOE, he seized his Victim by the Nose, declared he had intended to honour him with the Dignity of a BARONET; but now, says he, receive this Reward of your Insolence; so, applying his Royal Foot to the passive Posteriors of his late Friend, he expelled him the HALL, and went forth himself, muttering the Words *Scots Fiddle* with great Rage and Confusion.

" Bless

" Blefs me, cries a delicate Female, ftarting up, what an unpolifhed Wretch that SOLOMON, as he called himfelf, is! What Jargon the Creature fpoke! What a Solecifm in good Breeding, to quarrel thus before fo many Ladies of Quality! And what a hopeful Set of Animals the *Englifh* muft be by this Sample of their King's! But indeed when I was upon Earth, and in that Paradife called PARIS, I have often heard ENGLAND defcribed as the Seat of Barbarifm. Poor imperfect Imitators of our refined Cuftoms and Fafhions: Tho' they regularly refort to our Capital, and expend princely Fortunes there in Purfuit of Elegance and true Tafte, they return to their infular Confines a diverting Mixture of tawdry Glare, forced Spirits, and affected Eafe."

" Truly, Madam MONTESPAN, replies another Female, tho' you had for fome Time your *Grande Monarque* at Com-

mand,

mand, and from thence may fancy yourfelf a great Woman, I fee no Reafon you
have to make fo free with us, and efpecially before me, who was fo well acquainted with your Hiftory.—FRANCE,
indeed! did not my Hufband JOHN beat
your frippery *petit Maitres* till you became the Derifion of all EUROPE? Was
not he very near expelling the Great
LOUIS from his Paradife of PARIS, as you
call it? And did not his Name become a
Bugbear even to your Children?"

" As to that, Madam SARAH, fays the
Gallic Dame, I am no Politician, therefore won't fay much of the Matter; but,
for mere Fighting, poffibly thick Heads
and favage Hearts may have an Advantage—But you feem, Madam, to hint at
my Hiftory, infinuating, I prefume, your
own great Modefty in Contraft; a Point
of View, on Examination, not at all advantageous to your Ladyfhip; however,

I

I have too much Delicacy to enter upon
Particulars of such a Nature, and shall
only obferve, Madam, that to yield to the
Sollicitations of a powerful and amiable
Monarch, was lefs a Crime than to rob a
Nation, to impofe upon its QUEEN, to
defraud Merit, and extort Bribes, thereby fixing the indelible Stain of Avarice
upon your JOHN's Glory; who, to give
your Grace my Opinion freely, for all his
Military Prowefs, was but a pitiful Fellow to be the Slave of such a Wife."

"He had better be the Slave of a Wife
than the Slave of a *Madam*, like your Pa-
ramour, Mrs. MINX, retorts SARAH; and
if Heaven bleffed me with the better
Head of the two, why should not he be
conducted by me; but I plainly perceive
what low Malice is at the Bottom of this,
you and all your Weathercock Country
hate me, becaufe my Counfels brought
you fo low."

"Not

" Not at all, good Madam, replies her Adverſary, we think ourſelves much obliged to you for undoing all that your Huſband had done: From your Conduct may be derived the four happy laſt Years of that Reign which had been ſo troubleſome to us; ſo that if you would but lay down the Virago, and take up the Lady; ſoften your Deportment, give gentler Terms, and talk no more of that Phantom *Virtue*, (which you certainly had as little real Right to claim as myſelf) we might exiſt here upon tolerable friendly Terms."

" Friendly Terms with ſuch a B——! returns her Antagoniſt; if I was on Earth again I would give ſome Hiſtorian Ten Thouſand Pounds to gibbet up your Fame to Poſterity."

Here the Altercation began to riſe with ſuch Warmth, that in all Probability the Ladies would ſoon have proved Paſſion

to

to be inconfiftent with Politenefs, or even Decency, had not Swift fuppreffed the Flame of Contention by declaring abruptly, with a loud Voice, That if the Devil had any Refidence out of his infernal Regions, it muft be in the Tongues of fcolding Women. People have been angry, continues he, at my Reflections upon the Sex, tho' every Day proves their Failings to ftretch beyond the Power of Satire; no Language but their own envenomed Recriminations being fufficient to give an adequate Idea of them.

" Harkee, Brother Jonathan, replies Rabelais, will you never have done fnarling? There can be no Expectation of a Bifhopric here, therefore you have not Difappointment to crofs you; befides, you are full as great a Perfonage now as Oxford and Bolingbroke, who can no longer amufe you with dabbling in the Froth and Scum of Politics, as they did

on

on Earth : What then can be the Reafon
of your retaining that cynical Difpofition
which conftituted you the moft inhuman
Humorift that ever waved a Pen ? Your
Satire, like a two-edged Sword, cut which
ever Side it turned, and your unlimited
Ridicule tended to degrade all Human-
kind : What avails it then to admit your
Works to be, in general, a Pattern of Wit,
of Humour, of Penetration, of pure and
nervous Language, if Juftice obliges us
to condemn many of them as deftitute of
all Benevolence, and even of common
Decency, efpecially wherever you have
touched upon the fofter Sex ? But indeed
you were fufficiently punifhed for this in
the other World, by your Houfekeeper's
making a Raree-Show of you, when exhaufted Nature had at laft reduced you to
a State of Idiotifm—Prithee, Man, take
Example from me and my Neighbour
Scarron here ; laugh rather than rail;
ufe Ridicule as a Feather to tickle, not

as

as a Scourge to wound; pity where you reprove; neither write nor speak from Passion nor Interest, and acknowledge a Truth you always seemed unacquainted with, that *good Humour* is the only *true Humour*."

" Fine lukewarm Doctrine this, cries JUVENAL, as he started up; a delicate Phrase that same *good Humour* for tender-hearted, courtly Authors, who are afraid to delineate Vice in her full State of Deformity, left polite Readers may be shock'd—Is this supporting the impartial Dignity of SATIRE? Is this the Method for honest Rectitude to work a Reformation of Manners? Can the Feather of Ridicule take Effect, where Whips of Steel can hardly make an Impression? Who that has a Heart touched with true Zeal, who that is not callous to moral Feelings, can cloath his Face with Smiles amidst such Provocation as the corrupted State of Nature

ture throws out on every Side? He that
would fight the Caufe of Virtue fuc-
cefsfully, muft not engage her politic
Antagonift in the Ear, but purfue and
ftab her to the Heart—Dangerous and
irrational is it to trifle with inflammatory
Diforders, becaufe efficacious Medicines
are painful or unpalatable; nothing but
confcious Guilt can ftart at the Voice of
SATIRE, however indignant and fevere;
therefore no ill Confequence can come of
bold Truths and warm Cenfure; in which,
and in which only, dwells the true mental *Panacea* to reftrain pernicious Paffions; to regulate the various Principles
of the Mind; and roufe up Reafon to affume and maintain her Empire."

Here HORACE, with graceful Mildnefs, check'd the over-heated Zeal of his
Countryman, by remarking, That Reafon was never in greater Danger than in
Connexion with an enthufiaftic Imagination.

tion. " All thofe who have feen your
Productions, Friend JUVENAL, continues
he, muft allow them great Merit; but at
the fame Time lament that ungovernable
Rage which flames thro' them; SATIRE
was undoubtedly your Talent; an extenfive Knowledge of Men and Manners,
Dignity of Sentiment, and a moft inte-
refting Glow of Expreffion, place you
very high in literary Eftimation; but at
the fame Time the Eye of Delicacy turns
from you overflowed with Tears for the
many grofs Ideas which occur in your
Productions. There are Vices and Imperfections exifting in our Nature, which
cannot be brought within the Limits of
agreeable Defcription or ufeful Satire. To
rake into Filth is more likely to propagate
Vice, and to taint, than purify the Mind of
the Reader: It gives a large Majority the
Knowledge of what otherwife they would
not, and indeed fhould not, know. To
live in fuch a Time as you did, muft undoubtedly

doubtedly fill every fenfible Mind with
Indignation; but may there not be Enthufiafm in Satire as well as in Religion?
There may moft certainly: This hurried
you away, and your Mufe, actuated by
the Fervor of a heated Imagination, over-
leap'd all Bounds. It is but charitable
to believe you meant well; that your
Fury was neither kindled by Difappointment of your own Expectations, nor proftituted to gratify the malevolent Difpofitions of others; that you wrote from no
private or public Prejudice; that you did
not oftentatioufly defign to infinuate a
peculiar Purity of Manners in yourfelf;
but really faw, felt, lamented, and therefore rouzed yourfelf to chaftize the national Depravity you have fet forth.
Viewed in fuch a Light, you will ftand
much exculpated; yet even in this Cafe,
every benevolent Friend of Learning
muft wifh you had been poffeffed of as
much Patience to temper your Impetu-
ofity

ofity, as you had Spirit to expreſs your
Reſentment."

PERSIUS, with that grave Solemnity
which is the peculiar Characteriſtic of
his Writings, was preparing to give his
Sentiments as a Party concern'd, when he
found himſelf interrupted by the late
Mrs. MARGARET WOFFINGTON, who
declared, with ſome Vehemence, that
ſuch a Monopoly of Converſation among
Males, and upon ſuch inſipid Subjects,
was intolerable; while ſo many of the
other Sex, equally capable and willing to
uſe their Tongues, were obliged to ſit ſilent: " Here, continues ſhe, have I been
ſome Years in this heatheniſh ISLAND,
and, except ſome few occaſional Compliments from THE. CIBBER, I have been
no more noticed than a caſt Mantua;
notwithſtanding, I have ſome ſmall Reaſon to believe there are not many preſent more indebted to Nature than myſelf."——

self."—" True, ſtap my Vitals, Peg, returns Theophilus; but we are the oddeſt
Olio of Mortals here that ever were aſſembled—motley as an *Hay-Market Maſquerade*, but not half ſo polite or entertaining.—Smoke what antediluvian Figures
theſe old Greeks and Romans are; they
may have been wiſe Fellows and brave
Fellows, but they are quite aukward and
unpoliſh'd, ſplit me."

" Raviſhing Appearances, indeed, ſays
the Heroine, and their Women too, what
Figures! that Gianteſs Andromache, what
a Tower ſhe has upon her Head! enough
to ſmother a Dozen Ladies of Delicacy;
poſitively, there never was ſeen ſuch another Fright."—" Ah, ma Princeſſe, interrupts Cibber, who ſaw Hector frown,
and trembled at the Conſequence, what
would I give that we were now captivating
the Million, as we have often done, in Lord
Foppington and Lady Betty; I the Delight

light of the Women, you the Adoration
of the Men."———" No more, no more,
cries the afflicted PEG, with a Tragedy-
Tofs; what avails the Philofophy which
fome of thefe hideous mufty Fellows
have made fuch a Buftle about? They
never knew dear *Covent-Garden*, nor dearer
Drury-Lane; they never mingled with
pretty Fellows behind the *Scenes*, nor diftinguifhed themfelves by Repartees in
the *Green-Room*; they knew not the Ma-
nœuvres of Intrigue; the magic Twirl-
ings of a Fan; the polite Exercife of that
introductory Organ the Snuff-Box; the
graceful Difplay of a white Hand and
brilliant Ring; the filent Artillery of the
Eyes; the melting Languifh; the diftant
Leer; the fpirited Glance; the familiar
Nod; the fignificant Wink; and a thou-
fand other Appurtenances of genteel
Life—But all's over, and here I am, poor
Devil, infipid and forlorn as an old Maid
or a neglected Prude."

VOL. II.   F   Thefe

These Words, pronounced with particular Emphasis, and applied with a Sneer to a Female we do not chuse to name, for the Sake of some living, occasioned a tart Reply to the following Effect:—" You are always more forward in your Applications to me, Mrs. MARGARET, than becomes you; the Liberty of this Place gives you an Opportunity of displaying your Wit, as you think it, upon the Words *old Maid* and *Prude*; but I would have you to know they are either of them preferable to a mercenary Trull, that would sacrifice her Favours for Interest: For my Part, I wonder that such Creatures can have the Assurance to set up their Noses among Women of *Modesty* and *Virtue*."

" *Modesty* and *Virtue*, replies MARGARET! those Words have a very pretty Sound, truly; I have often repeated them

when

when I reprefented romantic, unfashion-
able Dames of Antiquity; but I could
never find out myfelf, nor learn from
any other Perfon, the precife Meaning of
them: Many People, I believe, pretend
to both, that have neither; and fome who
indulge little-fpirited Gallantry, are not
fo bad as feveral ftarch'd-up, formal,
fanctified Tapeftry Figures, that confine
Modefty to fet Features, and Virtue to
Licentioufnefs that efcapes Difcovery.——
But I hate grave Argument mortally; it
is as fure a *Prologue* to the Spleen, as a
dull Sermon, or a Stave of STERNHOLD
and HOPKINS; however, I fhould be glad
to hear your precife Ladyfhip's Notions
of thefe mechanical Accomplifhments
you feem to admire fo much."

" My Notions, replies the anonymous
Difputant, however juft, will undoubtedly appear ridiculoufly mechanical to one
fo oppofite in Thought and Action;

however, Madam, if you ever read Pamela, in her you faw a juft Pattern of
our Sex."

" Your Smelling-Bottle, dear The.
cries the Theatrical Lady, or I fhall moft
certainly faint: Pamela, ha! ha! ha! ha!
Hark ye, Harry Fielding; nay, don't
hide yourfelf, you old Cuff—you fhall
fpeak, and Truth too: You was fuppofed
to underftand Characters as well as any
Body; what's your Opinion of that fame
Mrs. Pam; was there ever yet, or can
there be, fuch a one? Come fpeak, nay, I
won't let you alone."

" Zoons, take Care of my Gout, Peg,
roars the cynical Humorift; I have left
Magiftracy in the lower World, and yet
this curfed Appendage of it ftill cramps
my Hands and Feet." " Well, but you
have not the Cramp in your Tongue,
replies fhe, and fo you fhall fpeak."

" Shall

" Shall speak, says the Justice; why, what the Mischief have I to do with Women's Disputes? As to PAMELA, she is indeed a tolerable Picture, a pretty Moppet of Imagination; but we may say of her Life, as a learned Bishop did of JONATHAN's GULLIVER, that the Story was well enough, but must be a confounded Lye; and that the Book ought to be burnt by a Jury of Females, as LOCKE's *Essay on Human Understanding* was by the Convocation of OXFORD, for tending to confuse and mislead with impossible Principles—For my own Part, the World and its Actors always appeared to me in so ludicrous a Light, that I chose rather to become a Philosopher of the laughing, than of the crying Sect; Cowards boasting of Courage; Lawyers, of Honesty; Divines, of Humility; Statesmen, of Patriotism; Hypocrites, of Religion; and Whores, of Virtue, is Food for Risibility not to be withstood: Nor was my Enjoy-

ment

ment selfish; I drew Scenes from Nature, juſt as Experience preſented them to View, and happily made all my Readers laugh with me. In regard of your Diſpute at preſent, I neither know nor care much about it. As to *Modeſty*, ſhe never was among the Number of my Acquaintance; and for *Virtue*, if you would receive Inſtruction on this Topic, let me recommend you to Joe Addison: But why ſhould you debate about the Matter, when you are both of one Way of thinking in the Main? To be worſhipped for an Angel, you, Peg, led the Life of a very Devil; and your *pious* Antagoniſt there, under a Veil of Sanctity, gave, by the Help of an Irish Footman, two *living* Inſtances of *her* Virtue."

This unpolite Familiarity touch'd both the Females to the Quick; and Patience not being among the Number of their Qualifications, they united againſt poor Harry,

HARRY, who made a most vigorous
Defence during a warm Altercation;
till happening to wish his Feet at Liberty, that he might apply them with
proper Effect, the enraged Viragos so
unmercifully stamp'd his Chalk-Stone
Toes, and so clawed his magisterial Phiz,
that PARSON ADAMS, under the
Hands of SLIPSLOP, made not a more
rueful Figure. This *Fracas* put a timely
End to the Meeting, for Party began
to shed inflammatory Particles among
the Members, and raised every Voice
in Contradiction concerning Right and
Wrong.—How far such a general Contention might have extended, no one can
say; CATO sided with the Prude, being,
as he imagined, a scandalized Woman of
Virtue; ALEXANDER enter'd the Lists
for ROXANA, as a Girl of Spirit; CER-
VANTES bristled up to see his Brother
Novellist mauled; and, like his own
QUIXOTE, fell on every one that stood

in

in his Way, while the Friends of Order were enrag'd at such Confusion, and especially PETER the GREAT; who declared, That all the Rioters, Male and Female, should be kick'd out, and for ever excluded the TOIRTAZAN. The abrupt Adjournment of this Assembly, as well as the Debates of it, bore near Resemblance to the POLISH Diet; much Talk, little Matter, great Bustle, and no Business.

" Well, Sir HUMPHREY, says the NAMREDAL, have I not presented you with a curious Set of Figures, both in Appearance and Disposition ? Matters seldom proceed so far as they have done at present; but there is very little Cordiality at any Time, so close do the darling Opinions and Passions of Mortals stick to them even here, notwithstanding there is some Degree of Punishment attending every Individual : And were it not, con-
                                    tinues

tinues he, that we SUBLUNARS are entirely subject to the NOIBLAN Restrictions
and Decorum, there would be as much
violent and uncharitable Contention
among us in the MOON as upon Earth."
From these Remarks, and a more particular Retrospect of the Scene we had
been present at, the NAMREDAL drew a
Number of moral and social Inferences,
which I would recite at large, only I
think them sufficiently obvious; and it is
but reasonable that, upon such Occasions,
every intelligent Reader should think for
himself; therefore, FELLOW TRAVELLER,
leaving you to such Speculation as may
appear proper, let us both take our Rest
till we are disposed to begin a new
CHAPTER.

CHAP.

CHAP. III.

Some Account of the NOIBLAN DRAMA—
Remarks on Theatrical Performers—AD-
DISON *introduced—The* ESTRALAM—
An ODE, &c.

AFTER attending the TOIRTAZAN,
nothing worthy Remark occurr'd
till the NAMREDAL commanded my Attendance to the ESTRALAM, or THEATRE.
On our Way thither I took Occasion to
inquire, if Theatrical Entertainments in
NOIBLA were similar to ours.

" No, says he; in the DRAMA here
one general Subject is proposed and uni-
formly pursued, without the Incumbrance
of any Episodical Matter; without Divi-
sion of *Acts* or Change of *Scenes*. This
Evening ADDISON entertains us with a
new Piece, called SALMINA ELENGALE,
the TEMPLE of VIRTUE. All CITIZENS
are Actors by Turns, which gives them a
just Idea, and a competent Facility of
speaking

ſpeaking in public with Propriety and Grace. To excell in ſuch Exhibitions is rather a Credit than a Blemiſh here; indeed the partial Laws and illiberal Prejudices againſt Performers in the lower World, have ever appeared to me unaccountable; ſince it is certain that, to make any tolerable Figure in ſuch a Character, many valuable Qualifications, both intellectual and corporeal, are requiſite; Underſtanding, to conceive; Senſibility, to expreſs; Grace of Perſon and Eaſe of Geſture, to engage and to adorn. As to its being taken up from mercenary Views; if all Ranks of People, except thoſe born to independent Fortunes, and even ſome of them too, were not actuated by the ſame Principle, it might be an Argument of Servility, peculiar and diſgraceful; but where Intereſt is the univerſal Spring of ſocial Movement, the very Soul of Action, why ſhould they be ſtigmatized for obeying the juſt and powerful

erful Voice of honeſt Gain? Nay, more,
why ſhould they be held in Contempt for
giving Life and Utterance to thoſe Productions which gain the Authors much
Eſtimation, tho' they write, as the Performers act, for lucrative Purpoſes.——I
know, continues he, that the ROMAN
Law gave Riſe to theſe Prejudices among
the ENGLISH; but with what Propriety?
It was made to check the Increaſe of degenerate and abandoned GRECIANS;
who, like the preſent effiminated Sons of
ITALY, were pernicious to a free and war-
like People. So far Reſtriction would
be highly commendable; yet, by the Information of HANDEL, who ſays he never
liked them, but in Compliance with the
Caprice of Faſhion, Numbers of thoſe
uſeleſs Animals are imported every Year
at an immenſe Charge, and maintained at
an incredible Expence. To me it is aſto-
niſhing that thoſe who ought to be the
Protectors of national Taſte and Manners,
ſhould

should cherish such Vermin, who vitiate even that in which they are imagined to excell; rendering Harmony as empty and unmeaning as their own Heads."

Being no Friend to the *Signiors* and *Signoras* that infest the *Hay-Market*, it is probable I should have made some additional Remarks not much in their Favour, but that my Guide seemed already in Possession of all I could suggest; therefore I contented myself with observing, That it was much to be lamented the *Opera* Subscription was not converted to the Support of an Academy, under the most eminent ITALIAN Masters, to instruct BRITISH Youth in the pleasing and useful Arts of Painting and Architecture; from whence the Subscribers, if possessed of any real Taste, must enjoy a much more delicate Satisfaction than from hearing beardless Heroes rage in the *Forté*, melt in the *Adagio*, caper in the *Vivacè*,

reason

reafon in *Recitative*, and expire in *femi-
demi Quavers.*

We now reached the ESTRALAM, and
the NAMREDAL conducted me to his Box,
(which was appropriated to him as Magiftrate, and was the only diftinguifhed
Station in the Houfe) capable of containing eight Perfons, and elevated about
three Yards above the other Seats, which
branch from it on each Side in an amphi-
theatrical Form, and fill up all the Space
to the STAGE; every Perfon is partitioned
from his Neighbour, and fo fituated as to
be in full View of the NAMREDAL, whofe
fuperintending Eye always commands
ftrict Decorum.

Inquiring the Reafon of this feemingly
unfociable Separation, my obliging Inftructor replied, That upon his Arrival,
bating abfolute Riots, the NOIBLAN
THEATRE was as liable to Confufion as
thofe

thofe in the nether World; but, fays he, I undertook, and have effected, a Reformation. As no two Perfons fit together, there cannot be any Chattering or Noife to interrupt the Performance; Attention does Juftice both to the Sentiment and Utterance; or, at worft, thofe who cannot relifh inftructive Entertainment, are prevented from interrupting fuch as can: by this Method alfo each Individual judges for himfelf; ill-timed hafty Criticifms, rifing not from Difcernment but from Paffion, is curb'd; and Opinions are kept in cool Sufpence, till a more proper Time and Place prefents itfelf for comparing them.

I could not but highly applaud this Regulation, nor forbear remarking how it would depopulate our THEATRES; where, like Enthufiafts, the moft go along with the Cry of a few noify Fellows that call themfelves *Critics*, whofe

whole

whole Stock of Knowledge confisting in a few mechanical Phrases of Applause or Censure, influences nine Tenths of the Audience; while they themselves are influenced by *gratis* Admittance, Intimacy with some of the Performers, or to flatter a handsome ACTRESS and their own Vanity, by supporting her at any Rate; with Insinuations that she is a *damn'd* fine Woman; and that they have *particular* Reasons for saying so. If the NOIBLAN Custom should be introduced, what would become of those who are wholly employ'd in Remarks upon the Features, Dress, and Deportment of others, all of whom are sacrificed to their own manifest Superiority? What would become of the soft Whispers and powerful Glances of Intrigue, which so attractively employ the Belles and Beaus? In short, a Playhouse, so metamorphosed, must be, to the Sons and Daughters of true Taste, almost as insipid as a Church; and, of Consequence,

the

the Productions of SHAKESPEAR or OT-
WAY will be as little admired as thofe of
CLARKE or TILLOTSON.

While we were in Converfation, the
Audience, leaning over their little Parti-
tions, enjoyed themfelves in the fame
Manner, till a Bell, ftriking five Times,
gave Notice to begin. Here the NAM-
REDAL prefented me a Tranflation of the
Piece to be exhibited, with this Remark,
That the Idioms of the NOIBLAN Language and that of ENGLAND are fo widely different, that I fhould difcover very
few of thofe Beauties which probably
adorned the Original; therefore, fays he,
you are only to regard the general Tendency and the Sentiments, and not to look
for the Stile of ADDISON in the Tranflation: According to the Cuftom that
every Author fhall introduce his own
Piece, he is approaching, and you will
now perceive of what Confequence Prac-

VOL. II. G tice

tice is to Elocution; for he, who could never utter any Thing declamatory in the
other World, having, by Cuſtom, caſt off
that childiſh Diffidence, or perhaps irrational Pride, which cloſed his Lips there,
is now become one of our moſt eloquent
and moſt powerful Speakers.

Here the admired Author of CATO
preſented himſelf with placid Dignity,
and, according to my Tranſlation, delivered the following Proſe PROLOGUE, for
Verſe is employed ſolely in thoſe Pieces
that are ſet to Muſic:

" Your Approbation—Oh NOIBLANS,.
ſo often cordially conferred, muſt ever
ever warm my Heart with the moſt ſenſible and delicate Pleaſure, Pleaſure which
nothing can ſo ſoon or effectually com-
municate as Praiſe honeſtly ſought and
candidly obtained; it is an undefiled In-
cenſe that ſheds balmy Sweetneſs over
the

the intellectual Feelings; for so noble an Acquisition Imagination plumes her Pinions to a profitable Flight, and Judgement labours to a laudable End. Among you the Syren Voice of Flattery cannot charm the Ear, nor the gilded Pageantry of Vice allure the Eye; ye are not Camelion Devourers of mere Sound and Show; the intermeddling Monster, Party, cannot gain Admittance here; nor the Delusive Meteor, Prejudice, lead one Fool astray—Writers have nothing to influence them but an honest Ambition of spotless Fame. What is there of Virtue I can offer, which is not known and practised in this happy ISLAND? Her celestial Charms are seen by all in their most striking Lustre, and are by all admired; yet, as Exercise is necessary to invigorate the corporeal, so is Contemplation to regulate the mental System; and the oftener we view those Beauties, which even the Wicked are forced to honour with their

G 2   Respect,

Refpect, the more fhall we be fired by them to meritorious Purfuits, the more fhall we purify and exalt our Natures.

"Upon thefe Principles I endeavour to remind, not to inform; as in a Mirror I prefent you with the Failings of another World, that you may be the better fatif-fied with your own Rectitude, and more fteadily determined to maintain it; for who, that has felt the Power of unble-mifh'd Innocence, and the Delight of felf-approv'd Virtue, would ever bend an Eye on the falfe Glare of groffer and inferior Enjoyments? My Defign, in its Nature, and in this View, I dare avow; the Exe-cution muft be referred to your Judge-ment, in whofe Approbation I glory, and to whofe Cenfure I fubmit."

Here he retired, and I was going to pay him the Tribute of noify Applaufe, according to the Cuftom of our World,

not

not only for what he faid, but alfo for the
Manner of Delivery, which was peculi-
arly graceful; when the NAMREDAL
ftopp'd me with this Remark, That the
Approbation of public Exhibition is always referr'd to the next Day; that Judge-
ment, uninfluenced by the prefent fudden
Agitation of the Paffions, may determine
with more Impartiality and Precifion.

ADDISON had no fooner concluded his
introductory Addrefs, than RICH's Pan-
tomimical Genius transform'd the STAGE
from a plain Hall to the Perfpective of a
delightful Grove; at the Extremity of
which appeared a tranfparent TEMPLE,
feated upon a craggy Rock of awful Appearance and very difficult Accefs. Within the *Veftibule* of the Temple fat three
graceful Females, reprefenting WISDOM,
VIRTUE, and TRUTH; the firft of which
Characters my Inftructor told me was per-
fonated by ELIZABETH of ENGLAND; the

fecond, by LUCRETIA of ROME; and the
third, by a Virgin of NOIBLA; for there
could not be found among all the SUB-
LUNARS, one who had not in fome Shape
or other offended TRUTH.

Several peculiar and agreeable Sym-
phonies now ftruck the Ear, Variety of
Inftruments being fo difpofed as to echo
one another from all Parts of the Grove,
in a moft natural and mafterly Manner:
Thefe having continued for ten or twelve
Minutes, the following ODE, in fingle
Parts and Chorufes, was performed to
great Perfection. As a Specimen of
NOIBLAN Poetry, I give the Original;
and, for Sake of Readers who have never
travelled to the MOON, nor ftudied the
LunarLanguage, fubjoin the Tranflation.

Trivenoc Elengal—Sforfan Ranzar,
Lanfe nedmel Salmina;
Wolul Ryclemen Retmel.

                              Setrod

Setrod terefmon Leverep,
Thoumno droffere notpam,
Ekor fal negramo Nethram.

Retexot felawar—Annive Rombu;
Calamanza Felquerez,
Demrofein Yllipa furoe.

TRANSLATION.

Thou fpotlefs Regent, Virtue, hail,
    May Mankind to thy Temple hafte;
Hold thou of FAME th' impartial Scale,
    And give to REASON perfect Tafte.

Let all thy gentle Laws obey,
    Thy Laws which perfect Blifs beftow;
To Mortals fmooth the thorny Way,
    And teach them all they ought to know.

The Di'mond's dimmer Luftre fades
    Before thy cheering, fun-like Eye,
Which gaily gilds Life's darkeft Shades,
    Bright Source of mental Liberty.

                       The

The ODE being concluded, VIRTUE opened the PLAY, or whatever you pleaſe to call it, as will appear in the ſucceeding CHAPTER.

C H A P. IV.

The TEMPLE *of* VIRTUE, *and various Characters, exhibited—A* BUCK, *a* GENERAL, *a* QUACK, *and a Huſband-hunting Girl introduced.*

"CHASTE SISTERS, in whoſe kind Affection I find my chief Support, it is not unknown to you what ceaſeleſs Pains I have taken to gain Proſelytes among terreſtrial Beings: Humbling myſelf to an almoſt unparalleled Degree, I have wooed them to the Promotion of their own Happineſs; yet ſo much are they influenced, and for the moſt Part overpowered by thoſe Boſom Foes, their Paſſions, that I have few real, tho' many hypocritical,

hypocritical, Admirers; Hypocrites fo
accomplifhed, that while they give me
the fevereft Wounds in private, exter-
nally they adore me; I have therefore
determined to make a public Trial, and
to that End have ordered FAME to give
a general Summons, promifing each Individual to grant what he may wifh or
want, which I imagine will have a more
powerful Effect, and draw more Suppli-
ants, than the bare Attraction of my own
native Charms, which all praife, yet few
endeavour to poffefs."

   " The Defign, replies WISDOM, is undoubtedly juft; for while Appearances
are preferred to Reality; while Mortals
confult Fancy more than Reafon; Appetite more than Prudence; and Paffion
more than Judgment, it is needlefs to
hope for many *Votaries* at the Shrine of
this TEMPLE, unlefs drawn hither by Delufion."

Here

Here Truth interposed, and said,
" She could by no Means agree to Mifreprefentation in any Shape; that unper-
form'd Promifes were palpable Violations
of her Dignity, infufferable Intrufions
upon her Prerogative; which is, continues fhe, fo extremely delicate, that the
leaft Infringement not only endangers
my Power, but even my very Exiftence;
witnefs the many Regions and the count-
lefs Multitudes; whence, tho' they owe
the moft perfect Subjection to my Dominion, I am almoft abfolutely exil'd: If once
I flack the Reins of Government, and let
Tongues go unbridled, thofe who only
fport with me at firft, will foon become declared Rebels, lofe all Senfe of Duty, and
ever after fcorn my Controul. For thefe
Reafons, in direct Oppofition to a moft
injurious Adage, Truth fhould appear
like herfelf at all Times, and in all Places,
juftly difdaining to be the Tool of falfe
Complaifance, or mercenary Views."

" Dear

" Dear Sifter, returned WISDOM, you cannot have a more fincere or more powerful Advocate than I have ever been; and it is with the utmoft Regret I fee you fuftain fuch Injuries, as all my Love and Influence cannot prevent; yet let me fay that, in the prefent Cafe, you are free from all Danger. Whatever your eldeft Sifter fuggefts, fhe fanctifies; her Views lead to a defirable End; and if fhe *feems* to fet you afide, in a general Promife of granting what may be follicited, it is only to eftablifh you more firmly; you fee her Power and yours declines with equal Pace; an Attempt to recover both cannot deferve Cenfure, fince Delufion, if it may be called fo, working to falutary Purpofes, is thereby rendered the Inftrument of Good. I know your nice, timid Nature fhrinks back even at the Shadow of Falfhood; which, however, cannot be more effectually encountered than by its own Weapons; therefore fear not, WIS-

DOM

DOM and VIRTUE will never injure TRUTH, no more than she can injure them."

Here FAME appeared, and acquainted the GODDESSES that innumerable Crowds were attending in Confequence of the Summons publifhed; who, if they were admitted promifcuoufly, would create incredible Confufion, and prevent the regular Progrefs of Bufinefs; VIRTUE therefore ordered that her Gate-Keepers, PERSEVERANCE and INTEGRITY, fhould admit but one at a Time; then directing FAME to take Place at her Feet, the firft Suppliant was introduced.

Upon Perufal of his Figure, I found him to be that very curious Animal an *Englifh* BUCK or BLOOD. With the ill-bred Affurance and confident Familiarity of fuch a brainlefs Creature, he addreffed himfelf in the following abrupt Manner, tho'

tho' the Place and the Appearances loudly demanded the moſt diſtant Reſpect:

" Rot me, Ladies, I am come here upon a very whimmy Occaſion; though, by the Bye, I have had a confounded troubleſome Tour, ſo I hope I ſhan't come of a Fool's Errand—But hold—eh—a pretty *Hotel* enough this—tho' not ſo taſty as the Temples, and Pagodas, and Dragons at KEW neither—but no Matter for that, the Thing's well enough, ſo I'll proceed to Buſineſs—Yet ſtay—upon my Soul my Head is ſo much upon the Tantwivy with the Batch of Burgundy I knock'd off among ſome Hearts of Oak laſt Night, that I had almoſt forgot to aſk which of you Ladies is Miſtreſs of this *Chateau*."

" I am, Sir, replies VIRTUE; and theſe are my Siſters, WISDOM and TRUTH." " Humph, ſays the BUCK, peeping curiouſly thro' an Eye-Glaſs —VIRTUE —
WISDOM

Wisdom—and—Truth—then, knock me up, I have been moſt egregiouſly miſtaken—I have heard you often mentioned, 'tis true; but, among People of Taſte and Spirit, you are always deſcribed as three curſed, ugly, preciſe old Maids; now, by the Bye, I think if you were a little while among us, you would make faſhionable Figures; and if I obtain what I come about, 'tis not Six to Four but I may introduce you to ſuch a Set of choice Spirits, that we ſhall ſoon be all of a Piece."

"Your Intention, Sir, returns Virtue, of making us as wiſe and as happy as yourſelf, is extremely kind; but, before we conſider it farther, pleaſe to let me know what unſatisfied Wiſh you have brought hither?"

"That you ſhall be told immediately, Madam, ſays he; I am what the World calls

calls a likely young Fellow; brisk, airy, full of Spirit; I can sit up six Nights without yawning thrice, and knock off six Bottles each Night; Tom Whip, the *Jockey*, Field-Marshal of the *Turf*, owns I ride as well as himself; Heelem, the *Cocker*, swears no Man makes better Bets; Hoyle I have at my Fingers Ends; then, for Wine and Women, Rochester and Buckingham were but Fools to me."

"Monstrous, cries Truth, interrupting him, I can forbear no longer; this Fellow, tho' sufficiently despicable, wants to represent himself ten Times worse than he really is—let him be driven from our Presence without farther Audience."

"Sister, replied Wisdom, you are too precipitate, we shall never gain any Proselytes by sudden and severe Resolutions; let us hear him out, and then proceed accordingly."

"Well

" Well faid, my little Sparkler, cries
the Buck, Curfe catch me if thofe roguifh
blue Peepers of thine, and thy good Nature, have not made me half in Love
with thee—Well, to go on with what we
are about; all my Acquaintance allow
that I am capable of cutting a capital Figure in Life, yet, for all my Qualifications, I am moft damnably cramp'd by
an old Grub of a Fellow, who calls himfelf my Father; he has fcraped and ftar-
ved himfelf into the Poffeffion of 2000 *l.*
per Ann. never lived like a Gentleman,
and, being determined to prevent me
from raifing the Credit of the Family,
allows me but pitiful Five Hundred
a-year; and what's that to a true Soul?
Mere Penury — a paltry humdrum Pit-
tance: Befides, the Cormudgeon talks
about my Extravagance, and mumbles
fomething of making a Will, that may
put it out of my Power to fell or mort-
gage after his Death: Now, what I wifh
is,

is, to have him decently tipp'd off before that happens, the sooner the better; and if you will bring it about, Ladies, why I shall be extremely your humble Servant, and always make you next Toast to the *Royal Family* and the *Jockey Club*."

" You have stated your Case, rejoins VIRTUE, in a very clear, tho' unfavourable Light; it is, to be sure, great Pity that so enterprizing a Disposition as yours should suffer any Limitation; but I know not how to assist you in this Affair, for your Father is a most intimate Acquaintance of mine."

" How! interrupts the Blood, is old Square-Toes a Poacher then? And does he keep Tid-Bits unknown to me?"

" Restrain your licentious Tongue, says the Goddess; his Industry, Prudence, and moral Life, the very Reverse of thy shame-

VOL. II.   H   ful

ful Diffipation, have recommended him
to my Efteem; what has tainted thy Heart
with fuch vile Ingratitude as to wifh that
Fountain dried, from whofe Current flowed thy Life? Why wifh thofe Eyes clofed
that love to look upon thee? And why
languifh for unnatural Poffeffion of that,
which, granted to thy prefent Difpofition,
cannot be a Bleffing, muft be a Curfe?
However, if you will work a thorough
Reformation; if you will exchange Extravagance for a prudent Spirit, and af-
fociate with Companions of more deferving Character, I dare promife that your
Father will equally fhare every Advantage with you while alive, and leave you
in full Poffeffion of his Fortune when he
dies."

" Hey Day, hey Day, cries the Suppliant; you preach juft fuch infipid Stuff as
fome of our Parfons; I'll tell you what,
my grave Madam, if I can't fpend my
For-

Fortune according to my own Difpofition, I muft be e'en content to wait, and raife Money at Fifty *per Cent.* till Dad knocks up in the natural Way.—Œconomy and Prudence! ha! ha! ha! ha! I fhould make a very fine Figure indeed with your Advice—fo Miftrefs Virtue, Lady Wisdom, and Mifs Truth, fince you have nothing better to offer, I may as well fhove off without farther Compliment."

" Hold, Friend, cries Justice; with Permiffion of the Goddefs of this Temple I grant thy Wifh; this Moment thy aged Sire lays him down in the Sleep of Death, and thou art now unlimited Mafter of his Poffeffions; but be affured, ere long, thou wilt have Caufe to wifh him alive again, when the Torrent of thy Vices has borne thee down, and left thee naked on the inhofpitable Shore of Poverty."

" No

" No Matter for that, fays the over-
joyed Heir—a fhort Life and a merry
one—now I can have a Match over the
Beacon Courfe, or back the Main for Five
Hundred, with any Lord of them all."

This fprightly Child of modern Merit
was fucceeded by one whofe Appearance
had in it a Kind of venerable Terror; a
dignified Ferocity.   Having made Obei-
fance to the Throne, he delivered himfelf
as follows:

" Moft amiable GODDESS of this TEM-
PLE, unufed as I am to the fmooth Polifh
of courtly Language, and fubtle Windings of Infinuation, receive an Addrefs,
blunt, yet honeft in its Nature, founded
on Sincerity, without Art.

" Know then I am, and have been
fince my earlieft Years, a Son of War;
many

many perilous Encounters, many Hard-
ships laboriously toiled thro', and mostly
successful in their Event, have raised me,
by Steps of just Gradation, to the Degree
of a *General*; in which Situation I have
extended my Country's Strength and
Glory to incredible Limits, and that with
the universal Approbation of those I have
had the Honour to command. Nor have
I acted upon interested Motives; a genu-
ine Thirst of FAME first fired me to great
Exploits, and has ever been the ruling
Principle of all my Actions; had it not,
I might have laid me down in the silken
Arms of Peace, and reclined upon the
Down of Luxury, there to indulge the
more ungenerous Passions in a Life of
shameful Indolence ; but, disdaining
aught so foreign to Public Good, and in-
consistent with the Dignity of my Nature,
I preferred Temperance to Luxury, La-
bour to Ease, and Perils to Safety.

H 3 " Let

" Let not this Account be deemed oftentatious Vaunting of my own Merit, fince it is literally juft; and the prefent Occafion requires I fhould offer fome Facts to fupport the Claim I lay to a fair, exalted, and lafting Place in the Records of FAME, that my Name may be engraved on ever-during Brafs, and not vanifh with the tranfient Breath of popular Applaufe; this granted, I fhall have attained my ultimate Wifh, and think myfelf thoroughly rewarded for all my Toils."

VIRTUE now took Occafion to obferve, " That tho', in her own Nature, fhe far preferred the Smiles of Peace to the Frowns of War, yet Military Merit was highly deferving in her View; for, continues fhe, what Character is more complicate, more difficult to perfect, than that of a *complete* GENERAL ? who muft have Refolution, to face the moft imminent Hazards;

Hazards; Humanity, to treat Enemies with Tenderneſs; Penetration, to foreſee proſperous Events; and Caution, to anticipate unfavourable ones: Activity, to cultivate Succeſs; Perſeverance, to ſurmount Difficulties; Sagacity, to project; Experience, to conduct; and Steadineſs, to execute his Schemes: Patience, to temper Impetuoſity; Vigilance, to ſeize Occaſion; Liberality, to engage Regard; Dignity, to ſupport Command; Diſcipline, to promote Order; and Condeſcenſion, to render Subordination as agreeable to all Ranks as the Nature of the Service will admit: This extenſive Portrait conſidered, in which View you place yourſelf before us, moſt certainly merits the Diſtinction you apply for: What ſay you, SISTERS, ſhall we order FAME to gratify his Wiſh?" WISDOM nodded Aſſent; but TRUTH objected as follows:

" SISTERS,

" Sisters, no one can more admire, or would sooner join in the just Reward of Merit, than myself; and it is with sensible Regret that I find myself at present under the Necessity of offering any Thing against extensive Deservings; but my Name, my Nature, and my Station in this Temple, all oblige me.

" What this *Veteran* has advanced in his own Favour generally, I cannot deny; but, as you have already remarked, there are many more Requisites essential to a perfect Child of Fame, than those he has set forth; that he has atchieved several great and arduous Exploits, in the supposed Service of his Country, I shall not contradict; but the Glare of *Victory* is often the Tinsel Covering of very melancholy Effects to that State it shines on: That he has preferred a Life of Toil to one of Indolence, I readily admit; but what

what were his Motives? *Patriotism?*—
No—a true *Patriot* will lament the Neceffity of War; he always fecretly rejoiced
in it, and did his utmoft to promote it.
Was he void of Intereft in his Views?—
No—witnefs the Devaftation fpread thro'
conquered Countries, by levying enormous Contributions; great Part of which,
inftead of fupporting or encouraging the
Soldiery, found their Way into his own
infatiable Coffers.   Has he given Life to
Merit?—No—thofe who *paid*, not thofe
who *fought beft*, he promoted.   Did he
always avail himfelf of Advantages for
the Intereft of his Country?—No—more
than once he has taken Bribes of the
Enemy, to forego fuch Opportunities as
might have been decifive.

" Thefe Things confidered, which he
cannot have Hardinefs enough to deny
before me; or, if he fhould, would not
therefore be the lefs true, tho' they do
not

not entirely exclude him from the Lifts
of Fame, yet do they fufficiently fpeak
againft the exalted Station he afpires at;
therefore, SISTERS, with your Concur-
rence, I fhall order him to be fet down a
very GREAT GENERAL, but a very BAD
MAN."

VIRTUE and WISDOM entirely agree-
ing to this Decifion, FAME entered him
accordingly; which feemed to chagrin the
Son of MARS highly, who went off muttering with great Indignation, " That
little better could be expected, when Females fat as Judges of heroic Actions."

The next who claimed Audience, was
an important Figure with emaciated Features, large Penthoufe Brows, a huge dark
Tye, a Suit of SPANISH BROWN adorned
with a Multiplicity of Buttons, a Gold-
headed Cane to fupport his meditative
Chin, and a peaceable Sword which had
never

never quitted its Scabbard: Having paid his Addreſs with truly claſſical Formality, this illegitimate Son of HIPPOCRATES, for ſuch he appeared to be, ſpoke to the following Effect:

"Unacquainted with the Titles and Decorum uſed in this TEMPLE, it is not to be wondered at if I ſhould inadvertently run into Soleciſms; but a general Profeſſion of Reſpect will prove, I hope, illuſtrious Ladies, a general Exculpation.

"I ſtand before you an injured *Profeſſor* of PHYSIC; one who has more enriched the *Materia Medica* than all the Faculty beſides; yet that Seat of Ignorance in *Warwick-Lane* *, jealous of my ſuperior Talents, has ſtigmatized me with the Title of a QUACK, and put my ineſtimable Diſcoveries upon a Footing with the *Sack Drop*, the *Sweating Powder*, and *Fiſtula Paſte* of WARD—the *Valerian*, the

* College of Phyſicians.   *Bardana,*

Bardana, and *Sage* of HILL—nay, with
the *Viper Drops* of ROCK, and such-like
illiterate *Pedlars* in MEDICINE; but scorn-
ing the common Dog-trot Pace of PHY-
SIC, I have severally studied ENGLISH,
SCOTS, IRISH, and WELSH Constitutions;
for each of which I may venture to affirm I have discovered the true *Panacea.*
For the first, I have my infallible Essence
Porteriæ—for the second, *Marmalade de
Oatmeleana*—for the third, *Balsamum Po-
taticum*—and for the fourth, *Spiritus Lee-
kicus:* Now these, Ladies, are of my particular, original Invention; yet, tho' I have
obtained Patents to recommend them;
have advertised till I can bear the Expence no longer; have wrote, as is usual
in such Cases, Letters of Thanks to myself; and have procured Affidavits of extraordinary Cures from more than ever
took them; yet all won't do, and for no
other Reason than that I have no Chariot;
for you must know, illustrious Fair Ones,
that

that much Merit lies in an Equipage, and there is very little Chance, in our Way, without it; therefore if, out of Regard to Mankind, you will affift me with a *Carriage* and *Pair*, or, to fecure all, a *Carriage* and *Six*, I make no Doubt of obfcuring not only my Contemporaries, but even all my Predeceffors in the Phyfical Way."

Here WISDOM, who had been fome Time whifpering with FAME, replied, " Friend, the Profeffion of which you pretend to be, is an Object of my particular Regard; and forry I am to find it fo often difgraced, and rendered obnoxious, by ignorant Pretenders; who, with blufhlefs Faces and unfeeling Hearts, augment the Miferies of Fellow-Creatures, to promote their own mercenary Views: Such a one, FAME fays, you are entered in her Note-Book, a Firft-rate

Man-

Man-killer; and therefore, inftead of gratifying your Wifh, we fhall give you into
the Keeping of *Honefty*, that you may do
no more Mifchief; in the mean Time
confefs yourfelf an Impoftor, or worfe
will follow."

Here the trembling Empiric endeavoured to apologize, by obferving, That
every one had a Right to try for Bread:
" My Father, I muft own, fays he, was a
Taylor, and indeed would have brought
me up in his own Trade, but my Genius
foared higher; fo I ran away, and got to
be Sweeper of an APOTHECARY'S Shop
(many great Men have rifen from fmall
Originals); from thence I attended an itinerant Phyfician for feveral Years, and,
feeing fome thrive that knew as little as
myfelf, I e'en fet up; but, LADIES, if it
is not an honeft Profeffion, I have another at Hand, which I can eafily affume;

I

I can give up HIPPOCRATES for WHITE-
FIELD; *Phyſical Preſcription* for *Methodiſt
Preaching*, and perhaps be no Loſer."

" Audacious Wretch, cries TRUTH,
dareſt thou profeſs thyſelf my Enemy in
the tendereſt Point of my Intereſts and
Affections, in Religion? Art thou equally ready to prey on the immortal as the
mortal Part? There are too many Vermin of thy Kind wandering about already, to the Subverſion of ſocial Order and
moral Good; therefore it is but juſt to
prevent thee from adding to the Number, ſo we doom thee to perpetual Impriſonment; and I could wiſh that every
Moral and Phyſical QUACK breathing
were equally in our Power. '

The diſappointed Adventurer was now
removed, with much Horror of Countenance, to his Captivity; execrating Ambition, that had made him look on his
Father's

Father's Goose, Needles, and Sheers in
so contemptible a Light; and regretting
the egregious Folly of a Rogue's seeking
Preferment in the TEMPLE of VIRTUE;
tho', added he, I have heard FORTUNE is
blind, and I hoped these Folks were so
too.

Next, a blooming Girl, of remarkable
Vivacity, presented herself, and was going
to address the Throne without any Symp-
toms of Diffidence, when VIRTUE antici-
pated her thus:

" Young Lady, I am glad to see one of
your Age and Appearance come to this
TEMPLE; I shall have a particular Pleasure in showing myself your Friend, and
you cannot any where find safer or more
gentle Protection; but give me Leave to
remark and condemn an unbecoming
Confidence you seem to be possessed of;
my Votaries may be *free*, but I do not
chuse them to be *forward*."

" Lack-

" Lack-a-day, Madam, replies the Suppliant, I don't know what you call *forward*, but all young Ladies of Fashion are eafy and familiar; and *Mamma* has often told me that fuch a fine Girl as me, fhould never be bafhful in any Company."

" There it is, fays Wisdom, fine Girls are fpoiled by foolifh Mothers, who are continually trumpeting Beauty in their Ears, without taking any Care of their Principles and Difpofitions; Affectation is taught for Addrefs; Impudence, for Spirit; and Intrigue, for Underftanding. I fuppofe now, Child, continues fhe, this kind *Mamma* takes Care that your Beauty fhall be ornamented with all the Changes of Fafhion."

" Oh yes, Madam, replies the Favourite, I am always in the very Tip of the Mode, and feldom mifs any public Place except Church; nay, we fometimes go there too, when we hear of a new-married Couple making their Appearance, to fee what the Bride is dreffed in, and how fhe looks. Now I talk of that, there was Mifs *Gauky*, a horrid ugly Neighbour of ours, made fuch a Figure——ha! ha! ha! ha! laft *Sunday*; no Tafte, no Life, but looked as mumchance as if fhe had been a Citizen's Wife thefe feven Years—and her Bridegroom, fuch a Hottentot! with his formal cut Bob, ftiff-topp'd white Gloves, and fuch a Quaker-like Suit, that the whole Gallery were in a conftant Roar.——Well, certainly, to People of Fafhion, fuch Creatures are high Entertainment."

" Very brilliant Notions you feem to have of Life, Mifs, fays Virtue, pray what Age may you be ?"

" Sixteen, Madam, returns this Daughter of Spirit, tho' I believe they cheat me
out

out of a Year or two; indeed Mamma
says I am fit for a Husband, and, to tell
you the Truth, I have thought so myself
these three Years; but the old Glumps
my Father calls me a light-headed Hussy,
as if *he* could know any Thing of Women's Matters; Mamma often calls him a
Fool, and bids him mind his own Affairs;
but he will be meddling, and so, forsooth,
I want to get out of his Way. Now,
there's a charming, delicate, sweet, fine
Gentleman, that swears he loves me better than ANTHONY did CLEOPATRA;
that he would, like him, lose the World
for Love, and a thousand other ravishing
Things: He is an Officer too, and wears
Scarlet trimm'd with Gold; and has the
finest Hair, speaks *French*, and dances
like an Angel; so I come here to beg that
I may have this delicate Creature for a
Husband, and that old Gruff may give
him all my Fortune."

There

" There cannot be, fays Virtue, a truer Friend to the Married State than myfelf; 'tis there I find my moft pleafing Refidence, and my moft permanent Joy; but as to many it is a Climate of undifturbed Serenity and true Repofe; fo to others, who unadvifedly and at improper Seafons journey thither, it proves an uncomfortable Seat of Perturbation and continual Storms; barren of every Comfort, and pregnant with every Ill. More appertains to a prudent Choice than is ufually thought of; Politenefs and a liberal Education are agreeable Qualifications in a Wife; but domeftic Œconomy, which you are too young to know, and Complacence, which good Senfe alone can give, are indifpenfible Requifites to make the Married State happy: But even fuppofe you are poffeffed of thefe, if the Object of your Regard happens to be worthlefs, and you have no Affurance to the contrary, the Profpect muft be gloomy;

my; let your Father's Caution direct
your Choice, and check that inconfide-
rate, youthful Impatience, which probably may urge you into a State of long
and bitter Repentance."

" What, repent having fuch a charming Man as the Captain, fays Mifs *Hot-
upon't!* impoffible; befides, I *know* he is
to be my Hufband; a very great FOR-
TUNE-TELLER faw him in three Coffee-
Cups running, and told me his Size, and
the Colour of his Hair, as exactly as if he
had been in the Room; fo you know I
muft have him, it is my Fate: But then
I want to have him *foon*, and I want to
have my Fortune too, that he may keep
me a grand Equipage, and all the other
Appurtenances of a fine Lady."

" Well, fays VIRTUE, to prevent the
ill Confequences which probably may at-

I 3   tend

tend the Oppofition of your Inclinations,
I grant your Wifh; but remember hereafter that your own precipitate Difpofition is the fole Caufe of whatever Incon-
veniences may enfue."

" Yes, yes, I'll remember, replies the
overjoy'd Suppliant; but a Fig for Danger, would not any Girl of true Spirit
*pleafe her Eyes, tho' fhe fhould plague her
Heart?*—Well, Ladies, I vow I am very
much obliged to you, and if you will honour me with your Prefence when I am
fettled, at my firft ROUTE, which I in-
tend to make fo grand that *all the World
will be there*, I'll do every Thing in my
Power to return the Obligation."

" A ROUTE, Madam! replies WIS-
DOM, if you had been tolerably acquainted with us, you would have known that
we are never feen at ROUTES."

" Not

" Not seen at a ROUTE! cries Miss, positively that's strange, and plainly shows you are not much among People of Quality; now, I doat on Persons of Rank, and when I am married I shall be one myself; so, dear Ladies, your most obedient humble Servant."

" A pretty Sample this, says WISDOM, of a ruined Favourite; who, by the Folly of a Mother, has been nursed up in Dissipation and Vanity, to the utter Destruction of a good natural Genius, and an amiable Disposition; but mistaken Indulgence so generally prevails, and Parents labour so much to create artificial Passions, that this Object, tho' pitiable, is not at all singular."

But I see the CHAPTER is of a sufficient Length, and a Pause may be as acceptable to the *Reader* as it is to the *Author*.

CHAP.

C H A P. V.

The TEMPLE *of* VIRTUE *continued* — *A*
DWARF — *A* YOUNG WIFE — *An* AU-
THOR, *and other Characters introduced.*

THE next Suppliant was a Man of
very diminutive Size, on whom
Deformity had exerted her utmost Power,
presenting himself respectfully. He remarked, " That he had been unfortunate
from his Cradle, despised even by his Parents, for no Cause but unavoidable Defects in Person : Indeed, continues he, I
have derived some Advantage from my
Misfortune, as it has imprinted upon me,
and caused me to pursue, an excellent
Maxim of SOCRATES, who advises daily
Contemplation in a Glass, that the Beautiful may make their Minds *worthy* of
their Persons, and that the Deformed may
render their Dispositions an *Apology* for
their Defects : Upon this Plan the whole
Tenor of my Conduct has been rather to
consult

confult the Pleafure and Advantage of my Fellow-Creatures, than felfifhly to reap either from their Harm: I have uniformly indulged a rational Sympathy, to weep with the Sorrowful; to laugh with the Gay; and to be ferious with the Grave: Folly, however opulent or titled, has never been the Idol of my Adoration, nor natural Failings the Object of my Cenfure; yet, with a Difpofition to embrace all Mankind, that would, if poffible, diffufe univerfal Happinefs, Mankind make me the cruel Return to fet me up as an Object of *Ridicule,* for no other Reafon but becaufe I am not bleffed with the natural Symmetry of Parts; my humble Petition therefore is, That hereafter I may not be treated with fuch illiberal Cruelty, nor fo often reminded of my unavoidable Misfortune."

" Hard indeed, fays VIRTUE, is thy Lot, my Son; yet while all have Eyes,

and

and but few Judgment, intrinfic Worth
will be fubject to the Sneers of Ignorance, where it happens not to be deck'd
out in the adventitious and tranfitory
Ornaments of Riches or Beauty: Had
ALEXANDER been in no greater Sphere
than thou art, thofe who deified his Power
would have made themfelves merry with
his wry Neck; let this lovely Reflection
comfort thee, That tho' Nature has denied thee Harmony of Shape, my Sifter
WISDOM here has bleffed thee with Delicacy of Thought, and Integrity of Soul.
The Infects of *Ridicule* will buzz, will
ftrike their unavailing Stings; but do
thou keep thy Courfe, nor ever caft an
Eye upon Objects fo much inferior to
thee, unlefs to pity the much more material Deformity of their Minds. It is
not in the Power of VIRTUE, WISDOM,
and TRUTH, to prevent the Sarcafms of
Malevolence; but we can and will enable
thee to bear them without Emotion; depart

part then, affured of our Favour, which
fhall fmooth the rugged Paths of Life;
which fhall raife thee above the partial
Power of FORTUNE; and, after Death
fhall have diffolved thy perifhable and uncomfortable Frame, fhall embalm thy
Memory as a beauteous Pattern for Imitation; while thofe who indulge their
Spleen at thy Expence, fhall moulder for-
gotten into Duft, no better, no more
lovely, than thine."

Here the Suppliant departed with that
delicate and perfect Satisfaction, which
VIRTUE alone can give to a Heart poffeffed of proper Feelings.

Another Female approached next, and
delivered herfelf thus:

" Ladies, I come to beg your Affiftance in an Affair of great Confequence;
you muft know I have been married juft

six Months; Mr. STRUGGLE, my Husband, was the tenderest Lover that ever
Woman had; and indeed, for the first
three Months, I thought him the best
Husband in the World; but I have now
been told otherwise by my Neighbours,
Mrs. CHATWELL and Mrs. TELLTALE."

" How, Madam! says VIRTUE, have
your Neighbours a better Opportunity of
knowing your Husband than yourself?"

" Yes, certainly, replies the discontented Wife, for they have been married
several Years, and know the World better than me; besides, now they have put
me upon it, I can see how other People
behave; there's Mr. CHATWELL, like a
good Soul as he is, gets up in a Morning,
dresses the Children, makes Breakfast
ready, and carries it to Bed to his Wife,
who very seldom gets up before Eleven
o'Clock, because she is almost always
breeding,

breeding, poor Woman : Now, though I have declared myself pregnant, my rude Bear has never once offered to do so for me, but bids me stir nimbly, and says that Exercise is good for my Condition — There's a cruel Wretch."

" Truly, says WISDOM, if this is your chief Complaint you have more Reason to commend your Husband, and value him as a Man of Sense, than to be uneasy."

" Man of Sense! cries Mrs. STRUGGLE, I don't see why he should have more Sense than his Neighbours ; nor why I should not be as well used as any other Wife—there's Mr. TELLTALE does not want Sense, yet he dares not say *Muff* if his Wife begins. The good-natur'd Creature won't help himself at Table because she says he's aukward ; and never keeps a Penny of Money in his Pocket but what she gives him ; nay, he won't even

even put on his *Sunday* Cloaths till he has
afk'd her Leave, and fhe may fcold the
Servants for three Hours together without a Check from him; want what fhe
will, go where fhe will, do what fhe will,
all's right: Tho', between ourfelves, fhe
was but his Houfe-Keeper, and, they fay,
no better than fhe fhould have been before Marriage; but fhe's in the Right of it,
give the Men an Inch and they'll take an
Ell; my Tyrant's a Proof of that; indeed
he gives me Liberty to get any Thing I
want, in Reafon, as he calls it, nor can I
fay he is ever out of Temper; but while
other Wives have more Power than me,
I am determined never to be eafy; fo what
I wifh is, that if a Man of Senfe won't be
obedient to his Wife, Mr. STRUGGLE
may be made a Fool as faft as poffible."

" That, Madam, is not in our Power,
fays WISDOM; befides, if it were, we
could not do you a greater Injury than by
com-

complying with your Wifh: The whole
of your Uneafinefs, and I believe it is the
Cafe of too many, appears to arife from
the contemptible Infinuations of *Bufy
Bodies*, whom you feem to confider as
Well-wifhers; but what Example of Credit can be derived from fuch as neither
confult Reafon nor Decency? Be affured
that every Woman, who invades the Prerogative of her Hufband, works her own
Shame as well as his. There are Lines
of Rectitude in the Marriage State to
mark out and limit the juft Sphere of Action; on either Side to pafs thefe, is to
run into Error. Power, as well as all
other Poffeffions, ought to be held in an
exact Medium; if it be made to prepon-
derate on the Male Side, it is ungenerous;
on the Female, prefuming; therefore
confider yourfelf as happy, that you are
not like thofe Neighbours you feem to
envy; depend upon it they do not advife
you from Principles of true Regard, but
from

from a Defire of exciting Quarrels; be advifed, and keep the Affection of a good and fenfible Man while you have it; remember it is a tender Plant, and cannot outlive the frofty Breath of Contention; cherifh it while you have it in full Bloom, nor ever expect to find a Guardian and Protector in one who can wear the Name without the Dignity of a Hufband."

" Well but, fays Mrs. STRUGGLE, if I don't *hold my own*, as the Saying is, I fhall be called fo many *poor tame Creatures*, that I fhan't be able to put my Head abroad."

" Fear not, returns WISDOM, you are juft beginning Life, and 'tis rather unfortunate that you have fallen into the Society of fuch termagant Goffips; but, fince you are come to follicit our Affiftance, I'll take Care to conduct you in a fafe and pleafant Path; not in a State of Sub-

Subjection, but sympathetic Complacence, which makes the *Hymæneal* Torch
burn bright, and beams perfect Happinefs around thofe Hearts wherein it is
cherifhed."

Notwithftanding that the Love of de-
fpotic Sway (fo incident to Female Minds,
and which had been fo much enflamed in
this young Wife, by the Arts of old Prac-
titioners in domeftic Ufurpation) feemed
to hold a ftrong Conflict with natural
Mildnefs; yet the weighty Remonftrance
of WISDOM had fuch an Effect as to fend
this Suppliant away, apparently well fatisfied.

The next in Succeffion was a fhabby,
pitiful Appearance, yet rendered laugh-
able by a grotefque Air of affumed Confequence, very ill adapted to his Figure;
which, if RIDICULE is at any Time con-
fiftent with Reafon and Humanity, is cer-

VOL. II.   K   tainly

tainly the faireſt Mark that can be ſet up for it.

This Son of Poverty, addreſſing him-ſelf, ſaid—" Moſt divine Ladies, more abundant in Beauty than the Sun's Ri-ſing, Setting, or Meridian Rays, I think I may pronounce myſelf a Man of good Deſervings, both as to my Abilities and Inclinations; yet, ſo it is, that I am often pennyleſs, while Knaves and Blockheads of all Sides roll in Plenty. Without Oſtentation I may claim Equality, if not Precedence of all my Contemporaries, in the Literary Way; yet, notwithſtanding the juſt Title I have to National Regard, thro' the Partiality, Ignorance, or Caprice of the World, I have much ado to ſub-ſiſt, and all for want of what is called a *Name*; without which the brighteſt Ta-lents are neglected, and the greateſt Me-rit is unprofitable: I come therefore to pe-tition, that, thro' your Favour, FAME may

eſtabliſh

eſtabliſh my Character, and at leaſt ſet me upon a Footing with ſome who deſerve leſs, yet enjoy more."

WISDOM obſerved, in Return, " That ſhe and her SISTERS ever lamented the Difficulties of Genius; that ſhe knew Merit was not always the Parent of Succeſs; but, ſays ſhe, that we may the better judge of your Caſe, let us have ſome Account how your Talents have been employed: It is an invariable Maxim with us never to eſteem any AUTHOR *good*, who is not alſo incorruptibly *honeſt*."

" If that be the Caſe, ſays the Petitioner, how very few can appear in the Liſt of your Approbation? Yet ſuffer me to hope I may be one; but let the Sketch of ſome Part of my Life, which I ſhall ſubmit to Conſideration, ſpeak my Claim more at large.

" My

" My Father, who had been the indigent, laborious Curate of an over-grown Living many Years, wanted Means to place me at the UNIVERSITY; however, by his own tender Attention, the Lofs was nearly made up to me: He made me a good Claffical Scholar, laid a folid Foundation of Moral Philofophy; gave me a pure and unprejudiced View of Religion; and fince, to indulge the political Genius of his Parifh, he read the News Paper as conftantly as the BIBLE, I had an Opportunity of knowing how Matters went in moft Parts of the World; a Branch of Study which, purfued with Moderation, he faid was highly ufeful—He died in my twenty-fifth Year, and left me nothing but my Head to depend upon.

" Launched into Life, Chance firft threw me in the Way of a *Noble Lord,* who condefcended to retain me as his SECRETARY; and indeed he very much
wanted

wanted one, being himſelf extremely de-
ficient both in the Matter and Manner of
Writing; yet his Propenſity to buſy himſelf in State Affairs, and to make a Buſtle
in the World, was as great as if his Abilities had been equal to the higheſt Station.

" In the Service of this Noble Lord I
wrote ſeveral *Political Speeches* and *Pamphlets*, by Means of which, as appeared
afterwards, he obtained a conſiderable
Employment; but finding when he was
ɪɴ Place, that he wanted me to contradict
and falſify all I had advanced when he
was ᴏᴜᴛ, I took the Liberty to remon-
ſtrate againſt ſuch mean Temporizing;
which ſo irritated his high Blood, that he
diſmiſſed me with no other Reward than
the bare Maintenance I had received, and
ſome unmeaning Promiſes of Friendſhip
occaſionally thrown out while in his Family."

" I

" I have often heard of that Wretch, says WISDOM, who, like many other empty, infolent Pretenders, has the matchlefs Affurance to boaft an Intimacy with me; but I have marked him, and fome more of FORTUNE's fcandalous Favourites, for public Detection; which fhall leave them no Retreat, but the pitiful Afylum of hereditary Titles."

" Accident, continues our AUTHOR, next threw me in the Way of an opulent COUNTRY SQUIRE, whofe Friendfhip I fo much engaged by writing a Song on the Chace, that, in the Zeal of his Heart, he fwore I was, except himfelf, the cleverest Fellow living, and therefore employed me as Tutor for his two Sons: In this Situation I had almoft become a Martyr to his Kindnefs; for Bottles and Punch-Bowls were as feldom off the Table as if the Houfe had been one of public Entertainment.

" My

" My Pupils I found to be naturally dull, but render'd more fo by the extraordinary Pains the Squire had taken to make them no wifer than himfelf. In Converfation he ufed to boaft that the eldeft fhould leap a five-barr'd Gate with any Man, or Woman either, for a hundred Guineas; as to the younger, he mark'd him out for a *Parfon*, having a good Living in his own Gift; for which Reafon, added he, the Lad muft have fome Linguo, and be a Bit of a Scholar; tho' you need not load his Head too much neither, for you know he can get fome poor, wife Fellow of a Curate cheap enough; and if he has a Mind to preach himfelf, why they tell me he can buy very good Sermons for Eighteen Pence or Two Shillings a Dozen.

" By liftening patiently to fuch Kind of Entertainment, and giving him his own Way, he grew fo exceffively fond of me, that

that he talked of getting me *Bishop'd*—
his Phrase for Ordination, and generously
said I should have Thirty Pounds a-year,
besides Bed and Board in the Family, till
his Son came of Age; upon Condition,
however, that I would not plague them
with long SERMONS; but make my Dif-
courses merry and short, with now and
then a Bam upon the COURT; for so far,
as hating the Administration, *he* was a
PATRIOT too.

" Presuming to remark the Improprie-
ty, nay, the Scandal, of a Preacher's submitting to any Direction but that of RE-
LIGION and his own Judgment, my polite Patron called me a Fool and a Block-
head ; which occasioned a Coolness that
at length grew into a downright Quarrel, and ended in our Separation; for,
getting a severe Fall a-hunting one
Day, and declaring that I would never
venture my Neck again upon so silly an
Occasion,

Occaſion, the SQUIRE openly declared he would no longer keep ſuch a Chicken-hearted Son of a B—— in his Family."

" By the Deſcription you give, ſays VIRTUE, this SQUIRE muſt be that igno-rant, inſolent Fool of Fortune, who, with brutal Heart, has ſo often aſſaulted me in the Perſons of innocent Country Girls: Well was it to eſcape from ſuch a Mon-ſter, whoſe ſhameful Practices muſt either give continual Pain to an honeſt Mind, or, by the dangerous Force of Example, bring his Aſſociates into his own con-temptible and abandoned State. Thus far, my Son, thou haſt highly merited our Favour; proceed, and if thou haſt uni-formly purſued the ſame Track, thou mayſt be aſſured of our Aſſiſtance."

" After thoſe already mentioned, re-ſumes the Suppliant, I met with a large Variety of Characters, too tedious to enu-merate;

merate; let it then fuffice to fay, that from feveral I might have pick'd up a comfortable Livelihood, could my Nature have proftituted itfelf to their Follies and Vices; but having always confidered a venal Pen as the moft dangerous Weapon in Nature, I could not be prevailed upon to fatirize *honeft* Men, nor *deify Brutes*. From this invariable Adherence to what I think right, a worthy Bookseller, who has ufher'd fome of my beft Pieces, unfuccefsfully, into the World, fays I derive my Poverty, and that I muft take fome *popular* Step to procure a *Name* before I can hope for even a tolerable Subfiftence. This is the Motive of my Sollicitation, and I fubmit the Cafe, with all Deference, to your Candor."

Truth having confirm'd every Article of his Relation, Virtue again applauded his Integrity, and at the fame Time commiferated

miferated his Situation in moſt pathetic Terms. " Whatever may be the Event of thy Endeavours, continues ſhe, for it is very doubtful whether we can command Succeſs in thy Favour, I will promiſe to fill thy Mind with a conſcious Satisfaction, a true Harmony, which the undeſerving Favourites of FORTUNE may languiſh for in vain. I am very intimate with CONTENT, who will, upon my Interceſſion, ſuit thy Wiſhes to thy Poſſeſſions: If to this FAME, who ſhall exert herſelf in thy Favour, can add agreeable Circumſtances, we ſhall all rejoice. Go then, adhere to thy Integrity, however unprofitable; be aſſured it will afford thee the moſt laſting Satisfaction, the moſt uninterrupted Serenity of Mind, and give thee Happineſs, which I only have the Power to beſtow."

The honeſt AUTHOR was retiring with much Pleaſure in his Countenance, when
WISDOM

Wisdom delivered herself to this Effect:

" Hold, Friend, some Words with you before you depart, and don't think that what I am about to offer is meant to pain, but to serve you; that you have *Genius*, I know; that your Success is far beneath your Merit, I lament; and that your Integrity has been inviolate, I allow. I am your Friend, and sure Friendship is never shown to more Advantage than in kind Reproofs; hear me then while I point out to you those Circumstances in which I think you erroneous.

"Dost thou not know that all Pride, and particularly Self-sufficiency, is utterly irreconcileable to my Dictates? That, by striving to magnify thy real Abilities, in Effect they are diminished? To aspire to a Superiority over thy Contemporaries, is commendable; to determine, to boast of,

or

or even to hint at such a Superiority thyself, is weak. Another Error I think thee liable to, is an obstinate Adherence to thy own Opinion, which thou takest to be Integrity; this has occasioned thee to contradict and run counter to the Generality of Mankind, who may be led by Persuasion, but not driven by Brow-beating: He who would instruct the World and live by it, must seldom appeal to Severity, but in every honest Way must humour human Nature; till, like heated Wax, it becomes fit to receive a due Impression. For want of preserving the Golden Mean between servile Compliance and dogmatical Opposition, thy Success has not been equal to what it might have been; wherefore, that the friendly Endeavours of FAME may be more effectual, let me recommend it to thee rather to resemble the pliant Willow, than the stubborn Oak. Chuse to wind about rather than knock down; that is, change Self-

Self-fufficience for Humility, and Contradiction for Perfuafion; comply with fome
of the Whims, that you may the more
powerfully combat the Vices of the Age;
correct with Smiles; then even the real
Objects of SATIRE will fuffer with Patience, and all Mankind will become thy
Friends."

This mild Rebuke, temper'd with fuch
falutary and friendly Hints, feemed to
have a very fenfible Effect upon our AU-
THOR; who, promifing ftrictly to obferve
the Admonitions, immediately retired."

Here the TEMPLE was fuddenly difturbed with a confufed Noife of—*I will
come in*—*But you fhan't come in*—*Confider
my Rank and Quality*—*Carry it to* COURT,
it won't do here—and fuch-like Altercation; at length a very portly Figure, with
a moft ponderous Wig, rufhed forwards,
HONESTY holding him faft by the Collar.
The

The Son of Law, for such he appeared to be, was going to open his Case at
large, and in due Form, when HONESTY
stopp'd his Mouth; however, with much
struggling, he mumbled out a Complaint, That, as PLAINTIFF, he had a
Right to speak first—No, no, replies his
enrag'd Antagonist, we'll have no PLAIN-
TIFF nor DEFENDANT here; as you have
so often kick'd me out of WESTMINSTER
HALL, I'll take Care to kick you out of
the TEMPLE of VIRTUE, whither nothing
but the matchless Impudence of a *Petti-
fogger* could have brought you. This
Resolution was immediately put in effectual Execution, to the no small Amusement of VIRTUE, WISDOM, and TRUTH,
all of whom had long known him for a
declared Enemy.

During this concise Scuffle a Number
of Characters pressed in, each eager to
petition first; but still one interrupted the
other—

other—*You come here!* cries one Female
to her Neighbour, *I wonder you are not
aſhamed to ſhow yourſelf, when there are ſo
many* ſubſtantial *Proofs that you never regarded* VIRTUE—*And what then, Madam*
METHODIST, retorts the Accuſed, *I have
no Body to care for, no Body to anſwer to,
but myſelf; I don't make a Cloak of* RELI-
GION *and a* HUSBAND *to cover dark Deeds;
I don't pray, and ſing Hymns for an Hour or
two, then cheat, tattle, and lye with a ſanc-
tified Phiz all the reſt of the Day, as ſome of
my pious Neighbours do.*—This Encounter
of two able Tongues promiſed to be not
only ſharp but of conſiderable Duration,
had not a teſty old Fellow ſnarled out—
*Pſhaw, pſhaw, here's Work with a Couple of
babbling, goſſiping Huſſies, that chatter away
as if precious* TIME *was only made for them
to waſte; but I, who know* Œconomy *better,
and want to be in the* ALLEY, *can't wait
trifling here; I muſt be diſpatched immediately*—*You diſpatched, old* Turnpenny, *cries*

a

a young Smart—*nothing but Sixpenny worth
of Hemp should dispatch such a Grub as you.
What can you possibly ask here? A Fellow,
who, in the Midst of Abundance, starves himself and his Family, and over-reaches all he
has any Dealings with—Aye,* retorts the
USURER, *and if it comes to that, what
brings you here, Graceless? A prodigal
Wretch, that squanders away his plentiful
Fortune in Follies and Vices. Well,* replies
the *Smart; and what then, old* Multiplica-
tion, *I make the World the better for me,
while you rob Mankind, and, as far as you
have Power, stop the necessary Circulation;
a few more such Scrapers would occasion a
national Consumption.*—This Altercation,
like the former, promised to extend a
considerable Length; but that the impatient Crowd grew so vociferous, and re-
criminated against each other with such
uncharitable and indecent Violence, that
VIRTUE, WISDOM, and TRUTH, not being able to bear the Anarchy, ascended

VOL. II.   L   thro'

thro' the Roof of the TEMPLE; upon which the whole Edifice, and its rocky Foundation, falling with a mighty Crash, overwhelmed the iniquitous Crowd in one juft and general Ruin.

After the TEMPLE of VIRTUE, which concluded with this Incident, we were entertained with a *petit* Piece, called the EUROPEANS*, written by BOLINGBROKE; which, according to the Tranflation, with the Characters, and who reprefented them, you will meet with in the fucceeding CHAPTER.

* The Reader is defired to remark that this, like the TEMPLE of VIRTUE, being only a Tranflation, cannot be expected to have the Spirit of an Original.

C H A P.

C H A P. VI.

Containing the several Scenes of the EURO-
PEANS.

PERSONS *in the* EUROPEANS.

Baron *Swizzle.*			*Handel.*
Mynheer *Vanderherring.*	All Suitors to Liberty.		*Dewitt.*
Marquis *de Capriole.*			*Lewis* XIV.
Don *Imperioso.*			*Philip* II.
Signor *Feminiani.*			*Senesino.*
Sir *Stedfast Hatebribe.*			*Lord Russel.**

Liberty.   Queen *Elizabeth.*
Property.   *Afra Behn.*

The Piece commenced with a Scene between
Liberty *and* Property, *as follows :*

Lib. WELL, *Property,* am I not in a
most troublesome Situation,
so many Admirers, and so few Friends?

Prop. A very sad one, indeed, Madam;
and I, your Handmaid, am in little better; no poor Creature was ever so bandied

L 2   about;

* Who was beheaded in *James* the Second's Reign.

about; fome affault me with Force, fome with Fraud; fome poffefs me with as little Regard as they have for their Wives; others love fo intolerably that I can never have any Connexion with you; fome venture their Necks, fome their Souls; in fhort, I am the univerfal Game, and hunted in every Corner of the World.

Lib. Very true, Child, we are both in a moft precarious Situation; you, indeed, are to be met, in full Health and Beauty, at fome Times, and in particular Places; but it is a Matter of very great Doubt whether I have at prefent, or ever had, any real Exiftence upon the Face of the Earth.

Prop. Oh yes, Madam, among the Greeks and Romans you made a very great Figure.

Lib. I know it has been faid fo, but the Matter will admit of much Doubt;

my

my Nature is extremely nice, and my Compofition elufive; there are two Monfters frequently miftaken for me, *Luxury* and *Licentioufnefs*.

Prop. What Family are they of, I pray?

Lib. Very near Relations of your own; the former moft immediately derived from *Monarchy* or *Ariftocracy*; the latter, from *Democracy*.

Prop. But how can fuch deform'd Monfters, Madam, poffibly impofe upon Mankind?

Lib. Merely thro' the Blindnefs and Prejudice of their own Paffions; luxurious Enjoyments lull the Great, and Licentioufnefs pleafes the Vulgar; the former know no Good beyond the Appendages of Grandeur, and the latter imagine themfelves fully poffeffed of me,

L 3   when

when they have unlimited Opportunities
of abuſing their Superiors.

Prop. Pray then, Madam, that I may
never miſtake you, give me ſome ſuch
Out-lines as may preſerve me from Deluſion; for without you I muſt be in a very
dangerous State.

Lib. Your Obſervation is juſt, and your
Requeſt reaſonable, therefore I ſhall ſatiſ-
fy you in as few Words as poſſible : If
you ever meet with a Nation where the
upper Claſs ſtudy to protect and encourage the lower; where the Great fill Offices of Government for Public Good
alone, without any pecuniary Profit; and
where their Dependents gratefully con-
form to legal Regulations, not from Fear
of Puniſhment, but from Conviction that
Obedience is neceſſary to the general
Happineſs; where Teachers of RELI-
GION ſtudy to regulate the Morals, and
not

not to trammel the Reaſon of their Flocks;
where the Military Genius is cultivated
not to ſerve ambitious Views, but to prevent foreign Invaſion; and where Practi-
tioners in Law prefer Juſtice to Gain;
there you may be ſure to find me.

Prop. Truly, by this Deſcription, and
the Obſervations I have made, you may
be long ſought after in vain—Ah, Madam, I could wiſh never to be ſeparated
from you; I am always ſafeſt under your
Protection; therefore I humbly requeſt
that, if you fix upon any of the SUITORS,
who are this Day to ſollicit your Favour,
you will caſt an Eye upon your faithful
humble Servant.

Lib. Doubt not my Friendſhip, *Property*; I ſhall be always glad to retain you
in my Service; tho', between ourſelves,
you often attach yourſelf very unworthi-
ly; however, you ſhall be preſent, and I
give

give you full Authority to fay what you can in your own Favour, without the leaft Referve.

Prop. That, Madam, is as much as I can poffibly expect—Soft, here comes a Vifiter.

Baron Swizzle.

Bar. Madam, the Imperial Eagle cow'ring at your Feet, by me' follicits your honourable Alliance.

Lib. Ere you receive my Anfwer you muft acquaint me, Sir, with thofe national Qualities which authorize this Addrefs.

Bar. Is it poffible your Ladyfhip can be unacqainted with the many and glorious Claims GERMANIA has to your Favour?

Lib. Even fo, Sir, for I never remember to have been in that Country.

Bar.

Bar. Amazing! we are all extremely intimate with your Name, and I thought, Madam, you had been very frequently amongſt us.

Lib. You are quite miſtaken, I aſſure you; it often happens that thoſe who talk of me moſt know me leaſt; but let me hear the Pretenſions of your Embaſ-ſy, and I ſhall give you an undiſguiſed Anſwer.

Bar. Pretenſions, Madam, our Preten-ſions lie in the moſt brilliant Military Fame, in which we outſhine all the World; in the Perſon of our Imperial Parent, who preſides to hold a political Equili-brium among the ſeveral States; and in that Noble Diet which takes Cognizance of all public Grievances, and rectifies them: Add to theſe the many invincible Heroes who have fought, who have bled, who

who have conquered, who have died in
Defence of your Ladyſhip's Charms.

Prop. Ah, Madam, don't believe a
Syllable this Fellow ſays; for my Part,
the wildeſt Indians cannot attack me in
a more barbarous Manner than his Countrymen.

Lib. Fear not, Child, fair Pictures cannot deceive me; to anſwer regularly, Sir,
I muſt take Notice that Military Fame,
as it is purſued in your Clime, ſtands
forth my greateſt Enemy; your Imperial Parent, as you ſtile him, is an inef-
fectual Pageant of Power, not able to ſupport me, tho' inclined to do ſo; for every
petty Prince, when he can link himſelf
with any other, from whom he may derive Aſſiſtance, fears not to oppoſe him:
The Diet, or National Aſſembly, you
boaſt, may now and then compromize
                                    ſome

some trivial Disputes; but does it form a constant Barrier between Oppression and suffering Industry? You cannot say so: And as to those Heroes who have bled in my Defence, according to your Report, it is an errant Mistake; Fighting, among your Countrymen, is a Trade; your Sovereign Princes are many of them so poor, that younger Sons must be sent into the Field of War for Maintenance, and a great Part of their indigent Subjects must become Soldiers for the same Reason: This dreadful Situation of Things makes it necessary in every Court to hold Cabals, which may promote Action, that your mercenary Troops may be taken into Pay, and let loose to plunder their Neighbours. Can you then call such as these my Defenders? However brave, however wise, however persevering, such Instruments disgrace rather than support the Name of *Liberty*; therefore, instead of venturing myself into so

inho-

inhofpitable a Seat of Depredation, I fhall advife even my moft diftant Friends to have no Connexions with a thanklefs People, who know no Friendfhip beyond the immediate Call of Intereft.

Bar. Madam, as Reprefentative of the illuftrious GERMANIC Body, I muft be bold to fay that you fpeak in Terms unworthy your own Delicacy and our Importance; therefore, unlefs you chufe to think better of it, I fhall publifh a Manifefto of the Indignity received, and doubt not but our Allies will affift to enforce Reafon.

Lib. Spoke with the true overbearing Spirit of your Country, the *ultima ratio Regum*; but think not I am to be intimidated by Threats, or gained by Force; both are fo repugnant to my Nature, that the very Mention of them removes me far from the Poffeffion of fuch Knight Errants

Errants as wooe in Thunder, and robe themſelves with Blood.

Bar. This is the firſt Time I ever knew that the Sons of Valour could be diſagreeable to a Lady.

Lib. Nor would they, Sir, were Valour only ſhewn in a juſt Cauſe.

Bar. Well, Madam, I am ſorry it has been my Fortune to come upon ſo unſucceſsful an Embaſſy; however, take Notice, that whoever is favour'd with your Smiles, may chance to lament the Slights I have received.

Prop. Oh, Madam, I am rejoiced he's gone; the rough Bear threw me into a horrid Palpitation leſt he ſhould have been downright rude.

Lib. Of that there was no Danger, for even my greateſt Enemies preſerve an

external

external Respect—Oh, here comes another—You, Sir, are the DUTCH Plenipo,
I presume?

Vanderherring.

Van. Your Ladyship's Discernment cannot err; by me the UNITED PROVINCES
offer their Respects: It is well known that
they shook off the *Spanish* Yoke out of an
inviolable Attachment to you, and from
thence we originally lay Claim to your
Patronage.

Lib. And so far, Mynheer, your Right
is well founded; to disdain and cast off
Oppression is the highest Merit in my
Sight; but has your future Conduct kept
Pace with such a glorious Beginning?

Van. Madam, I hope it has; we have
never suffered Monarchy to creep upon
us; indeed the STADTHOLDERSHIP seems
to bear Superiority; but we have always
taken Care to cramp it so, that, upon due
Exa-

Examination, it will be found little more than a Name: Add to this our unbounded Spirit of Trade, our national Œconomy, and that certain Consequence of both, our astonishing Opulence: With whom then can *Liberty* find a more pleasing Residence?

Prop. Aye, Madam, this Gentleman talks to the Purpose; I may venture to recommend him and his Countrymen as very particular Friends of mine.

Lib. I know that Recommendation, and shall consider it with the rest.

Prop. Ply her close, and I warrant you, Mynheer. *(Aside.)*

Lib. At the Time of shaking off the Spanish Yoke, my Spirit animated the Cause; I was amongst you; and in the Support of Republican Principles you

have

have fhewn yourfelves my Profelytes;
but, avoiding Scylla, you have fallen
into Charibdis; you are not Slaves to
Power but Avarice; Gain is the Tyrant
that lords it over your Hearts, and directs
all your Actions; how can you be free
that are fo fwallowed up in the Gulph of
private Property, as to render your State
ufelefs to Friends, and defpicable to
Foes? Individuals are opulent; the Government poor, irrefolute, and diftracted
with Diffention. Temporizing and Eva-
fion are your Policy; Encroachment and
Monopoly, your Aim; Proffeffions·with-
out Performance, your Practice. How
then could I propofe to myfelf a Refidence of Pleafure or of Safety among thofe
who, by every Method, are accumulating
private Wealth to allure their ambitious
Neighbours, and have no public Spirit to
fecure Refpect: In a Country which is indebted to a neighbouring Island for its
Independence, and which could never
have

have supported itself in the Midst of many envious Enemies, but through the continued Protection of so powerful an Ally? which, notwithstanding, they have treated with such Ingratitude, that I should prove myself guilty of a Weakness little short of Self-destruction, to rely upon any Promises from you that were not bound with Gold.

Prop. Now, Mynheer, for a genteel Come-off, the DUTCH are famous that Way. (*Aside.*)

Van. Pardon me, Madam, if I presume to say that the Charge of Ingratitude to our Insular Friends is rather premature; they certainly have our good Wishes, and they want no more; they are sufficient in themselves to support the Necessities of their State; why then should we run ourselves into Difficulties and Perils to give them Assistance? Your Ladyship cannot

VOL. II.　　　M　　　but

but know that Self-defence is the moſt powerful Obligation; That, duly fulfilled, we ſhall be always ready to aſſiſt our very good Friends the ENGLISH.

Prop. Well ſaid, Sir, that will do. *(Aſide.)*

Lib. I am not to learn, Mynheer, that Plauſibility is a Characteriſtic of your Country; but tho' you may plead, that to grant your Friends Aſſiſtance is unneceſſary, pray how do you apologize for being ſo induſtrious to furniſh their Enemies with Materials offenſive and defenſive?

Van. As to that, Madam, we make no Difference; Trade will ever follow the beſt Market; and as Trade is our Support, it is natural enough to carry Merchandize where it will have the quickeſt Sale, without any unfriendly Meaning: Beſides, Madam, we ſhould

not

not be placed *entirely* on the *Debtor* Side;
pray, did not we do you and ENGLAND
very fignal Service in fending over our
PRINCE of ORANGE to refcue you from
Popifh Tyranny?

Lib. Had that been a national Piece of
Friendfhip, it would have cancell'd many
Faults; but your Countrymen wanted to
get WILLIAM out of the Way, who was
too great and good not to have many
Enemies, tho' he preferved your State
from Ruin; and the PRINCE was as defi-
rous of leaving a thanklefs People, who
always cramp'd his Operations, and ftrove
to fully his Fame; hence the happy RE-
VOLUTION in my Favour appears, with
refpect to you, rather the Child of Chance
than of Friendfhip.

Van. Are you then determined to reject
my Solicitation?

Lib. Moft certainly.

M 2

Van.

Van. Why then it is in vain to multi-
ply Words and lose Time; look you, Madam, we have hitherto been able to make
the lower Class of People believe you re-
sided constantly amongst us, which answers the same End as if you was really
on the Spot; nay, to my Thinking, much
better; for you seem to have such consci-
entious Scruples about Friendship, and
Gratitude, and public Spirit, that I think
you would be a very troublesome Guest,
so e'en fix where you will for *Vanderher-*
ring: HOLLANDERS know better than to
prefer Shadows to Substance, so farewell.

Prop. I profess, Madam, I cannot help
thinking you too scrupulous.

Lib. There it is; like the Generality
of Females, you are prejudiced in Favour
of the most assiduous Lovers, tho' the
Affection of such is seldom found or permanent; but I must be more cautious, for

a

a voluntary Surrender on my Side would bring Ruin upon all my Friends; your Cafe is different, becaufe being entirely valued for your Influence, where that prevails moft you will naturally like to be.

Prop. Very true; but I like your Ladyfhip's Service fo much, that I could wifh never to leave it.

Lib. Your Defire is reafonable, but vain; the Nature of human Affairs will not fuffer us to be often or long together, left we fhould too firmly fix the Power of my poor unfettled Sifter HAPPINESS.

Prop. If that be the Cafe, Madam— foft, I'm interrupted.

Marquis de Capriole.

Marq. Madam, I'm thrice three Times your Ladyfhip's moft obedient and devoted humble Servant; the Brilliancy of

M 3   your

your angelic Charms muſt counterwork
your Name and Nature, and captivate all
Beholders.

Lib. Your Country, Monſieur *Marquis,*
is a Soil fruitful in Compliments.

Marq. Right, Madam, Politeneſs is the
Characteriſtic of FRANCE; a Country fa-
mous alſo for every great and amiable
Qualification.

Lib. True, Sir, if we take *your* Opinion of the Matter.

Marq. My Opinion! Your Ladyſhip
cannot but know the Truth of my Aſſer-
tion from inconteſtible Evidence; why,
Is not ours the leading Language in *Europe?* Do not our Faſhions regulate the
general Taſte, and are we not a Terror to
all the ſurrounding States?

Lib. If you call this latter Influence
worthy or amiable, I am yet to learn the
true

true Meaning of thofe Terms; and let me tell you, that the Influence of your Language and Fafhions is more owing to a ridiculous and fervile Complaifance in other Nations, than to any real Worth in themfelves.

Marq. Pofitively your Ladyfhip differs widely from all the polite Female World, which muft be owing to fome Prejudice; but, to remove the Cloud from before your bright Eyes, let me invite you to that fecond EDEN, VERSAILLES; where Beauty meets with higher Regard and more Adoration than on any other earthly Spot.

Lib. What Beauty, my Lord?—The Beauty of falfe Appearances? How is it poffible that I, who always fhow my own Face, and fpeak juft as I think, fhould make a tolerable Figure where all the Females wear mafquerade Faces, and all the Men fallacious Hearts?

Marq.

Marq. Thefe Matters, Madam, you take merely from Report; Experience, no Doubt, would foften this moft unfavourable Profpect—'Tis true our Ladies, from a Defire to pleafe, and confcious that Nature is liable to a precipitate Decay, do apply external Ornament; and certainly, where Features want Bloom to enliven, or White to render them delicate, Reafon allows Art to be commendable.

Lib. By the fame Rule, Sir, Reafon might place Affection upon a beautified Moppet: This ftrong Attachment to artificial Charms, fhows that your very polite Nation pays little Regard to intrinfic Worth, and feldom looks fo far as the Heart, where only real Beauty is to be found; for which Reafon we view your Females, in general, as we do Buildings of gaudy, outward Show, without any Marks of Tafte, Convenience, or Richnefs within.

Marq.

Marq. Well, Madam, suppose this should be the Case, (which, however, I cannot be unnatural enough to admit) your Appearance must be with the greater *Eclat*; and tho' you should be envied by the Women, you are sure of being sole Arbitress among the Men.

Lib. Then I must not come near the *Court*, for there dwell my most inveterate Enemies; look ye, my Lord, Flattery, the usual Female Bait, won't do here; Openness of Expression and Sincerity of Heart are much stronger Recommendations to me; you are, it must be allowed, a plausible People, prodigal in Profession, penurious in Performance; placid in Looks, designing in Action; fond of Military Fame, regardless of honesty: Your Court is a Fountain of Dissimulation, which spreads Infection thro' all Ranks of People; the Root of Oppression, which shoots forth Branches thro' each Depart-

ment

ment of Government; and a Magazine of
Combuſtion to ſet the World on Fire;
how then can you have the Aſſurance to
ſolicit my Preſence? You ſay Prejudice
miſleads me; 'tis falſe, I have viſited your
Country *incog.* ſeveral Times, and have
wept Tears of Blood over the enſlaved
Millions I ſaw there; I did but peep
abroad in the Perſon of HENRY IV. and
a RAVILLIAC was ſoon found to ſtab me;
ſince then I have ventured occaſionally
into your *Parliaments*; but each ſucceeding *Grand Monarque* has watched ſo cloſe,
and ſo aſſiduouſly compaſſed my Deſtruction, that common Prudence forbids me
even to enter into ſo hoſtile a Climate.

Marq. I dare ſay, Madam, our preſent
Grand Monarque, were you to enter upon a
Negotiation, would ſhow himſelf much
leſs your Enemy than you imagine.

Lib. Aye, there it is; your Succeſs in
Negotiations has been ſo extraordinary at
different

different Times, that you would lead me
into the Road of Impofition; but I am
prepared againſt all the Powers of Inſi-
nuation, being very well aſſured that
French Fidelity has but an imaginary Exiſtence, and that thoſe who have leaſt Dependence upon it are moſt likely to remain in Safety; beſides, my Lord, had
you been at all acquainted with me, you
muſt have known that my Nature and
Conſtitution are diametrically oppoſite to
the overbearing Power of any Monarch
upon Earth; it is an Abſurdity to imagine
I ſhould coop myſelf within the Limits
of one Man's Will.

Marq. Your Ladyſhip here again, pardon my Freedom, conſiders the Matter
in a partial Light; where can you ſhare
Power or Royal Favour to more Advantage than in an Union with the FRENCH
MONARCH, who can caſt never-dying
Laurels

Laurels at your Feet, and grace your Brows with Beams of unrivall'd Glory.

Lib. Thefe, Sir, are Ornaments of trifling Value to *Liberty*, who difdains all the oftentatious Gifts of arbitrary Power; who has no true Enjoyment but in the undiftinguifhed Happinefs of a whole People; in the mild and impartial Diftribution of neceffary Laws; and in the tendereft Impofition of indifpenfible Taxes; as thefe Points cannot be hoped for in a political Conftitution like yours, it is, I fay again, vain and abfurd to defire my Prefence.

Marq. Give me Leave, Madam, to remark, that, when I undertook this Embaffy, I expected more Refpect to my Country, and the dignified Character of its Reprefentative; but your fecret Attachment to a certain ISLAND is well known, and, like other Female Follies, may beget Repentance; while GALLIC Power

Power and Fame, unincumber'd with those dark and heavy Prejudices which seem to govern you, shall tower beyond your Reach, and soar to Immortality.

Lib. Ha! Monsieur the *Marquis* has dropp'd his cool philosophical Politeness.

Prop. No Wonder, Madam, for you anatomized his frippery Nation pretty severely; and Dissimulation detected, among *French* Politicians, always turns to *Rhodomontade.*

Lib. No Female, sure, was ever tormented with such Suitors.

Prop. Nor any Suitors, Madam, better match'd in a peremptory Mistress; Soothing and Threats, Smiles and Frowns, seem all alike to you.

Lib. Seem! nay, they really are so, I assure you; yet, for all this, I could wish
myself

myself in an agreeable and permanent Situation.

Prop. And I too, Madam; well, who knows, one of those to come may possibly deserve your Favour.

Lib. If that should be the Case, depend upon it I shall not be over nice in my Choice, nor too rigid in the Articles of Settlement—Oh, here comes the formal SPANIARD, confident in his own vast Importance.

Don Imperioso.

Don Imp. It is with Pleasure, Madam, I approach you as the Representative of SPAIN; Pleasure founded upon probable Assurance that you, who have had Discernment and Prudence to reject the indigent GERMAN, the avaricious HOLLANDER, and the fantastic GAUL, will listen with Condescension to my superior Claim.

Lib.

Lib. No Doubt, my Lord, an Audience is as much your Right as that of any who came before you, and you may expect an equal Impartiality.

Don Imp. On that I ſhall reſt Succeſs: 'Tis not unknown to your Ladyſhip that our Nation laboured ſome Ages under the Diſgrace and Hardſhip of *Mooriſh* Captivity; yet, at a Time when we ſeemed loſt beyond Redemption, an inextinguiſhable Regard for you rouſed our great Forefathers from their ſlaviſh Lethargy, ſo enflamed their Hearts, and ſo nerved their Arms, that a total Extirpation of the *Infidels* enſued, IBERIA once again ſhining like herſelf.

Lib. My Lord, I remember the great Event with particular Satisfaction, as it is my peculiar Nature to wiſh every Nation the full Poſſeſſion of its natural Rights, and an Exemption from all foreign and domeſtic Oppreſſion.

Don

Don Imp. Truly great and amiable; no Place on Earth, but that Nation I repre-sent, can do Justice to such exalted Worth; let me then, Madam, lead you thither, and lay the amazing Treasures of both INDIES at your Feet.

Lib. Alas! vain Man, were there no other Objection, what thou hast now mentioned as an Inducement would alone deter me — The INDIES! I turn my Eyes on them with Horror — You men-tioned the *Moorish* Captivity as an Hard-ship; did they, though branded with the Name of Infidels, so wantonly and cru-elly use the Iron Rod of Power amongst you as your Forefathers did among the unpractised, unsuspecting INDIANS? Did they in cold Blood, with fair Faces too, cut off Thousands for the Sake of cursed Gold? What Right had your Discover-ers, driven by Chance among the unhap-py MEXICANS and PERUVIANS, to me-

ditate

ditate and profecute their Deftruction?
Providence had given them their Country as a natural Inheritance, what Privilege had your CORTES and PIZZARRO
rapacioufly to deprive them of it? Superior Power fhould have taught you Mercy: If you had more Wifdom you fhould
have pitied their Weaknefs, and not im-
pofed upon it; you fhould have taught
them Commerce, and not inftructed them
in the Arts of Inhumanity and Plunder;
their Right to Life and Independence is as
inconteftible, and ought to be held as fa-
cred, as that of the moft polifhed Nations;
and nothing but the moft illiberal Partiality could ftigmatize them as Barbarians
for afferting thofe Rights, and refenting
the Infringement of them.

Don Imp. But, Madam, in the Caufe of
Religion we cannot be too warm.

Lib. Religion! what Religion? The
CHRISTIAN? Mildnefs and Perfuafion

VOL. II.   N   are

are the Means she uses, and the only
Means she justifies; but you, with Interest
to inspire your Zeal, array'd her in Frowns
and Terrors; even your own internal Policy exhibits her with the most gloomy
Aspect; Pride, Ostentation, Indolence,
and Enthusiasm are the reigning Charac-
teristics through all Degrees of People,
which render my Residence among you
utterly impracticable.

Don Imp. But, Madam, if you are to
be received on the most friendly Terms,
and to hold equal State with the highest
Ranks in our antient Kingdom, some
Defects may be overlooked.

Lib. Farther Solicitation is in vain; I
cannot be happy at the Expence of
others, nor selfishly enjoy the Smiles of
Comfort, when Wretchedness appears on
every Side.

Don

Don Imp. Wretchedneſs, Madam! Happineſs and Miſery take their Riſe from Compariſon; thoſe who have never known better are content with the humbleſt Enjoyments of Life; artificial Paſſions, both in a national Capacity and a domeſtic one, are created by an improper Indulgence; this our political Conſtitution prevents, by maintaining a juſt Subordination, from whence only can be derived the eſſential Reſpect to ennobled Characters.

Lib. Aye, there, my Lord, you have ſaid the whole; your Nobility ſuppoſing themſelves to be made of ſuperior Materials, conſider the lower Ranks as mere Utenſils for the Support of their Pride and Convenience. This Kind of Subordination I pronounce Slavery, nor will I ever come where Prieſts tread upon the King, and the King upon the Nobles, and the Nobles trample the People underfoot.

Don

Don Imp. Madam, 'tis well; but take Notice that Obſtinacy may bring late Repentance; you have been treated with Reſpect and Cordiality; ſince theſe will not prevail, united to my Couſin FRANCE by a FAMILY COMPACT, we ſhall, I doubt not, reduce your Ladyſhip to Terms leſs advantageous than you might have obtained by mild Negotiation.

Prop. Oh, dear Madam, I tremble to think of this *Spaniard's* becoming your Enemy, you know what a vindictive People they are.

Lib. I know them well, they never were my Friends; therefore I have loſt nothing, nor will I fear their becoming Tools to their ambitious Neighbours, which muſt be the whole Effect of their FAMILY COMPACT; a Deſign more likely to do me Good than Harm, unleſs all other States ſhould become totally indifferent, or blind to their own Welfare.

There

There are certain Bounds in political
Connexions, to paſs which creates Envy
and Danger; ſuch, if I miſtake not, their
Combination will prove.

Signior Feminiani.

Fem. I eſteem myſelf happy, Madam,
in being appointed the Inſtrument of
Mediation between your Ladyſhip and
ITALY the Bleſſed; a Clime moſt favoured by Providence in the Temperature of
its various Seaſons; a Nation ſo improved
by Art, ſo beautified by Taſte, and ſo enriched by Elegance, that Travellers view
us with Amazement.

Lib. 'Tis true, *Signior*, but the Admi-
ration and Regard of moſt Travellers are
not bent upon Places and Things of
greateſt Conſideration, real Value cannot
be determined by their Paſſions.

Fem. Suppoſe not, Madam, yet undoubtedly ROME and its adjacent Coun-

N 3   tries

tries have commanded Respect thro' the Annals of many Ages.

Lib. Once, I admit, the Inhabitants of your Country deservedly found an exalted Place in the Records of FAME; but the former Lustre strikes a Shade from the present degenerate Sons of ROME; who, with slavish Ignorance, submit to the absurd Dominion of a proud Churchman, and his Council of full-gorg'd *Ecclesiastics*, who support Religion by Ostentation and temporal Authority, not by Scripture or Reason; who themselves hold fast the Goods of this World, while they delude their unhappy Flock with shadowy Promises; or terrify them with impious Threats, in regard of a future Existence, as if the Supreme Director had reserved no Power to himself, but the mere Ratification of their *Absolutions* or *Anathemas*: No more then mention what ROME *was*, seeing how changed she *is*, and how miserably fallen.

Fem.

Fem. This is a Point, Madam, we are taught never to difcufs too nicely, the Confequence is dangerous.

Lib. And therein are ye the greateft of all Slaves; why were fuch noble Faculties implanted in the human Mind, if not to confider and digeft whatever relates to its Dignity and Intereft ? Why has the UNIVERSAL PARENT made it free, if Man ufurps the Power of tyrannizing over it; but as I know the Stubbornnefs of rooted Prejudices, I fhall enlarge no farther upon this Topic; and befides thefe I have many other Objeċtions to refiding amongft you.

Fem. Is it poffible, Madam, that you fhould diflike a Country where the Elegance and Dignity of *Architeċture* commands Attention, and imparts the moft elevated Pleafure; where *Canvas*, glowing with the mafterly Labours of fo many excellent Artifts, calls up, alternately, every

Paf-

Paſſion of the human Heart; and where *Muſic*'s powerful Voice, in Strains little ſhort of celeſtial Harmony, raiſes the enchanted Soul to the Abodes of Bliſs.

Lib. Theſe, Sir, as agreeable and wonderful Efforts of human Genius, I admire; and would always, under the Influence of Reaſon, cultivate them with Care; but muſt at the ſame Time conſider them only as Ornaments, not Eſſentials of Humanity. WISDOM and VIRTUE, the true Beautifiers of the Nature and the Life of Man, are very ſeldom found amongſt you; you ſubſtitute that poor Phantom TASTE for the ſolid Principles of Morality; you are not only Slaves to your Superiors, but Slaves to your own Paſſions; your licentious Effeminacy renders you contemptible, and your entire Devotion to Externals, worthleſs; return then, and know that LIBERTY diſdains the Friendſhip of thoſe who worſhip Shadows for Subſtances;
and

and either do not know, or will not regard, the intrinsic Worth of a well-governed and well-cultivated Mind.

Fem. O rude and *Gothic* Notion of Things! truly, if your Ladyship is of this Way of Thinking, you are too rough, too untractable for the Delicacy of our *Southern* Climes; and it will be much more agreeable to report your Answer, however ungenteel, than to introduce so great an Enemy to the polite Arts.

Prop. What, the smooth and gay *Italian* gone also; at this Rate, Madam, I do not find that any Suitor is like to win your Esteem.

Lib. There is but another, how he may recommend himself, I know not yet; here he comes, and seems to carry some Prepossession in his Appearance.

Sir

Sir Stedfaſt Hatebribe.

Sir *Sted.* Madam, my plain Manner of Addreſs, without any Aſſiſtance from external Ornament or Equipage, may appear ill adapted to the Occaſion; but, in my Mind, Reſpect ſhows itſelf to more Advantage without ſuch flimzy oſtentatious Appendages; I am, I hope, an honeſt ENGLISHMAN, and in that exalted Character prefer my Solicitations.

Lib. You could not have named one more agreeable. Pray, Sir, of what Family are you?

Sir *Sted.* A Family, Madam, but little known, and not very numerous, that of the HATEBRIBES.

Lib. Are you of that valuable Stock? It is a Name I know and honour.

Sir *Sted.* So I hope, for we have always been moſt inviolably attached to your Lady-

Ladyſhip; that implacable Enemy of yours, CORRUPTION, has taken great Pains to win us over; PROTEUS never tried a greater Variety of Shapes; ſometimes like a *Lord* of the *Treaſury*, and then as one of *Trade*; a *Secretary* of *State*, or of *War*; a *Commiſſioner* of the *Cuſtoms*, or of the *Exciſe*; a *Biſhop*, or a *Judge*; a *General*, or a *Penſioner*; yet all in vain: We have always ſpoken as we thought, and done as we ſaid; we never bent the fawning Knee to Power; nor ſacrificed the Intereſt of our Fellow-Subjects to promote our own: Indeed we have often ſtruggled to no Purpoſe; but if you, Madam, would fix your conſtant Reſidence amongſt us, the Glory of BRITAIN muſt ſhine with unrivalled Luſtre, and our Happineſs ſurpaſs that of any other Nation upon Earth.

Lib. I agree in your Opinion, and no Perſon can have a more friendly Inclination towards BRITAIN than myſelf; it is a Country where, tho' I have at different

Times

Times met with some ill Usage, many
steady Friends have exerted themselves
in my Cause, and my Castle of *Magna
Charta* has always proved a safe Retreat;
yet 'tis true there are many Circumstances
in the Political Constitution very unpro-
mising to my Happiness, if not totally in-
consistent with it.

Sir *Sted.* I am sensible, Madam, of too
many Defects; however, if you will make
me acquainted with those you consider as
most offensive, I will represent them to
your Well-wishers, and no doubt they
will use all honest Endeavours to rectify
them.

Lib. So will they merit and obtain my
Favour: To enumerate all the Particulars which give me Pain, would swell the
Catalogue to a tedious Length; let it suffice to say, that I feel a particular Grief
at the enormous Multiplicity of Laws,
which rather tend to obscure than dispense
Justice; a Multiplicity which seems to
say

say that your *Parliaments* have been studious to establish and promote a Trade, or a Profession which derives its chief Advantage from inextricable Principles; and furnishes so many evasive Windings to a crafty and litigious Adversary, that Honesty, whether pursuing him or retiring from him, can scarce work its Way thro' the dangerous Labyrinth, unless Wealth becomes its Guide.

Sir *Sted.* Truly, Madam, I have often lamented this Case myself; but, by Neglect and Accumulation, our Laws are become an *Augean* Stable, in which nothing less than an *Herculean* Reformer could accomplish the necessary Change.

Lib. I fear it would require an HERCULES indeed, while there are so many interested Defenders of their present State; yet I will not despair, a truly independent SENATE would be truly patriotic; and to such a Body the framing useful Laws, and enforcing a due Execution

of

of them, muſt be the firſt and moſt intereſting Point of Conſideration.

Sir *Sted.* The Friends of your Ladyſhip would undoubtedly act upon ſuch Principles; but I am ſorry to reflect that, while ſo many *Placemen* are choſen Repreſentatives of the People, Government and its Dependencies muſt have a prejudicial Influence.

Lib. That Complaint, I know, is general and juſt; yet an eaſy Remedy lies in the Power of thoſe who complain: It has been propoſed to obtain an *Act*, which might exclude Servants of the Government from Places in the *National Aſſembly*; but how can ſuch a Law be hoped for, while theſe conſtitute the Majority in that Aſſembly; nay, why ſhould it be ſought for, when a much eaſier and more effectual Remedy is in the Hands of the *Electors?*

Sir *Sted.* That, Madam, I ſhould be glad to know.   *Lib.*

Lib. Your Principles intitle you to
know every Thing which tends to the
Good of your Country. Let every Place
then which deputes a Reprefentative, at
the Time of Election exact a Promife,
upon Honour, that the Perfon chofen
fhould not, on any Pretence whatever,
accept a Place or Penfion. If it were poffible that fuch a Reprefentative could afterwards violate his Integrity, a Law now
exifting would vacate his Seat, and his
Conftituents would have an undeniable
Argument for rejecting a Perfon fo void
of Truth and Honour.

Sir *Sted.* The Practicability, as well as
general Ufe of this Hint, Madam, ftrikes
me; but then it faid that, without fome
Profeffors to inftruct our Law-givers in
the different Branches of political Knowledge, the Senate muft ever be imperfect.

Lib. Not at all; a Military Council
might be appointed to prepare all Matters

ters relative to the Army, for *Parliamentary* Ratification; another for the Navy; and so on through all the other Departments of public Affairs. Besides, the *Aristocratic* Influence in your Government is hateful to me: Your PEERS, not content with forcing all their Sons and Relations into the Lower House, point out other Persons to be chosen by the People; and, in the Character of Landlords, Lords of Manors, &c. proceed even to compel *Electors* into Compliance with their Recommendation, by threatening to deprive Dependents and Tenants of their Bread, who refuse to prostitute their Votes to them; and all this in direct Opposition to that essential Law of the Constitution, that a PEER is by no Means to enter into, or influence, the Election of a Member of the Commons. I am not, as some have misrepresented me, an Enthusiast; but this unsufferable Intrusion overbears all Patience.

Sir

Sir Sted. No Wonder, Madam, as from this our Conſtitution and your Intereſt are likely to receive the moſt dangerous Wound.

Lib. Nor does my Uneaſineſs ſtop here: No one can reſpect Royal Prerogative more than I do, ſo far as it ſheds real Dignity upon the Monarch; which Effect it cannot have, unleſs the Nation's Happineſs is included in it. The Power of proroguing Parliaments appears to me in the Light of a dangerous and cenſurable Privilege; a PRINCE ſhould undoubtedly have the Power of ſummoning the National Council upon any Emergency; but its Receſs from public Buſineſs, and its ſtated Times of Meeting, ſhould lie in the Determination of its own Members : Had that been the Caſe, CHARLES the FIRST would not have had the unhappy Privilege of enraging his Subjects, and of ruining himſelf; nor, under ſuch a Regulation, could any STATESMAN, conſcious of Crimes and

Mifdemeanors; fo eafily frame the Means
to fcreen himfelf from public Refent-
ment: You will find that every blunder-
ing or corrupt MINISTER, whofe Infamy
is immortalized in Hiftory, has taken Advantage of this Privilege in the PRINCE
to gain Time for his Defence and Se-
curity.

Sir *Sted.* Even fo, Madam; and we
have another pretty Afylum too for fuch
hunted Foxes when they are almoft run
down, the Shelter of Nobility with a Penfion; but I dare fay your Friendfhip and
Perfeverance, granted to the Solicitation
of unbiaffed Friends, together with their
difinterefted Attention, will in Time remedy fome, if not remove all the Grievances that have been mentioned.

Lib. So glorious a Profpect, joined to
my natural Affection for BRITAIN, fires
me; nor fhall fome unavoidable Infults
deter me from giving you my Hand in
Friendfhip; my Companion PROPERTY
too

too fhall attend my Steps, and, if there fhould not be Knaves or Fools enough to banifh us, it is in our Power to create you Refpect abroad and Happinefs at home.

Sir *Sted.* Madam, I glory more in obtaining this Condefcenfion, than if I had been cover'd with Laurels gather'd from the Conqueft of a World; I am happy in reflecting that, when I lead *you* to my Country as a Friend, I give her the greateft Blefling fhe can enjoy.

Prop. Madam, I give your Ladyfhip Joy of fo prudent and agreeable a Choice.

Lib. I hope it may prove fo in its lateft and moft remote Effects; come then, my Friend and Companion, let us proceed without Fear or Sufpicion, fince we cannot have a better Guardian nor a fafer Guide than an *uncorrupt* and *uncorruptible* BRITON.

Here

Here ended the EUROPEANS; a Piece formed upon general Hints, and therefore better calculated to set the Mind at Work upon the several Subjects, than perfectly to gratify it.

The Audience separated, and the Volume ends: There remains no Room for the Criticisms that passed between the NAMREDAL, Queen ELIZABETH, SHAKESPEAR, and Sir HUMPHREY, upon the *Dramatic* Action of NOIBLA, which gave Occasion to many Strictures upon that of our World.—Much curious Matter also, of various Nature, is left untold, and many Kingdoms of the Moon are yet unvisited; if you like your Journey, my Fellow-Travellers, when the Season for renewing our Expedition returns again, I shall not fail to meet you; and in the mean Time I heartily wish you all the Good you wish yourselves.

The END *of the* SECOND VOLUME.